Prolc

HE HAS taken about four pills but as something stops him taking another. S this suicidal road. Something.

Jake Hawkins puts the lid on the bottle and places it back on the bathroom shelf. He goes to the lounge and sits. His phone is on the coffee table but he doesn't pick it up. He's sick of picking it up, sick of it ruling his life.

He thinks how the world is changing, it always has and it always will. But it's complicated change now. It's overloaded change. It's change that is too fast. Where the basics of human existence are being put under pressure and almost squeezed out. Where once the past was left where it was, now it can come back, it can return, people, times, places, they can all come back. Whenever they want.

The things that used to be confined to history can impose on your now life and just screw it up. In a way that, before now, it never really could, not so easily.

You are no longer free of your past. You can be found, you can be stalked, from a million miles away, from decades ago.

Another notification flashes on his smartphone but with the drink and the pills he cannot even begin to make out who it is from, let alone what it says.

It will be her. But which her? Which one of those women who abandoned him all those years ago will it be and does he care anymore? If he cared he would not have opened the bottle of pills with the intention of swallowing them to oblivion.

But since he has stopped popping the pills and gulping the whisky, maybe he does care.

You didn't really want to go through with it, really, did you. (rhetorical, the inner voice always is).

What do they want, these women? You want to know, you want to find out even though they fuck with your head, fuck with your head just like I do, just like I always did.

Jake Hawkins. That is my name. That much I know.

He opens the balcony doors. He lights a cigarette, a habit he had given up years ago but still cannot resist the occasional binge even though he hates the taste now. Thank God or he would be back on 60 a day.

His chair in the balcony awaits him and he clumsily, half-drunkenly, wearily plonks himself in it and inhales the cigarette deeply. He can make out the shimmering lights reflecting from the Thames through trees whose leaves are rustled by the wind, sending out whispers of calm, their sound soothing him. Nature, natural, unfettered by technology, by mankind, by people. The rustling of the leaves and the sound of the river drown out the echo chamber of people and the city and the apps and the social media that got him into the state he has been in tonight.

What do they want? Redemption? From me? From what? From themselves.

In the old days, you had to live with the mistakes you made years and years ago. You moved on, there was no easy way to track back. Now people could, they could find you again, try to repaint, try to rewrite it, with just one click on a phone app. Words that had hurt, they want to delete, images they left behind they want to airbrush, sounds they left in your head they want to edit out. Because now, they just can, so easily. Or at least they think they can try and in trying they make themselves, or hope to make themselves, feel better.

What do they want? What do you want? So many choices, so many options, too many. Overload.

Jake chucks the now burned down cigarette over the balcony. It has gone into the ether. Not properly stubbed out but it will burn itself out, burn itself away. Just like people eventually do.

He hears the leaves again. The sky is clear, he can see the moon, he can hear the river lapping. No voices now, just the sound of nature and the real world. His phone is in the lounge, his laptop he switched off hours ago. If he wasn't so fucked by the drink and the pills he would seek out a book and sit here and just read. Like he used to. But he will do that tomorrow, sober, tranquil, clear-headed. Free.

October 1989
Dear Jake
I hope you are well.

Things have not been getting any better for me since I last wrote to you and I am quite frightened. Scared. Terrified. Must not be too alarming or melodramatic. But let me explain.

Salime´s behaviour gets evermore bizarre. Though he is talking to me again now, we went two whole weeks without saying a word to each other. I tried, I kept asking him what was wrong but he just blanked me. Buried his head in his newspapers and books. I just got those looks, you know, as if I was in the way, a nuisance, a burden.

Then he would do his disappearing act for days on end. I would explain that I had been worried about him when he had not come back to the apartment. "There's no need for you to worry about me," he would say. And that's all he would say.

But what's really strange is, I think all this is playing havoc with my mind. It's small things, like buying milk and eggs. I know I bought them but then Salime will come from the kitchen and say, there is no milk or no eggs. And I know I bought them the day before so I go and look in the fridge and sure enough, we are out of milk or cheese, or whatever. Maybe I never bought the milk or whatever. I only think I did. He says this is all part of my mental condition.

As you know he says he is going to treat me, psychiatric treatment to help me banish the ghosts and issues of my past. Well I'm still waiting. I ask him when the treatment is going to start but he says he has many cases he is dealing with and that it is best if I take time to adjust to living in Paris. That way, he says, the treatment will be most effective.

And then there are the calls to the apartment I told you about. Heavy breathing and always when I'm in the apartment alone. Some pervert I suppose.

He tells me I should stay in the apartment and not go out too much. He doesn't say why. I mean, I cannot stay cooped up in the flat all day long. I have to go out for things and he expects food to be shopped for.

Anyway, one night a few weeks ago I followed Salime. He said he was going out to meet friends for a drink in the Latin Quarter. I don't know why I followed him.

I suppose I just wanted to get out anyway, just for some fresh air and following Salime gave me a good enough reason.

I kept a fair distance from him and covered my head in a scarf. I nearly lost him a few times. But I managed to keep up with him. Then he stopped and went in a doorway. He had said he was going to a bar but this was no bar, it looked like the entrance to a block of apartments.

I crossed the street. I saw him press a buzzer. It must have been one of those you can unlock from inside because as he pushed at the door it opened and he went in. I hung around for a while and looked up at the windows to see if I could see him looking out, or maybe a light would go on. There is a café opposite and tables near the window. I decided to go in and sit there with a coffee and wait for him to come out. I kept my eye on the door, hardly ever averting my gaze. But no-one came out.

After an hour I ordered another coffee and got through 20 cigarettes, all the time watching the door. But nothing. It was getting late and I was getting tired, the café was preparing to close so I decided that he must be staying there for the night.

I walked back to the apartment. He is seeing someone else, he's got a woman on the side, I thought. I had suspected this anyway, what with his long disappearances. But I would have thought he would have been going to the other side of Paris, not screwing some woman only a few streets from where we live.

But here is the strangest thing. I got back to the apartment which was in darkness. I switched the light on and, well he gave me the fright of my life...there he was, Salime, sitting in the dark smoking and drinking whisky. He stared at me with his usual look of anger and then his face broke into a big, big smile and he asked me how I was and where I had been.

I just said I had been out, for a walk and a coffee. And then the smile stopped and he looked very serious, almost angry and accusing and said:

"Jean, why do you lie so much? Everything you say is a lie."

I didn't know what to say. Eventually I said, what do you mean everything I say is a lie?

He just stubbed a cigarette out, slammed the now empty glass on the table and got up. I swear Jake, he was coming in my direction but then he turned and went out.

I shouted after him, asking where he was going now, at this time of night (it was almost midnight). But all I heard was the slam of the door. The slam, of the door... I think that's the title of a song, or maybe the lyrics, I can't remember though, not at the moment, as I write this.

Anyway, last week, things were great between us. His mood just changed. We went shopping together and he bought me a bracelet and we had a lovely romantic meal in a gorgeous bistro and he talked animatedly about his work at the mental health clinic. He said he was relieved because he didn't think he would now lose his job as the cuts at the clinic had already been implemented and his job was safe for now.

The evening ended with us, you know, going to bed (I'll spare you the details, Jake) and he was as passionate as the first time we met.

I felt great the next day and he went to work, giving me a kiss before he left, and I really felt we were a normal couple, me, his English girl living with him in Paris.

Then, just this morning, the day I write this letter, he accused me of throwing away his expensive cologne which costs 100 francs a bottle. I had been clearing out the bathroom the day before and got rid of a lot of rubbish, old deodorant sprays etc. But I know I would not have thrown away his cologne.

"You must have, otherwise where else is it?" he shouted.

I honestly don't remember throwing it away. Honestly Jake, I would never throw away something like that, especially since he had only just bought a new bottle and it would have been virtually full.

Then he said something to me, as he was putting his coat on to leave for work. He said: "You are destructive Jean, very destructive."

Then he smiled and said: "It's not your fault, I suppose. We are how we are brought up. It is all to do with childhood."

Then he left.

I'm just fed up Jake. I love him but everything with him is so strange and unpredictable. Volatile. I do still love him but I don't know how long that can last.

Maybe I should not say this because I think, or I hope, you have moved on. Moved on from us. But I just remember how simple things were between you and me even though we never got it together in that sense.

Remember the rave in Brighton?

And the rave at the back of King's Cross where we first met?

I can't believe all that happened this year, only months ago. It seems like a lifetime ago. Happy days in Earl's Court. I do miss England and London especially.

You asked if I had heard from my mum. I had told you I had tried to get back in touch with her, with a letter, after all this time. To try to at least stay in touch even if we have never been close. I sent the letter about a month ago but I have heard nothing. I tried to phone a few times but it just rang and rang and she doesn't have an answer machine.

It's sad what happened but, well, nothing to say. I cannot dwell on what happened at home. I hope she is OK and maybe if I come back to England I will go and try to see her. It's always a problem when you are an only child, as you will know. If I had a brother or a sister, I could check up on her through them.

Anyway, how are you, how is your life? Anybody special at the moment? If there is, she is a very lucky girl!!!!

Anyway, Jake, I would love you to come to Paris. Salime does not know we keep in touch and I have your letters locked in the little brown suitcase.

We would have to meet as far away from the Latin Quarter as possible. I'm sure he would not mind, maybe I am being silly, why would he object to me keeping in touch with a good friend and having him stay? But we could meet well away from where I live. I think that would be best. I don't want to provoke him and anyway, I don't really want you getting involved in things here. I want to see you on my own, relive the good times, eh? Give it some thought, I would love, no, need to see you soon. Maybe I need rescuing.

Got to go. We're out of milk. Again!

Look forward to hearing from you soon, lots of love. Jean

LATE 1989

An aeroplane descends over west London as the five o'clock night-time curtain of the day comes down. He looks from the window on the top floor of the flat in Nevern Place, in the heart of Earl's Court. He has a perfect view of the Earls Court Road with traffic snaking through, people going in and out of cafes, restaurants and pubs and backpackers trudging along looking for somewhere cheap to stay.

He places her letter carefully back in the envelope and sets it down on his desk which faces the window so he can sit here, peer out and watch life go by. He lights a cigarette and wonders which direction Paris is from where he sits. How is she, have they had another row, could he get violent, hurt her physically? Has she got the milk?

What a difference a few months make. When she had first gone to Paris to be with Salime, she promised she would keep in touch and she did.

At first her letters were so positive, they sickened him. It was like she was rubbing his nose in the fact that she had made her choice – Salime over him, Paris over London – but he had tried to be happy for her. And, he had reckoned, she would get bored with telling him how wonderful her life and Salime were and the letters would dry up and contact would eventually be lost.

She could have been just another fragment of his life that in the months and years ahead, would become a hazy memory to be reminisced about in middle age. She would have been a part of that second summer of love, of raves, of blisteringly hot weather, someone, among many, he had met in his first year in London.

Now, after this letter, he fears and, maybe, hopes Jean is crying out to him. I would love to, no, need, to see you. Maybe I need rescuing.

The words stay in his mind, interspersed with swirling thoughts and visions. Were those final sentences a cry for help or something flippant, throw-away lines, a way of ending a letter?

He remembers how Jean was always quoting titles or lines from songs. Maybe you can rescue me. Another song title or lyric he was meant to get.

He sits in Cromwells, the pub across the road from the flat, with a pint of lager. There are a couple of Aussie girls sat opposite who keep looking over. He reads her letter again, for the fifth time, studying every sentence, every comma, trying to imagine her speaking those words, trying to work out the tone. Was it casual, was it calm, was she writing collectedly? Or was she hysterical, in a state of distress, crying even? There was very little that was positive about Salime apart from the time he took her shopping and bought her the bracelet.

So what about when she followed him? Was it another woman? But how did he get home before her when she says she had stayed watching the door for so long?

Why his mood swings and what about the tearing to pieces of her character? Everything, you say is a lie. You are destructive Jean.

And then the stuff about her childhood.

He takes a sip of beer and concludes that Salime is quite possibly a psychopath. You would want to think that wouldn't you. His inner voice speaks, as it always does.

What does he know about Salime Douali? Only what Jean has told him.

Salime Douali is 25 years older than Jean. Jean Ridley. He is dark, lean and handsome. He's deep and gentle (her words) he's not like any man I've ever met. He had pointed out that at only 24 she had not met that many men, had she, how could she compare?

Now he has to think of how he will reply to her letter. What will he say, should he dwell on her problems, ask her questions? And, of course, there is the bigger question: Should he go to Paris?

For a few minutes, it dawns on him that he can just screw this letter up, set it alight and burn it all away. Why should he care? What is the point, what can he do? She had chosen this life, and she could choose to get out of it, walk away, take a plane back to London. Back to London, back to him. And as soon he thinks those words, 'back to me', he knows why he will not burn this letter. The flames are still burning in his heart and while-ever they do he will still want to know about her, how her life is going, for better or for worse.

The time to walk away was the first time he met her, the signs in her eyes, the tone of her voice, moments, glints of possible trouble, unfathomable things she said, the way she had said them. But then you fall deeper, move in closer, the flashes of a smile, the feelings of warmth, the electrical current between two people that will always keep them connected.

CHAPTER ONE SUMMER, 1989

A FEW hours ago they had been dancing, entranced, zombie-like at a rave at the back of King's Cross. Acieeed, Acieed. A night of pills, strobe lights of red, blue, gold and green, of pounding, head-exploding beats, bottled water and sweat. The sounds and sensations of the summer. The summer of 1989.

He is now spooned against her naked body in bed. Shards of blazing June sunshine laser-beam through the gap in the curtain and he desperately needs to piss.

He carefully creeps out of the bed trying not to disturb her and gets to the small bathroom of this tiny flat. As he pees he tries to rewind his memory to the night before, or rather a night that segued into morning. This morning.

He hears the creaking of the bed, she's getting up. He wishes his pee to hurry up and stop so he can grab a towel and cover up before she sees him but just as this hope leaves his head, she is behind him with a hand cupping and squeezing his bare buttock.

Morning, she says in a whisper, her mouth pressed to his ear.

He stops peeing and feels a hard-on developing. She grabs him and they return to the bed and make love again.

You don't even know her, you can hardly remember her face. What does she look like? The inner voice interrogates him, it always does.

She doesn't stay after that, once it is over she dresses, gives him a long, lingering kiss and says she has to go. He asks her if she would like to see him again, which seems a silly question since they've just spent the night together. She says she does. He asks, do you have a number, can I give you mine?

She stops at the door.

Jake, do you have a spare key?

What, for this place?

Yes.

Can I have it?

He goes into the desk drawer where there is a spare key and hands it to her. Why does she want a key? To get in. Why does she just want to get in?

He watches her place the key in a compartment in her bag. Then she blows a kiss and leaves, shutting the door carefully and quietly behind her.

He opens the sash window and waits for her to descend the steps and walk out onto the street. She turns right at the end of Nevern Place, the direction of the station.

When she is out of sight he makes the bed and smells her on the covers. A light perfumed smell, clean, feminine and sweet.

He goes to the window and lights a cigarette and looks out. Wow, what a night. The place feels lonely, he feels empty, a Sunday lethargy wilts his body, questions stab at his mind, a need to take a walk, get some air and think overwhelms to the point where he urgently grabs his jacket and gets the hell out.

You popped an E, you danced manically, the warehouse was a mass of gyrating, sweating bodies. You were not off your face, but you were pumped up with adrenaline, the excruciating drum beats of the music took hold of your senses and screwed them up into a little ball and cast them away.

You went outside where drinks were being served. She was talking to Kim and Jodie, your neighbours back at Nevern Place. They introduced you to her. Kim and Jodie walked back into the warehouse, but you and her got talking. She was flirty, gave you another E. You left with her to go to a party in South Kensington. The party was a blur of more drinks and E. After a while, and you have no idea how long, she said she lived in south London and ought to get going to catch the last tube or the night bus. But you said she could stay at your place. You were not inviting her because you planned to sleep with her. You said you would take the floor and she could have the bed. But then it gets hazy, drugs and drink combined, collided, creating a smog in your memory. You got back to Nevern Place, you began putting cushions on the floor for you to sleep on but she said she didn't mind sharing the bed with you. Who made the first sexual move? You cuddled, it just happened, wandering hands, inhibitions lowered by the E and the drink. She slept with you and you hardly knew her. A bit of conversation about the north, how long you had been in London, you went running – so did she – and her name was Jean, Jean Ridley from Liverpool but these are all the details you know of her.

And you've slept with her, fucked at least twice. Now she has the keys to your flat but you have no address or telephone number for her. Why did she want the keys, why did she not give you her number?

CHAPTER TWO

HE HAS not heard from her for weeks. Every night he has come home in anticipation. Will she be there; would she use the key? Nothing. It had obviously been a one-night stand, she had moved on and now, so must he.

People come into our lives, sometimes they stay around, become familiar, permanent fixtures. Others are short-stay, even this short, just one night. No time for emotional attachment, just a crude physical act of making love in a loveless, emotionless encounter. AKA a one-off fuck. No harm done. Sowing wild oats, plenty of time to be plunging into the meaningful seriousness of something more long-term like falling in love. Barely in his life, but now completely out of it. Swallowed up by London, this vast sprawling city that he is only just beginning to get to know. She is probably in the city, living her life, meeting new people, normal things. But she might as well be a million miles away. He has no way of contacting her. Maybe their paths would cross, by accident, by coincidences. Maybe not.

Do people remember everyone who comes into their lives, no matter how briefly or do people, like events, like places visited only once become evanescent? How long before she has left my mind? Will I still think of her, remember her by the end of this long, hot summer? Will she have left my mind like she left my flat forever? Will I still think of her even by Christmas?

Time reveals all. But now, right now, he is back on his own and as he sips a pint in Cromwells, he looks out of the window onto the Earls Court Road and sees people walking along, passing through. Backpackers, travellers, people moving along just as time does. A face, a place, real at the time but eventually erased from memory by time itself. The wave of emptiness that had hit him when he had not heard from her after a week, two weeks has been replaced by a feeling of equanimity. Easy come, easy go.

CHAPTER THREE

THEY HAVE no idea where they are going. They just follow the convoy down the M25 in the car Kim and Jodie have hired. It has been billed as the 'biggest party ever' and its location is known only by the car at the very front. They had rung the number of the Sunrise poster and were given a location as a starting-point. When they got there they were told to follow a car. It was one of a convoy of vans, cars, motorbikes. Now they are turning off the M25 and coming into long, winding roads with endless views of countryside and forest sprawled before them. The sun is slowly sinking behind the hills, lightness is dimming as if it is being turned down ready for the night ahead. He looks behind and sees cars following theirs, snaking back further than he can see. They move slowly up a hill, reach the top and there they see it and begin to hear it. In a field, less than half a mile away. He can see the flashes of laser lights stabbing at the ever-darkening sky. He winds down the window and as they get closer they feel the throb of the bass line pumping out of ginormous speakers.

They are finally at their secret destination. The miles and miles of motorway and never-ending winding country roads have brought them to where they want to be. Passengers become revellers as they stream out of vehicles and swarm to the epicentre of the rave. Inside the main arena is a mass of gyrating bodies.

The E begins to work its magic.

Everything begins to move fast, some magnetic force pulls him up, higher and higher, a charge surges through his body, he is moving through the air. He tenses up, feels like he might fall off something but he's not scared, he just holds on, holds on. The sensation eases for a few minutes then like a wave it crashes over him again, he is clammy, sweating and trying to sip some water but can't. The music sears into his consciousness, slashes of riff, beats of base reverberate through his body, locking it, then releasing it, then locking again. He is in this wonderland of sound, colour and a sea of togetherness, he is synched into a throng of shiny, smiley happy abandon. D-d-d-d dance the night away are the only words he can make out and the d-d—d sends new spasms of euphoria charging through his veins. This is A A A A-cid.

Then Black Box scream out Ride On Time. Smoke billows out, illuminated by the strobe lights which freeze-frame the windmilling bodies.

And he thinks he has seen her. A flash, a freeze-frame, like a million flash bulbs going off at once. Her face again, a picture frozen for just a few seconds. And he sees her again. Then her face disappears and then he sees her again. Bang, boom, bang, boom.

He tries to get to her, moves forward, squeezing through the crowd to where he thinks she is. He looks up, looks ahead, sweat pours from him. He tries to get to that face in this crowd, reaching out, moving on weak legs, the noise and the lights seem to will him on, energy-charge him, fuel his mad determination. He keeps going, through the bodies but it's beginning to feel hopeless. He stops, tries to see, turns around, peers, strains his eyes and all he sees are hundreds of faces, smiling, happy, crazy faces. But not hers. Not Jean's.

He sees her again; this time it is a few weeks later at a rave in Clink Street not far from Tower Bridge. He tries to find her after seeing her face in the strobe lights. He barges through people, hell-bent on getting to her, touching her trying to make her feel real.

He comes to a door that leads him down a set of spiral stairs, into the bowels of the place, the only light coming from the street lamps bathing in.

At the far end of the room he hears a cigarette lighter flicker and it lights up a cigarette. He sees a flash of a face and then the figure is just a silhouette. He moves towards it, closer and closer. As he gets nearer, he hears deep, needy inhalation of tobacco, sees the hot, red glow of the cigarette, smells the smoke being exhaled. As he gets closer still, the cigarette is tossed to the ground, still lit. As he gets ever-closer, he thinks he will be able to make out the figure, put a face to it. But there is nothing, no-one. Nobody here. He picks up the cigarette, careful not to burn his fingers. It is receding rapidly, already about halfway down. He takes it over to a window where the light is better. He stares at the cigarette and around the filter is a red ring of lipstick. It is burning itself out now, getting close to his fingertips as he holds it and stares until he is forced to drop it. He stubs it out with his foot, vigorously, almost petulantly.

CHAPTER FOUR

HE DECIDES to give the E and the raves a rest and starts to question whether the whole scene is really for him. He has been to one just about every other weekend over the last few months and is not sure whether he is getting bored by them or is just tired, or too old, or both. He has started a new job as a researcher on a current affairs magazine. The work is demanding, challenging and immensely fulfilling. He feels he should use his weekends to rest, slow down, walk and read.

He realises he's been doing less and less reading, especially at weekends. There was a time when he devoured a couple of novels in a week, but he has read nothing of late.

Your mind is empty save for the regular returning thoughts of her, of that night and where she might be now.

Thoughts of her cartwheel through his mind again as he lies in bed exhausted from the rave.

Will I ever see her again? Will I come home one day and find her, sipping a glass of wine, waiting, waiting for me.

Why would she come now? It was weeks ago, forget about her, move on.

The inner voice commands, it is stern, it tells him she was a one-off, a casual encounter who had never meant to mean anything to him. But it still nagged at him, the question: Why did she ask for the keys? To let herself in.

It has been a long day at the office and after work he drops by Waterstones in High Street Kensington to stockpile a few books, ready for the more relaxing weekend he has promised himself.

Back at the flat he places the carrier bag full of books on the desk, takes off his jacket and puts it on the back of the chair then takes out one of the books and settles into the chair. The light is still good from the summer evening sun.

He opens the book but instead of reading, he glances over to the bed. The cover on one side is pulled back. He always made his bed in the morning, he had this morning, hadn't he?

His eyes freeze, his mind whizzes.

He goes to the bed and touches the mattress. Cold. He sniffs the linen. Trying to smell her. Sniffing for clues, as if some atrocious crime has been committed. He knows her smell, thinks he can smell it now. He checks the pillow, sniffs, then looks for hair, blonde hair, her hair. This is a pointless exercise in this dim light so he flicks on the main light switch and looks again. Searching, closely like a forensic scientist combing a murder scene. But there is nothing, not to the naked eye, maybe a magnifying glass would reveal some finite clue.

You might just have forgotten to make it. Or might have been in a rush. You may not have had time to pull the blanket onto the other side. This is plausible, this is the likeliest scenario.

He pulls the whole sheet right back to check the full length of the bed. She might have dropped an ear-ring, left a dirt mark with her feet.

But there is nothing.

He looks round the flat to see if there is anything out of place, everyday objects he always puts in exactly the same place that are not where they should be. He checks the kitchen for droplets of water in the sink, the shower for hair, the toothpaste to see if any has been used (He had only just bought a new tube).

But there is nothing. Nothing else out of place or unusual or suspicious.

What are you looking for? Are you looking because you really, honestly think she has been here or are you looking because you want her to have been here?

It doesn't matter. There are no more clues and maybe the partly made bed isn't even a clue either.

Fuck, fuck, fuck. He has to stop this obsession with her. He goes to the window and opens the sash as far as it will go. He lights a cigarette and sits on the window ledge.

The Earls Court Road is gushing with the early evening tourists, travellers, locals. How many people pass us by, how many people do we see that we will never speak to? The catch of an eye, the momentary glance, the passing each other by, camera shutter-speed awareness of other people who look at us and we at them and who we will never know or even speak to.

It's getting late and a breeze chills him as he puts out the cigarette.

He pours a small whisky, turns off the big light and puts on the desk lamp. He opens his new book and immerses himself into another world, other people, other times.

15

CHAPTER FIVE

TO HIS shame he has never read Kafka. A few nights after the unmade bed mystery he arrives home and sees a book on the bed. He looks around the flat, listens, frozen. Is she here, here right now? That is not his book. He can see the title, The Complete Works of Kafka. He can see from here it is fairly dog-eared. He can hear only the hum of the Earls Court noise and the gentle drone of the fridge in the kitchenette. He can see no other signs of someone here, no discarded coat, or jacket or shoes. He says loudly, Hello, Hello.

Silence is the only response.

He takes off his jacket and ritualistically puts it on the back of his chair and goes to the bed. He picks up the book, paperback. He flicks through, its pages are nicotine-yellowed by time, by age. He turns over pages, slowly, looking for scribblings or highlights.

It smells musty, so strongly, that it makes him sneeze. How old is this book? The page where it tells you who published and when seems to be missing. Who had bought it, who had read it, how many hands had it passed through, how many pairs of eyes had read its words, joined up its sentences, absorbed it and interpreted its meaning?

An unmade bed he was convinced he had made and now a book he knows is not his. Had it been placed there as a cryptic message, a sign? Or had it been left behind in a rush to leave, forgotten?

As he sits on the bed with this book in his hand, he suddenly hears heavy, torrential rain, it sounds like someone is throwing frozen peas at a metal bucket. He opens the window and looks down onto the Earls Court Road. People are standing in doorways to shelter or darting down the street to get out of the deluge. Cars slush through the water that has turned the road into a stream. He usually feels happy and secure and glad he is at home when the rain is heavy. But now he wants it to stop, so he can go out, get away from the flat, from this room, from this bed, from this book, from all this mystery.

He puts his jacket on, zipping up to the collar and goes out. He braves the downpour, dashing across the road to Cromwells. Over a pint, he takes out a notebook and pen and writes her a note. A note to Jean.

Dear Jean

Please, if you have been here, or rather you are here if you are reading this, please tell me you have been, that it is you. The book. The unmade bed. Tell me you are OK. Do you want to see me? There is no commitment required, we can just be friends, go for a drink. I am not angry with you for coming into the flat. I just need to know it's you. It would be nice to see you. Why not wait until I come back? I'm usually home by six.

Yours
Jake

In the morning he puts the note in an envelope marked JEAN in thick black letters and places it on the bed. She could not miss it. He positions it between two of the oblongs that make up the pattern of the quilt, between two lines of stitching so that he will know whether it had been moved, even by a fraction, even if she places it intricately back where she found it to make it look as though it hadn't been touched. He puts the Kafka book next to it. He makes sure the window is secure so a draft or gust of wind cannot blow it even slightly out of place. The trap is set.

Hyde Park is thronged with people soaking up the July sun which even at 5pm sears down. The city is hot, sweaty, humid, the air heavy, you can feel it weighing down on you, enervating you as you move, as you wish you could just bask joyfully in its warmth. Girls lay topless, some in the full scorching glare of the sun, determined to acquire a Mediterranean-style bronzed body, others take sensible respite from the heat under trees. Office workers read the Evening Standard which carries some scandal involving Dame Shirley Porter and Westminster Council. There is something in the air, not just the heat, that threatens, that says this is not to last. The weather never stays the same.

He walks through the park on to Kensington Gardens, on to High Street Kensington and then turns left down the Earls Court Road, the drone of the traffic pounds and the smell of petrol fumes gives him a slight headache, his throat is dry, his clothes heavy. He looks forward to an ice cold beer sitting out on the window ledge and watching the world go by.

No Cromwells tonight, it is too hot and there is nowhere outside to sit.

These thoughts are just a backdrop melody in his mind though.

At the forefront, her. Will the letter have been moved, or gone? Has she answered it?

On the landing, he puts his ear to his door. Nothing. He opens the door and shouts, Hello, Hello.

He goes in and closes the door behind him. He looks on the bed. Kafka has gone but his letter is on on top of the pillow.he feels inside the envelope and takes out a piece of paper. It is his note but there is a reply at the bottom.

Dear Jake,

Give me just a little more time.

Jean x

Her laconic message is encouraging at first, but after much pondering; infuriating, mysterious, and meaningless. He wonders what she needs 'just a little more time' for. Could she not have added some sort of explanation as to why she was coming into his flat? Why do you need a little more time to see someone? Someone you may not know very well but who you have slept with and who you might see fit to get to know a little better.

Days after he finds no sign she has been in the flat again – no abandoned books, no unmade bed. But at least he knows, has had it confirmed, she has been here, the bed unmade by her, the book left by her. At least he is not, after all, going mad. It bothers him, though, that she comes to the flat. Someone he met only once, even though sex had been involved, someone whose face is fast fading from memory, who he has not seen or spoken to for weeks, has access to his home.

Work is going well but he wishes it was a bigger magazine with more people. There is just him and three others, comprising the editor, a writer and another researcher.

He has had a drink with them all, just once, but there are no big drinkers except for Paula who is a researcher, in her late 30s and frumpy.

It is hardly the glamorous, cut-throat world he believed journalism would be and he needs to meet more people. Now he has cut out the raves, weekends are solitary, he walks, he runs, he reads and drinks in Cromwells. There are girls he makes contact with in the pub but it never leads to anything. Friends are few and Kim and Jody have gone back to Australia.

Much of the clientele in Cromwells are travellers, just passing through and usually in groups. He also notices a lot of couples travelling together.

He considers that he ought to go further afield to do his drinking. Maybe South Kensington, although he imagines the girls there would be quite stuck up and only interested in guys with cash. He has cash but he's not in their Yuppie league.

He looks at the flat, which isn't a flat, it's what is called a studio. Bed in the main living area, a tiny kitchen and small bathroom. He loves the place but wonders if he will ever live anywhere in London that is bigger. A proper flat with several rooms and everything completely separate.

For now, this will have to do and he is settling in in Earl's Court. He is happy to do as he pleases, whatever and whenever that may be. He decides the best way of meeting people is through work and he needs to start looking for a job in a bigger company.

He walks down the Earls Court Road on the way back to the flat. He opens the door, switches on the light and sees it immediately.

An A4 envelope with his name written in handwriting he recognizes as hers. He feels the envelope and then opens it. Several folded A4 pages.

Her story. He doesn't want to read it and be disappointed. He puts it on his desk and gets a tumbler of whisky, lights a cigarette and sits back. Now he reads, now he will find out, he hopes.

He was running away, her father did not need to shoot the young guy who was fleeing after breaking into their home. He shot him twice in the back, dead.

Dave Ridley had dreamed of being a star. When Jean was a kid she saw little of him – he was out most nights touring the working men's clubs of the north belting out 1960s Motown songs, hoping to be discovered, hoping to escape working in a factory. In fact, he felt trapped. Jean's mother had fallen unexpectedly pregnant. Dave told Carol to get a termination, they were too young, he had plans, he would get a better life for them both, he would become a star.

Carol had always longed to be a mother, thought Dave's dreams were just that and refused to get rid of the baby. The chasm between them grew and when Jean was born Dave hardly wanted to know, immersing himself in his performing. An unwanted child, a burden, a barrier to the life of glittering fame and fortune Dave Ridley thought would one day come.

When Dave saw a way of making extra money through selling drugs, it was irresistible. He gave up his job and it meant he could live the nightlife – the clubs, the women on the side and the money from drugs.

On the few occasions he was at home, the rows were played out violently in front of a little girl not wanted. Carol was drinking heavily, letting herself go and when Dave came home he came home to an ugly woman whose only ambition in life had been to have a fucking kid. How low you set your bar, he would say to her. Is this – pointing to the young girl – all there is?

When the audiences cheered their applause after his ballads had brought tears to their eyes, Dave knew this was the world in which he wanted to live.

The scally knew where Dave lived and he knew where the drugs would be. He knew where to look – Dave had befriended him from one of the clubs and took him back to the house one night. They scored and the scally saw where Dave kept his gear.

Days later with no cash and desperate for a hit, the scally broke in one night. Dave Ridley heard the glass being broken. He reached under the bed for the weapon no-one knew he had. He had bought the gun after the house had been broken into before, although he had never used it.

A guy at one of the clubs told him he could get the shooter and that if he was dealing drugs he should have one.

Dave descended the stairs, the scally saw him and made a run for it. Dave shot him once and then again. Neighbours came rushing out, someone called an ambulance, Dave Ridley got as far away as possible and, once arrangements had been made, fled to London, never to be seen again.

Carol's drinking got worse, another man moved in, the daughter she had always wanted, the only good thing to come out of her life, had become resentful, hateful towards her and the life she had given Jean.

The man's name was Peter and he made no attempt to love or treat Jean as his own.

Her father had deserted them, he had sent birthday and Christmas cards with money inside for a year or two but this eventually stopped. Jean suspected he had not made it to superstardom and was probably shacked up with a woman and another kid somewhere in London, penniless and drunk. She tried to imagine him as a star, she kept an eye out for him on TV and in the papers. When she listened to the Top 40 chart show on Radio One on a Sunday evening she hoped his name would be said, his song announced, even if it was only just a new entry at number 39 or even 40. Instead it was The Specials, Wham! Spandau, Duran Duran who took all the glories. Maybe Boy George is really her dad dressed up like that and with another name. She loved Karma Chameleon and would pretend, for a while, it was her dad singing. Boy George is my dad.

And then the music would stop and the reality hit.

And the cruel kids in the playground would chant: Your daddy didn't want you, yer daddy didn't love you. That's why yer fucken daddy left.

Then the riots kicked Toxteth when it was already down, when a childhood could surely not have got any worse. 1981, first Brixton then other cities burned, too. Cars blazing in the stench of hatred, the no hope that came from unemployment billowing through those working class streets, fanning the flames. Night after night of rioting, - hurled, stones, bottles, petrol bombs. She was a kid of the street, she saw it all. Where's yer fucken daddy? Yer daddy didn't want yer, yer daddy didn't love yer. That's why yer fucken daddy left.

One night Peter came home steaming drunk. She was sat up watching some TV, her mother long gone to bed, the gin almost knocking her out.

Peter sat next to a by-now teenaged Jean on the sofa. He put his arm around her. She knew something was not right immediately – he had never shown her any affection. Before she knew what was happening, he had pulled her face to his and he tried to kiss her. She managed to get up and free herself of him.

Yer dirty fucken bastard, yer fucken arsehole.

Yeah, and I bet youse are like yer fucken mother, a fucken frigid bitch.

Go fuck yer fucken self cos no-one ad fucken fuck youse yer perv.

In her teens she worked hard at school, teachers told her she had a talent for writing and she decided she wanted to be a writer. What kind of writer, a writer of what? She didn't know. She got a clutch of O and A Levels, studied at college and then in her 20s decided she would go to London. As far away as possible from the glass and dog dirt-strewn streets of Toxteth. There had never been anything for her in Liverpool, from the day she was born. She had few friends and lived within herself.

This was her story. And when she had finished this story, she wrote:

So Jake, I'm a bit messed up. I'm trying to get on with my life, I'm doing a writing course here in London and waitressing jobs. I did get a letter from my father a couple of years ago. He told me he was in London. He gave an address, of course I went there but there was no sign of him, the woman living there had not heard of him.

I came to your flat during the day because I waitress at night. I live in a horrible shared flat in Clapham on a really rough estate. There's screaming and shouting all day long, so I just wanted somewhere to go for some peace, to read and sleep. I should have told you, I should have got in touch but sometimes I just can't face people. The raves are my escape, they give me a feeling of togetherness with so many other people who don't make any demands on me. The E takes me out of myself, the music just sets me free, shakes off my past and makes me feel like everyone else. Normal, no baggage, nothing weighing me down. Everyone is the same. Nobody is labelled. Everyone is just as one.

And then I met you and I don't usually sleep with someone I hardly know. I suppose the E and the adrenaline just kicked in. And, of course, I liked you.

Well, I've told you all this because it is good for me to write things down. Maybe I should talk more, too. Now you know all this about me, my background, I wonder whether you would really want to get involved with someone, someone like me. I think maybe you are too nice, too focused in your life that the last thing you need is someone like me. I think we could, at best, only be friends and not get too deep. But I would like to get to know you, if you still want to get to know me.

Write me another note. I'll come to the flat – but I would prefer you not to be there – and if you say you think it's best we don't see each other again, I'll leave the key and I won't ever come back and I'll just disappear and you can just wipe me clean from your mind and move on and I will do the same. And maybe it's best that you decide to do this. But it is up to you. There is a song, Together in Electric Dreams. That could be me and you. Only together in electric dreams.

But if you say you want to see me – and it's good news!!! – I'll come by at the weekend. I promise.

Yours
Jean
X

CHAPTER SIX

SHE SIPS the wine, tiny sips he notes, as he looks at her face, her beautiful face, her blonde hair shines, almost reflectively, her eyes sea-blue. They are in Bistro Benito just round the corner from the flat. He has never been in but it always looks cosy from the outside. They are served by the owner, a very short rotund Italian who calls Jake sir and Jean mad-am.

They talk about her writing course and books she likes reading – Kafka, as he already knows, is one of her favourites.

I don't understand people who don't read, she says.

My mother never read and neither did my father. I know you read a lot Jake, I've seen all your books in the flat.

He tells her he is a voracious reader, never watches television, hates the cinema but likes the radio.

She smiles, a warm smile that he now remembers from when they met at the rave.

He asks if she is still living on the estate in Clapham.

Yes, she is.

It's a shared flat with a couple of other girls and I think one is on the game. They both do drugs. The estate is full of dealers and low-life. Just round the corner from Clapham Junction. But it's fairly cheap. But I need to look for somewhere else.

She grabs his hand and holds it. I'm so glad you wanted to see me again. And, well, I'm sorry for going into the flat and not waiting for you. I shouldn't have done that.

He tells her it is Ok and he will help her find somewhere else to live.

And then it hits him. She could move in. Into Nevern Place.

Hey, she responds, Jake you're so kind but let's just get to know each other before we start living together.

He nods agreement as she fishes in her bag and takes out the key to the flat.

Here, take this back.

No, I want you to keep it. Go to the flat any time you like. And wait for me.

He tells her she can stay the night but she insists on getting home.

As he sees her off at Earls Court station he says, when will I see you again?

Ah, that's a lovely song, I love that song.

He frowns. She smiles.

The weekend. I'll come to the flat, Saturday afternoon. I know where there's going to be a big rave.

The rave is in Brighton and she tells him she has the whole weekend off and she wants to stay overnight in a cheap hotel on the seafront.

The heat hits you as you come out of Brighton station. They make their way towards the seafront with hours to kill before the rave.

Thousands of people pack the beach, someone's ghetto blaster plays Gloria Estefan singing Don't Want to Lose You.

Jean is wearing tight shorts and a t-shirt, sex on legs, he thinks and he is thrilled when she takes his hand and they walk along hand-in-hand like established lovers, the two of them, an item.

They find a cheap hotel in a side-street off the seafront, she asks for a double room. They leave their rucksacks there and go back onto the seafront, the heat hits like a blast from an oven as soon as you step outside.

Lunch is in a fish and chip restaurant on the seafront and after a few beers he makes her laugh with his impromptu impression of Neil Kinnock as they seem to lighten up with each other before going back to the hotel to change and get ready to go to the rave.

The kid comes running out from nowhere, the car screeches to a halt but hits him, lays him out cold on the road. Jake dashes over, the kid is just a few feet from him.

Where are you going, come on we have to go, Jean shouts from the pavement.

Other people arrive, including the kid's mum and dad. The mother screams hysterically, someone rushes to a phone box to call an ambulance.

He is getting in the way and a policeman comes over. He rejoins Jean on the pavement.

Come on, we have to get going.

He is dumbfounded.

A kid's just been knocked over, we ought to make sure everything is OK.

The policeman's here now, there's nothing you can do. Come on.

She marches ahead but when he catches up with her he says, weren't you concerned for the kid? We were the first on the scene, and you were just going to go on ahead and not try to help?

She stops. Anger crumples her face.

Do you want to go to this rave or not?

Yes, we'll get to the rave, I just wanted to help the kid.

He feels quite shaken, unsure of whether it is seeing the kid get hit or her angry reaction making him feel this way.

They walk on in silence. The bum-bam-bum of the rave music gets louder but he is in no mood for it.

Jean gets into it, pops an E and joins the throng throwing themselves about to Ride On Time.

He stands around and sips a beer, feels awkward. Two images in his head: The kid being hit by the car and his body flopping to the ground.

And her face when she had asked him if he wanted to go to the rave.

There is something strange about her, you know it. Something not quite right. You don't want to be here. You had not really thought about whether you wanted to get involved with her when you had read her letter. You just steamed in. Is she too screwed up, should you have ended it before it began?

They return to the hotel in the early hours. They get into bed in silence. He lays there waiting for her to fall asleep. But about five minutes later she says, put your arm around me, give me a cuddle. They kiss passionately for a minute and then she turns away and falls asleep.

You would have preferred to have spent the evening eating in a nice romantic restaurant and then walking arm-in-arm along the seafront. You would have liked to talk to her more, get to know her better.

The rave wasn't the right place for that to happen.

Late morning, they crawl out of bed.

She says she wants to stay another night – she isn't working until Monday evening. He tells her he is due in work.

Phone in sick Jake, no-one will know. Please, let's stay another night, I'd really like a nice relaxing day and then go for a nice meal and a drink tonight. Please, go on, live a little!

You shouldn't call in sick, you should go back to London, you shouldn't be so reckless over this girl, this woman. You still don't really know her.

They stay another night. The day is spent walking along the beach, he buys her a kiss-me-quick hat and candyfloss and they take a ride on a fairground carousel. She laughs and smiles the whole day, he has never seen anyone so happy.

In the evening they find a cosy restaurant just off the seafront, their appetites fuelled by the sea air, the walking and the heat.

Why did she react like she did when the kid got knocked over?

This nags away in the back of his mind, the image of her angry face intermittently flashing before his eyes. But now he can see a beautiful happy girl, woman, who wants to be with him, in Brighton, on this scorching hot night.

You are falling for her...falling, falling deeper and deeper.

The sky is a blaze of pinkish orange as the sun begins to sink. The swish of the tide comes in and is soothing and the temperature begins to abate with a refreshing sea breeze cooling their faces and blowing Jean's luscious blonde hair as they hold hands and walk.

Then she stops. He looks at her, almost a silhouette now with the golden orange of an ever-darkening sky in the background.

She holds out her arms and pulls him to her and kisses him, full-on lovers' kissing. They only stop when two young guys clap loudly and one says, you're in there mate.

CHAPTER SEVEN

A FEW weeks after Brighton he persuades her to move into Nevern Place. After seeing her flat on the estate in Clapham he tells her there is no need to live like that, running the gauntlet of drug dealers and muggers every time she comes home late at night and living in a soul-less, damp-ravaged flat with two other girls who looked as rough as sandpaper.

She is reluctant at first, saying it is too soon for them to live together.

He tells her to give it a try and if it doesn't work out he will help her find another place, maybe close by in Earls Court.

She moves in with her two rucksacks packed with clothes, CDs and books. She also has a small battered brown suitcase that looks like a prop from some 1930s movie. She tells him her grandmother used it to carry books to school when she was a girl and that she treasures this little case.

The case is heavy, there must be something inside it. He notices it also has a lock on it.

He asks her, what you got in here then?

Oh, nothing, just a few things.

She takes it from him and puts it on the other side of the room, behind a chair.

What's in that case? She doesn't want you to know.

Over the next few weeks, they live as a proper couple, cooking cheap pasta meals together, drinking a bottle of wine each evening while Fairground Attraction, or Simply Red, or Phil Collins (all her favourites) play in the background. When they are not in bed they read, or sit on the window ledge smoking, watching Earl's Court go by or go out for a pint in Cromwell's.

He loves that when they are in the flat and planning to go nowhere she likes to lounge around in just her bra and panties and sometimes naked. He comes home and sometimes finds her leaning out of the window with a cigarette and wearing only a top, naked from the waist down. It turns him on and she is always compliant when he comes and grabs her, puts his hand between her arse cheeks and arouses her into an early evening bout of fucking before he showers and they open the wine.

Happiness, this is it. A beautiful girl, wine, cold beers and a 1989 summer of searing heat. London seems sexier than ever, alive, they are enjoying the final months of the decade, the decade they grew up, turned from teenagers into adults and made their way in the world. Thatcher's Children.

How long will this last, is she really the one? You've been in London less than a year, maybe you should be playing the field, not getting in too deep.

On the way home one night he walks down the Earls Court Road towards Nevern Place and peers up at their little flat. Our little flat. The window is open as it has been for months now in this seemingly never-ending, blissful summer. Our Place. My Girl. From those lonely January and February days of knowing no-one and wondering the streets of this city, of killing time reading books and newspapers in railway stations, of sipping pints in pubs on his own, of having his mind pranged constantly by home-sickness and doubt about this place, now he has found happiness and someone. Someone like him. The Earl's Court has been kind to him, its streets have accommodated him as a stranger, a new arrival and have kept him going through these bitter months and now it has given him the happiest days of his life so far. He feels alive, he feels he belongs.

Maybe it's all too good to be true. You still don't know her, you need to get to know her, don't count on all this lasting. The summer of 89 will not last forever, its candle will be blown out, and the rave will come to an end.

CHAPTER EIGHT

AN AZURE sky, a soft early-morning breeze fanning through the window, a tepid shower to refresh, ready for another hot, sweaty day and a sleeping beauty in his bed having a lie-in as she has no work today. He dresses, grabs his bag and kisses her, his lips just a touch, gentle and with love. She stirs and smiles.

He will not see her again for days, though he does not know this when he leaves the flat and sets off for work.

The note, and that is all it is, is there on the bed when he gets home.

Dear Jake

I'm really sorry, I've got to go away for a few days, two, maybe three, something has come up. I've got your work number, I'll try and call you soon.

Love Jean

PS Jake, are you really happy, is this you? Maybe you should ask yourself who you are, what you want.

He looks in the wardrobe and drawers. Most of her stuff is still here – she has taken only one of her rucksacks and, of course, the mysterious, precious brown, battered suitcase.

He takes a beer from the fridge, lights a cigarette and sits on the window ledge.

Cryptic questions, the briefest of notes, little explanation, a tenuous promise to phone, a vague timescale, 'two maybe three days'. All she can spare in words and time after everything they have enjoyed these past few weeks, the peace, the tranquility, the togetherness, getting to know each other, long nights wrapped up in each other. Now this, a hand grenade lobbed onto the path he thought they were both treading, the path to...well he doesn't know where but why could it not last just a little bit longer, just for weeks, for months, just enough time to make it meaningful?

He needs to get out of the flat and after chain-smoking five cigarettes decides to go for a run.

Up the Earls Court Road, dodging pedestrians, into High Street Kensington, a hesitation as he thinks about running through Holland park but decides to run up to Kensington Gardens, as fast as he can, weaving around the shoppers and tourists. Then he is there, into the green and open land of Kensington Gardens, running at a pace now, and starting to sweat, his mind racing with the questions, her questions, are you happy, is this what you want?

Maybe you should ask who you are. Her favourite song invades his head, It's Got To Be Perfect, Fairground Attraction, a soundtrack to her questions, but he is determined to run it off, run all this out of his mind and when he runs across the gardens and into Hyde Park his head begins to clear, her questions stop interrogating him, the song ends and his inner voice speaks once more.

You've got to calm down about all this, you've got to take it more casually, this is probably not going to last forever.

The weekend arrives and she has not returned, there is no call to his work, the 'two, maybe three' days have just turned into five.

The rave is in a warehouse under the Westway, just off the Portobello Road. The organisers have created a fairground theme with slides, a carousel and bouncy castles. The vibrations of the bum-bam-bum-bam of the music shoot through his body and, fuelled by an E, he dances manically in the sea of bodies, out of it on pent-up aggression and surplus energy and he moves, and dances until the sweat flows off him. He takes off his t-shirt, as other guys have, abandoning inhibitions, riding on a helter-skelter of emotions that he cannot really describe because right now, nothing matters anymore and when Ride On Time comes on he finds a new energy building up. He squints as tears flood his eyes and he realises he is crying.

Her name is Pili, French, brunette, hippyish, Beatrice Dalle looks.

He is back at her place after the rave. She lives in a shared flat in, of all places, Soho, at the back of Old Compton Street. She is already up sipping coffee when he opens his eyes in this stranger's bed.

She smiles and brings a mug of coffee to him. He sits up in bed and realises he is naked. He places the mug on the bedside table. He sees his clothes discarded on a chair. He gets up and promptly dresses.

You can take a shower if you like.

That's Ok, I'll have one when I get back to my place.

Dressed, he sips the black coffee and says, Soho must be a great place to live, everything on your doorstep, vibrant.

It is good for work, work is close.

What do you do?

I'm a peep show model, you know the ones where the man puts one pound into the slot machine and I am there, naked and play with myself.

Right.

You had better get going after you have drunk your coffee. I have to go to work soon and need to take a shower.

He puts his cup down and grabs and kisses her. This lasts for a few seconds and then she gently pulls away.

His coffee is finished and he asks her if she wants to go out for a meal sometime.

No, I am very busy, I work most nights.

Do you want to see me again?

No, Jake, you are very nice, but I don't want to take it any further. It's nothing personal, I like you, but I just never get involved. I like to meet a guy, have a good time, fuck and then finish. This is my life for now.

Ok, no problem. Well, I had better get going, let you have your shower.

She smiles, opens the door and pecks him on the cheek.

In her strong French accent, she says, au revoir, be lucky Jake. Au revoir, you too, take care. As he walks down Old Compton Street, he vows he will never crave one-off sex.

He feels drained, emotionally empty, the memory of sex with Pili is hazy and now feels pointless, shallow and loneliness envelops him. It's the same feeling he had when Jean had left the flat on the morning after the night they had met. Never before had he wanted a long-term relationship more than he does now, something solid, tangible, reliable, continuous. Love. It's got to be …. Perfect. Her song, her familiar, comforting sound. To lie in bed with her now, to be in Nevern Place now with that fucking song playing…he had got sick of hearing it at one point but now he so wishes, so yearns for her, the flat, the sound, the song, the music, the everything about her.

As he walks from Soho to Earls Court he thinks about the weeks Jean and he have had, before she went away. He yearns for her to come back, for nothing to be wrong, for there to be no mystery, no secrets, no lack of trust. He wants a glass of wine, a comforting bowl of pasta, he wants to hold her in his arms and never again let her go.

Her going away, her absence, the one-night stand with Pili is submerging him into love, falling, falling in love for this woman who has come into his life in small, brief nuggets and when he went to the rave, and when he slept with Pili, it was his harder edge getting back at her, trying to prove he could move on. But the centre of him is soft and his centre, he knows now, is his real self.

The inner voice seems to have taken the weekend off. It seems to have nothing to say other than: *You don't know this woman, can she bring you happiness, with all her mystery, with all her troubled past? She may not want what you want, she may not see it like you see it, she may not feel the same way.*

He has answered her questions. Is this what you really want? Yes, without any doubt. Who are you? I'm a normal guy, I like a few beers, I'm just me. And I want to share my life and care for and love somebody who loves me.

CHAPTER NINE

MONDAY, BACK in Nevern Place she sits on the bed reading her Kafka book.

A bottle of wine on the table to be opened along with two glasses. A pan of pasta sauce is boiling and spitting on the stove for dinner. Their dinner. They make love for most of the evening, stopping only to have sips of wine and cigarettes – the pasta is abandoned.

She is sorry she had to go away – she went back to Liverpool to see her mother but it had not gone well. Her mother is drinking more than ever, the house is filthy, her bloke lazes around all day, drinking, jobless and hopeless.

He says he is sorry and hugs her tightly, to protect her, to keep her close, to make her feel loved.

I'm not sad, Jake, this is the life my mother has chosen for herself. I think she still blames dad, but she's had years to move on, to get over it. Instead she just wallows in pity and drink with a man who just uses her for sex and somewhere to stay. You know Jake, I cannot ever remember the time when my mum must have been normal, you know, happy, and with it and functioning. I made the effort to go and see her but there were no hugs or kisses. I knocked on the door and she just said, oh, it's you and let me in as if I had just come back from popping out to the shops for something and had never been away and not seen her for months. But she's chosen this and I can't stand seeing her like this so that's it. I don't think I ever want to go back to Liverpool. The city is so sad after Hillsborough, all I can think of is those poor people. But the city, oh I don't know, what with my childhood and everything that has happened there. I don't think I want to see my mother again.

What, you're never going to see her again?

Exactly. She's chosen her life and I've chosen mine.

But she's still your mum.

No she isn't. She's never been my mum, not a mum I can remember. She's cold, she's drunk, she's lost it. Well she's lost me now. No wonder dad fucked off all those years ago.

He refills their glasses and lets her onslaught continue.

How can you be like that to your own daughter? Is her life so meaningless that she can't even try to mend all the … all the broken bits there are between us? You know what, I wonder what sort of life dad is living? I wonder if he's, I don't know, living the life he wanted, whether he escaped her and went on to live a great, happy life? Here, somewhere in London.

She rummages in her bag and takes out a birthday card.

He must have thought about me. He stopped sending me a birthday card in the years I was a kid when he left us. This was on the sideboard at home. At least mum kept it and didn't open it and destroy it.

She hands him the card, he opens it. To Jean, happy birthday to my darling girl, Dad. Xxx

He hands it back to her after looking at the postmark.

Well he's still in London, he says, it's got a London postmark.

He is sure she knows this but she goes quiet, like it hasn't registered.

A moment later she looks at him and says, in a voice that is despairing rather than excited, he's still in London Jake, somewhere. Somewhere, he's out there in this big city. He could be anywhere, he could be close, maybe I've seen him in the street, maybe he has seen me.

London's a big place, he says, and when did you last see him? Would you recognise him?

It is something in her face that tells him she does not want to find her father.

Staring away from Jake with tears in her eyes, she says quietly, if I found him, my dad, I wouldn't need him, would I?

Need who?

She stares into space, then looks at him as if landing back down on earth, like she has been to another place.

Nobody, she says softly, nobody.

She swigs the rest of her half-full glass of wine straight down and goes to bed. He stays up a little longer, finishing the wine more slowly and smokes a cigarette at the window.

It's late and there are only a few stragglers down the Earls Court Road.

The sky is clear, the moon on its back, the hum of the London traffic goes on, a train rattles its way underground as he stubs out the cigarette and drains his wine glass. Tomorrow is on its way.

CHAPTER TEN

THERE ARE four M&S bags on the bed when he gets home. Jean is making pasta.

He asks her what is in the bags.

Prezzies for you. I've got you some new clothes.

Bag one, a blue cardigan.

Bag two a pair of trousers, green and clearly for an older person.

Bag three four plain shirts and a few ties. None of them, the ties, nor the shirts, would he have been seen dead in.

Bag four, an assortment of belts and braces. She wants him to look more mature, she says. He wears the clothes of a teenager. He protests, I'm 23 not 93. She tells him to try the clothes on. Horrendous is the only word he can think of to describe how the clothes look on, especially the cardigan and trousers.

You look good, more sophisticated, she insists when he returns from the bedroom to the kitchen where she is taking the pasta off the flame.

Jean, why do you want me to look 30 years older than I am?

I don't, but you dress like a teenager.

I have two modern suits for work and I like jeans and t-shirts. What next, a pipe and slippers?

She slams the pan down on the draining board and sits on the bed with her head in her hands.

Hey, what's the matter?

She is sobbing. He hadn't meant to hurt her feelings. She wipes her eyes.

If you don't like them, I'll take them back

What to say next. He cannot say he likes them really, or that he will wear the clothes.

She gets up from the bed and grabs her jacket and leaves, slamming the door. He rushes to the top of the stairs and shouts for her to come back. The response is the slamming of the outside door.

Irrational, illogical, unfathomable behaviour, she's crazy.

But he calms himself down and then beats himself up for being so unkind. She bought them for him, out of kindness, and here is throwing that kindness in her face.

But why does she want you to look older? These are clothes for someone 40 years older than you. You still go to raves for Christ's sake.

She returns about an hour later, hurt still etched on her face. He says he is sorry, that he should not have been so ungrateful. The next day when he comes home from work the bags of clothes are gone. She tells him she has taken them to a charity shop.

Days go by and he waits for her to talk about looking for her father. But there is no mention of him. Surely she must think about him after he sent her a card after all these years.

As for the two of them, they are just ticking along, going to work, eating, drinking, reading, having sex much less frequently, symptoms he supposes of the novelty of living together dissipating to be replaced by an air of uncertainty, certainly on his part. A cloud seems to be looming.

As they read, he looks up from his book to see her staring into space, distracted by inner thoughts, her inner voice maybe. She looks frightened, sad, troubled.

When he asks her if she is Ok there is always a pause followed by a slow 'yeah…fine'' which she says without diverting her eyes from where she is looking.

She's not, you know she's not fine, her mind is awash. With what? Something is imminent, this isn't going to last, this little love affair, if that's even what it is. It's simmering, in the heat of this summer of 1989. You still don't know her, really know her. There is so much to doubt, so much not known, there is no certainty to hope for. It's just a matter of time.

It comes one night, comes as wine courses through them like a flame travelling along a wire that sets off a detonator.

The fragility of this, her and him, is about to be blown to pieces in an uncontrolled explosion.

He looks out of the window onto the Earls Court night and up at the clouds as darkness begins to fall thickly. The clouds move round, circular, like the hands of a clock, only, it seems to Jake, anti-clockwise. It's like being on a roundabout, hardly moving, but moving nonetheless, but going the wrong way. They are going the wrong way, round and round.

He comes from the window. She is sprawled on the bed, her fourth glass of wine in hand.

He picks up and begins to read his book but he can feel her stare, almost a smirking stare. A look he has never seen on her yet it appears natural.

When he looks at her, she says, what do you really want Jake, I mean really want? From this life? From this world?

He puts his book down and stretches out to grab his cigarettes from the desk and lights up, her stare fixed on him.

Where's this come from, what's brought this on?

It's a straight-forward question, which bit are you finding so fucking difficult?

Fucking difficult. Why the fucking, why the sarcasm?

He drags deeply on his cigarette, sips some wine and says, but this is deep. What does anyone want from life? To be happy, I suppose.

As soon as he has spoken, he knows how feeble it sounds, how feeble she will take it.

Happiness. Happiness. What the fuck's that?

She gets up and grabs the pack of cigarettes from the table and lights up. She gulps the rest of her half-full glass of wine and pours another, banging the bottle down.

Then she begins to sing.

If you're happy and you know it clap your hands. If you're happy and you know it clap your hands. If you're happy and you know it and you really want to show it, clap your hands. Come on Jake. Clap your fucking hands.

The last part is shouted, come on Jake, clap your fucking hands.

Perhaps you've had too much wine. It's getting late, time for bed.

She looks at him with contempt. Then, in a slow, slurred voice she begins singing again, I am H.A.P.P.Y, I am H.A.P.P.Y, I am H.A.P.P.Y, I know I am. I'm Sure: I am. I am....H.A.P.P.Y. I am H.A.P.P.Y, I am H.A.P...P...Y. I am. Happy. Loved and...saved. I know. I am. I'm. Sure. I am. I am H.A....P...P...Y.

There are a few long minutes of silence, she stares into the corner of the room at the side of him, her face so beautiful, her cerulean eyes sparkling in the candlelight. He looks to the corner she is staring at.

On the floor the brown battered case.

What had her mother done to her? And her father? The scars of her childhood were the expression on her face, that beautiful face. He goes to her and puts his arms around her, kisses her hair lightly. But she is cold, rigid, her body lifeless, unresponsive.

He takes his arms away, he needs to get away from her, from this situation. He goes to the bathroom and swills his face with cold water.

You cannot go on like this, this woman is too complicated. It is not her fault but you have got in too deep. You are too young to take this on.

When he comes back into the room, she is sat with her grandmother's old case on the bed. It is unlocked and she has taken a red and blue notebook from it. Her diary.

I want you to read this Jake, I mean read it as if it is a book. When you have read it, please, do not be angry with me. I should have told you, weeks and weeks ago. But it was only because I wanted you, fell for you, wanted this, you and me, to work, that I didn't.

She hands him the red and blue book, it is mainly blue but at the bottom it is red, like a litmus paper that has had two chemicals spilt on it that have reacted with each other.

After Jean goes to bed, wine-filled and dark, he stays up and drinks some beer in the kitchen with a cigarette. He stares at the diary. It is a thick A3 ringbound notebook. The notebook of her thoughts, feelings and fears, he thinks.

I want you to read this like a book. I should have told you. What did she want him to read that she couldn't tell him to his face? There was only one way to find out.

He opens the book and sees her hand-writing in purple ink. The letters are small, she writes neatly and is economic with spacing. He sees his name but he is tired, tipsy and cannot make out the words.

He finishes his beer and decides he will sleep on the sofa. He will read the diary tomorrow with a clear head and a prepared heart and mind.

CHAPTER ELEVEN

HE SITS in Cromwells, a beer and cigarette on the go and the diary on the table.

She wants to be a writer. These are the words she has written, wrote, these are the words that are about to break your heart, make you wonder who you are, break the painful reality that sometimes what we want isn't the same as what others want. And people, well they are not always who they seem.

You were warned, there was always much, much more to her, you had doubts, she made you feel insecure, but you carried on, getting deeper and deeper.

A journal. Of my meeting Salime Douali by Jean Ridley

I've never written a diary before. This is my very first entry. And I've decided to do it because today I am so happy, the happiest I've been since I came to London in January. I'm working as a waitress in an Italian bistro in Lambs Conduit Street. And a man has asked me out. A very sophisticated man, French, who comes into the bistro every day and sips a few glasses of red wine, smokes small cigars and reads Le Monde before turning to a novel, he's always got a book on the go.

He's been coming to the bistro for a few months now. He is always smiling at me and I flirt with him when I take his order. I ask him what the book is he is reading and he tells me it is some French author who he loves, has read all his books, many of them several times. I can't remember the author's name. Anyway, as he was leaving tonight, he asked me out. "Would you like to take a meal and a drink with me?" he asked in a luscious French accent. My next night off isn't until Friday but I say yes and we agree to meet in a bar in Soho. He tells me his name is Salime and I tell him mine. After we agree our date he kisses me lightly on the cheek and gets up to leave.

I cannot stop thinking about Salime. How handsome he is – dark foppish, slightly greying hair. Yes, he is much older, but I think he is one of those men who probably gets more and more handsome as he ages. And he is French! Possibly quite well off given the way he dresses and he eats out most nights (The Bistro is upmarket and quite expensive) and he always leaves me a generous tip.

I have slept with two or three guys in the last few months – some that I've met at raves, one who worked here at the bistro as a

40

waiter. They were all around my age. But they never lasted, I never wanted to get too involved. I just wanted to have a good time and that was all these guys seemed to be offering.

But Salime. Well he has promise, I think. Maybe he's going to be my sugar daddy. Well, any daddy would be nice since I've never really had one.

What else to put in my diary? House prices are pushing up wealth in the South East (Evening Standard, I read it on my way back from the Bistro) and Kylie Minogue is in the charts with Je Ne Sais Pas Pourquoi. I'll ask Salime what that means on Friday when I meet him.

Hours before I'm due to meet him, I try on various outfits and curse at the limitations of my wardrobe which I've hardly expanded since I left Liverpool. Remember, he's sophisticated, so nothing too tarty, I tell myself. Remember he is mature, so nothing too…immature, I tell myself.

LATER

I have the most divine evening. We start in a café bar called The Pelican – French – in Covent Garden where we have cocktails. Then in The Windows Of The World restaurant high up above Park Lane with panoramic views of the city, the room is bathed in candlelight with a man playing a piano. It is like something I have only ever seen in the movies.

The conversation starts with Salime asking me to tell him about myself. I do not tell him about my past, my growing up. I cannot really imagine he would understand my world, where I come from and anyway, it is painful and complicated and I do not want to put him off.

I concentrate on my future and tell him what I want to be, how I want to live. I tell him I would like to be a writer, not necessarily fiction, but maybe biography and that I am taking a course in London in between waitressing. I tell him I love books, too. And keeping fit, running and swimming. And raves. And I immediately wish I hadn't mentioned raves. It makes me sound so young, too young and he picks up on it.

I am writing very roughly what I remember Salime saying. I hope I do justice to his eloquence, the beautiful way he weaves sentences together to express himself.

Salime: "I think the rave scene is, how to put it, getting too commercialised in this country. It has become an industry with the drugs and paraphernalia. You know the rave scene started off with a group of young people, here in the UK, who were unemployed, so went to Ibiza and organised parties every night on the beaches. Then someone had the idea of bringing it back here and there it began. In the early eighties, I think."

I ask about him. He is a psychiatrist back in Paris, he loves art, books, of course. That he is a psychiatrist makes me uneasy at first. Will he be studying me, will he spot flaws in my character that have resulted from my past? I don't want to give him a picture of a down-at-heel woman who comes from a broken family and whose childhood was so crap. And then he says something quite profound.

"I like the finer things in life, Jean. I am a libertine, but I don't like cheap thrills, I don't like cheap things. I like to spend my time and money wisely because there are so many things in…in this life that you can spend your time and money on and, well, they are all, to use a horrible English word, crap. I love this city, as I do Paris, but I see some of the more conventional, classical aspects of it disappearing and being replaced by tackiness and, er, cheapness and things that do people no good. Take drugs. I am not against drugs, I take them myself infrequently but I have to have the best. London is awash with cheap drugs for the poor and for the young and this is terrible. And then there is the drinking, people drinking themselves to oblivion.

"Why, what is wrong with them, what is wrong with their lives that they want to obliterate it? I like moderation, I like to take my time, I like to savour, I like to make sure that when I am reading, I read slowly, to take in and understand all the words. I don't even like fast cars. I don't like anything that tries to save time, to beat time. I like slowness, slow, not fast. Life goes too quickly, so why rush everything, why cut the corners? I want to see and experience everything at a pace that gives pleasure and knowledge. It's about taking your time, Jean, for everything, reading, writing, working, whatever. It always takes time if it's going to work, if you are going to have success and happiness. Time. I'll drink to time and using it wisely."

He lifts his glass to a toast. He says his words slowly, for emphasis and I find it soothing. I find it sexy, yes, I think I find it sexy.

He stops talking, takes a sip of wine and then places his hand on top of mine.

"Ah, par-don, par-don Jean, I am speaking too much. Once I get going I never know when to stop."

No, really, I tell him, I am fascinated, and I really am.

"I tell you what. I lighten the, the load, as you say in English. Look, I like peace and quiet, good wine, as you see every day in the bistro, I like my books, I hate the television and I don´t like pop music. But if you like television and pop music, this is Ok with me because who am I to tell people to like the same things as I like? So, do you like pop music?"

To lie or to be honest? I like some of it but not all and as for television, I haven´t seen any TV since I came to London, I tell him.

He smiles a warm smile. I expect him to ask where I am from but instead his smile stops and he looks at me with his deep brown French eyes.

"Can I ask you a question Jean?"

Of course

"Are you in love with anyone?"

I tell him no, I´m single, have had a few boyfriends but nothing serious. I say this a little too fast, too defensively.

I´m surprised by his response: "Why? You tell me you are 24 and yet you have never had at least one serious relationship, one where you thought, perhaps wrongly, that this person might be the one? You have never been in love? This I find very difficult to believe of such a beautiful woman like you."

It´s not aggressive, but it drills deep into me, turns me inside out.

I tell him no, I have never been in love with anyone and 24 is still very young, too young to get too involved.

He lights one of his small cigars, inhales deeply, then exhales almost with a sigh. "I suppose you may be right. But age is just a number, so, well, I don´t know."

It´s time to turn the tables on him. Has he ever been in love, is he in love?

"Ha, ha, of course it is my turn to answer the questions. No, I have never been in love. Yes, I have thought that maybe I was in love but it turned out not to be the case. You see I don't really know that love exists in the way people think it exists. Sorry, this sounds very confused, but I think the whole concept of love is confusing. It is why it is so problematic. I think love can be a barrier to enjoyment, to self-expression, to who you really want to

43

be. It is too binding, yet it has no real definition. But, I suppose, well, maybe the right person has never come along, maybe…maybe there is someone out there who would turn on the taps of love and I would experience it and feel it. Hmm, maybe."

He picks up his glass, drains it of the wine and pours us both some more. Then he smiles, he puts his hand on mine.

"Ah, Jean, I am talking about the past, the past is where it belongs, somewhere else, not here, not now. The future, the future, not the past."

He said "The future, the future, not the past," in an almost musical whisper.

He changes the subject and we talk about books and when we get onto Kafka and talk so animatedly the time just shoots by.

He tells me he is putting me in a cab and hands me ten pounds which I at first decline, but he insists. As we wait for the cab, he continues to smoke and I ask him what Je ne sais pas pourquoi means. "I still love you," he says. I wait for him to ask when we can meet again. But he hails down a taxi, opens the door for me and says: "See you at the bistro next week."

The cab door slams. I look back and he is waving and smiling.

He is like no other man I have ever met. I yearn to see him again, I wish he had arranged to meet on Sunday, for a walk in the park, to hear him talking again in his sonorous voice, in his wisdom.

After the weekend:

Every time the door of the bistro opens I look and hope it is him. But it's a bit early today when I have these thoughts and hopes, he usually comes in after the early evening rush. My head is in the clouds, I'm concentrating on nothing else and it affects my work.

Ginilo, the manager asks me for a quiet word.

"Jean, you've made two mistakes today. You took the wrong wine to table number four, they asked for Chardonnay, you took them red. And table number seven was a disaster, you took the orders from table one. Please, please, we cannot afford to upset our regulars and it is so unlike you. Are you OK?" I say yes, I'm just a bit run down today, a bit dizzy and promise I will try not to make any more mistakes. Ginilo is a nice guy, it takes a lot for him to reprimand staff but obviously my mistakes have been big. I've got to get a grip and stop thinking about Salime.

I put him out of my mind and get on with my job until I realise, it has got to the usual time when he comes in and he isn't here yet. The door opens again and it's just a couple. Fuck them, why can't they be him.

I'm thinking this as I carry a pile of plates into the kitchen and walk straight into a customer who has just got up from the table, sending the plates crashing to the floor and splashing mess all over the middle aged gentleman's crisp white shirt.

Ginilo rushes over, I apologise and start picking up the plates. The customer is incredibly calm as Ginilo wipes his shirt with napkins, apologises profusely and tells the man that the meal is on the house.

The shift ends, Ginilo tells me to take a few days off but I can't do that. What about Salime? I insist to Ginilo that a good night's sleep will put me right, it won't happen again and he can take the cost of the free meal and the plates out of my wages. (I cannot afford this, but I cannot afford not to be at the bistro if Salime comes in).

What a fucking day.

A few days later.

He comes in the bistro, all smiles and acknowledges me and takes his usual table, he has his usual wine and pasta which I serve him and whisper how much I really enjoyed Friday night. It brings a beaming smile to his face and he whispers: "Let's do it again. I did not know whether you had a good time or not."

I ask him when. I tell him I am free again this Friday and it's a date.

The restaurant is busy tonight so I don't have time to speak with him much but I periodically glance over, hoping he sees me and takes his eyes from his book.

He does a few times but I stop glancing over at him as I know he takes his reading seriously. Him coming in tonight lifts my mood and my concentration levels and I don't make any mistakes in my work. Salime is good for me, good for my state of mind!

Friday again.

We meet, this time in a cosy wine bar in Mayfair, he has warned me it is very upmarket and only smart people get in. I blow almost my whole wages for the week on a new outfit and shoes.

At the restaurant Salime is wearing a dark blue suede jacket, a white open-necked shirt that is open by three undone buttons to reveal he has a very hairy chest. He smells lightly of cologne which I like. He studies the drinks menu.

"Do you want to drink red or white wine?" he asks. I say I don´t mind but since it´s hot outside we should start with a chilled bottle of white.

He tells me this is an excellent idea and orders from the waiter.

We exchange pleasantries such as, how was your week.? (Salime had not be in the restaurant and seems to be spending less time there since we started going out) I push him to tell me a little bit more about himself – I get in there quickly to avoid him probing any deeper into my background – and he seems slightly peeved, even defensive.

"Well, what do you want to know Jean? You want to know all about my childhood, or from when I was 18?"

I say, how about his age, whether he has been married, any children? How long is he staying in London, will he go back to Paris, how long has he lived in London?

"A lot of questions," he says almost as a sigh. "I told you before, I have never been in love, so no, I have never been married."

I feel stupid, of course, he said he had not found love. I feel very young, very immature at this moment. Stupid, stupid, fucking stupid. Think before you speak.

I am relieved when the waiter brings the wine, the situation feels, well, awkward. Maybe I should have carried on with small talk before ploughing straight in with my questions. I don't know but Salime seems slightly agitated tonight, the vibes are not good, they are like he does not really want to be here.

Salime is asked to try the wine and he takes a small sip, swishes it around his mouth and tells the waiter it is fine, abruptly.

Our glasses are filled, the waiter leaves us. Salime takes another sip, takes his cigars out and lights one.

"OK, so you want to know all about me?"

Only if you want to tell me, I smile.

He reclines in his chair and takes a drag of the cigar and blows the smoke out slowly which he watches drift into the air. He finally looks at me.

"I´m not married, no, I have never been married and I have no children. Why? A good question. But why do any of our lives turn out the way they do? I suppose I never found the right person

46

for me, or maybe I'm just not suited to the commitment that marriage requires.

"I grew up in Morocco, in Marrakesh. An only child. I saw what marriage can do to people if it is not right. I saw it in my parents. My parents only stuck together because of me and because that is what you did in those days. We went to live in Morocco because of my father's business, my mother had never wanted to leave Paris and had not wanted to uproot me, I was only five years old at the time.

"My father was a, how do you say, domineering figure, he imposed himself on my mother in terms of how he wanted the family to live. I don't think there was much consultation with my mother about anything my father decided to do and I think she resented it. Resented it with all her heart. There were never rows, never violence or confrontation but as I got older I could see it in her eyes, the way she looked at my father, the way she looked at him especially when he was talking or pontificating. They were eyes full of resentment, they were eyes that expressed agony and regret that my father had decided what our lives would be. I cannot imagine my father discussing with my mother the pros and cons of moving to Morocco. If he had decided, then that was it. No discussion. No opposition, not even an attempt to find out how my mother really felt about such a dramatic uprooting.

"She hated Marrakesh, hated the stench of it, hated the poverty that greeted you every day in the Souks and the rabbit warren of streets.

"Once we went back to our house in Paris for a few weeks' holiday.

"I couldn't really remember what Paris was like, I was only five when we left and this was the first time we had come back and I was by now ten. I fell in love with the place, it felt like home. Well, it was my home, really. And when we returned to Marrakesh, I became homesick for Paris and I could see my mother felt the same way and I realised that this was what had always been in her eyes, the resentment at having to live in Marrakesh, the yearning to live in Paris where she had lived all her life and a good many years while married to my father.

"Anyway, I digress, but you can see why I probably avoided marriage rather than it just being my fortune that I would never meet anyone I would marry. You see Jean, it is impossible, marriage, because it only works if two people want the same things. And they may start out wanting the same things, but then time starts to erode because they begin to want different things. And then it becomes about sacrifice – someone has to win and someone has to lose in a marriage because as people change, it's impossible for them to go on wanting exactly the same things.

"My mother and father are a good example, but walk around London, look around this bar tonight and look at the married couples. In each of these relationships, someone is getting their own way and someone is having to make a sacrifice. Some will make that sacrifice believing they are doing it out of love. I'll do anything, they tell themselves, in the name of love. They really think it's love. And the person getting their own way, they think it is being done because the other person loves them.

"But, as I say, time takes over, people realise they only have one life, and they're not getting any younger. Then they begin to question what they are doing with their lives. And they start to worry, start to believe that they are in fact wasting it. And that's when resentment sets in, that's when the strings that tie the relationship together become frayed. I've seen it in friends, too.

"The human spirit, the human conscious will always wonder what life could have offered them as an alternative. How their lives could have been so different. Different if they had not met this person, different if they had met someone else. Different if they had not fallen in love too quickly and too deeply. As age wears us down, we tire of the other person, we resent them and what we've sacrificed. And it works both ways. Even the one not making the sacrifice feels the guilt, feels the wrong choices were made. Look again around this room.

"You can see the couples who have just met, full of the unknown, the thrill, the excitement, the excitement of someone new, who they do not yet know. You can see those who are having affairs. Again, the thrill, the furtiveness of what they are doing. But then there will be the guilt, the guilt of cheating and the resentment that they settled with someone who they never committed to but have to stay with because of money, or children or because they want the best of both worlds – stability AND excitement. But it's always about compromise. I said to you the other night, life is the future, not the past. But most human beings are welded to their past and the mistakes they think they made back then.

"So no, I am not married and I don't think I ever will be or ever want to. Oh and your other question, my age. I'm 50."

I nearly choke on my wine. He CAN NOT BE FIFTY!
But Salime, you don't look anything like 50. You're so....young-looking, handsome.

"So how old would you say I am?"

"I don't know, late 30s, early 40s."

"Oh you do flatter, Jean," he laughs. "Well, I am very flattered, but no I am 50 and it is just a number. I have never had a mid-life crisis, I do not worry about getting older, I am fit, I live well. I live better now than when I was in my 20s. I run, I climb, I take care of myself. But I don't worry about my age."

You're a really perfect guy, aren't you, Salime Douali, Jake thinks as he decides to speed read the further entries, about his love-making prowess, his luxury apartment in Mayfair.

Then there are the entries about him planning to go back to Paris and how, when he's settled down in a month or two, he wants Jean to follow him.

She writes: I cannot believe this man has asked me to go to live with him in Paris. My dream man, living with him in Paris. Is this really going to happen? It's like a dream.

The next entry is in January 1989 and she writes: "I have not been keeping this diary up to date. I have been so busy at college, balancing this with my job at the restaurant.

I need to write, I think this is what has been wrong with me for so many months. Anyway, after Salime had asked me to go to Paris with him, he told me he wanted to go back for a few months before I joined him.

I moved out of the hostel in Queensgate and found a shared flat in Clapham. It's lousy, on a rundown estate behind Clapham Junction station. There are two other girls there who do drugs but I don't see too much of them, we have not really been acquainted let alone formed any sort of friendship.

I am lonely, Salime has been back in Paris for months now. He writes to me once a month and says we will have to delay my coming out to him because of complications and work commitments.

He also thinks I need time to think things through. I wrote back to him saying I was certain it was what I wanted to do. I also told him I should tell him more about myself, my past, my childhood. So I did. I didn't go into too much detail but I wanted him to get a fuller picture of me. I owed him that. Once I had posted it I spent days regretting it.

He would be put off me, use his psychiatric skills to assess me, it would put me in a different light.

When he replied, I was perplexed.

Dearest Jean

Thank-you for your letter. I was very sad to read of your childhood and of your past. I was also very surprised that you had such a tumultuous upbringing because you do not convey this in your persona. You seem quite happy, quite balanced.

But then you also seem to be in awe of me, you seem to elevate me, you seem to see me as someone who can make everything OK in your life. I have said to you that I am not the marrying kind, for all the reasons I told you in our long and lovely evenings together.

Jean, I do want to help you though. And I am reconsidering when will be best for you to come here – maybe sooner than I had planned, but I do not know so do not build up your hopes. I have a rather unconventional life, both here and when I am in London. It may not be what you are used to or familiar with.

You do not know who I am, we do not know each other very well. I asked you to come to Paris because I like you, and because, now that I know what you have been through, I want to help you. This I can probably do, but this is all, please do not expect any more. I know we made love on the last few nights before I left London. I hate the term making love. We fucked, we had an orgasm, we had mutual pleasure, I hope I opened your mind to sexual adventurism, that making love is not what sex is about. It is about pleasing each other, love does not come into it. Remember, I fucked you, I did not love you or make anything resembling love to you. You need to know this. You really need to know this and take your time to think about what that means in terms of what you are looking for.

Next time you write, I want you to spend at least three hundred carefully written words to explain your decision, if it is still to come to Paris. I must know you are here with a full understanding of what I have to offer and what I don't. I will take care of you, I will help you, I will fuck you. That is what I am offering and you must decide whether that is what you want. To be helped, to be protected, to be fucked.

Salime

I have to read it over and over again to make sense of what he is saying. I have to be certain that if I decide to go to Paris I give him a full and convincing reasoning behind my decision. Three hundred very important words.

To be helped, to be protected, to be fucked. Did this not amount to love?

It's February, well into the new year, 1989 and I have still not replied to Salime's letter although I have written several but screwed them up, didn't send them. Every attempt just came out girlie, fawning, not convincing. In fact, I just don't want to write anything. Even these few short words in this diary just do not say what I really want to say, if only I knew what I wanted to say. What a fucking sentence. To bed. Girl at work has invited me to a rave at the weekend. I'm going to go, pop some Es, get off my fucking face and forget everything. Just for a few hours. 1989 can only get better. But I do not know, do not really care.

March 1989

Feeling low, been to raves every weekend and coming down from the E is fucking horrible. Today I feel maudlin and decide I really must write to Salime. I have heard nothing from him and this is probably because he feels he has put me off with his last letter.

I write: Dear Salime, I am not going to write three hundred words explaining why I still want to come and live with you in Paris. I have tried, I have really tried but the words will not come, or not ones that I think adequately express how I feel. All I can say is that I am looking for the things you are offering. Some would say that offering to protect, and to help and, well, to fuck, is a form of love. You may not wish to call it this and I understand. But I feel we have something, I feel we are both free spirits, maybe slightly damaged, but I think we can fix each other. I could come to Paris and join you and see how things turn out. There would be no commitment on either side and if, at any time, you felt the situation was not working out, or if you were unhappy for any reason, I would not be a burden on you. I would leave and come back to London. I have already been through so much in my life. I want to take this chance. If it doesn't work out I believe my experience has made me strong enough to deal with any subsequent fallout. I am sorry I have taken so long to write to you, I took your advice about taking time, taking it slowly and I have given this all my deepest thoughts and the more I think about it I cannot think of any reason not to give it a go. I hope your offer still stands. I hope you will write to me soon, I miss your letters, I miss you. Jean.

April 1989

What the fuck is he playing at? It's weeks and weeks ago since I sent him my letter saying I would be coming to Paris. Or rather that I wanted to come to Paris. If he had had second thoughts, decided he did not want me there, could he not at least have sent me a letter saying so?

They say absence makes the heart grow fonder. Absence and silence make the heart just, well, fucked off. I feel this, I feel anger, then I have a drink and I just feel melancholy, feel like begging him to let me come to Paris to be with him. All my hopes, all my....oh fuck, I just don't know what to write, what to think. Fucking answer me, Salime, write a fucking letter, put me out of my misery, one way or the other.

Please, please say yes, please, you beautiful grown-up, mature man. My saviour. My love. I know you do not like that word.

Oh why write words nobody is going to read? Why write this stupid fucking diary? It isn't even any good. I ought to be writing some poetry or try writing a novel. Yes, a novel. That's what I want to be, isn't it, a writer. To make things up, to create a different world, with different people, to use my imagination, to write something that entertains, takes people away from their own miserable lives. This is why people read, isn't it and this is why I want to be a writer, isn't it? Is this a good reason for wanting to be a writer? Do you need a reason? Please Salime, write, write, write to me, for fuck's sake, write to me, anything, anything at all.

May 1989

My diary is different. Most people write daily entries but I only do it about once a month or when I feel like it. I think most of my days are so mundane, so uneventful that I have not enough material to write every day. Well, I'm not writing my diary but I am writing my novel. But it's kind of an autobiography, it's about me but in a way it isn't because it's about my imagined life with Salime. So I don't know what is happening with him and whether I am going to Paris so I decide to write what I imagine and I suppose what I hope would now be happening. It is fantasy, but it is fictional so I can say, yes, it is a novel, I'm writing a novel because everything is imagined even though the protagonist is me and the main characters – Salime and me – are real. It's just that I am writing a script that has not been said, in real life. So I am writing my novel. I cannot control my real life but I have absolute control over my fictional life. I can fucking make anything happen I want to – even if it is not real. Maybe one day Salime can read it and read about what might have been even if it is only through my eyes. I can just make my life up as I go along. It's what we do anyway, isn't it? Interpretations, seeing others in our own way that is often wrong. It's why everyone makes so many mistakes in their lives, because they see things from their point of view and this just obscures reality, obscures how other people really feel and think because we cannot know what is in their minds. It's all just perception and humans so often get it wrong. It's why relationships and marriages break up, it's why wars start, it's why people get angry. Because we get it wrong, we don't really understand each other's minds. We can't. So I will just make it up. As I go along. I will invent a life, my life, I will put my heart and soul into this invention. Because there is no point in making the effort in the reality, in the real world. Because I will get it wrong, I will make it up and think it is correct, just as we all do.

June 1989

This proves to be a mixed month. I have all but given up on Salime, although he is always on my mind and I continue to write my book about our imagined life. Mixed because two things happen. I meet a guy called Jake, a Yorkshireman, at a rave in King's Cross. He's a year younger than me. He is very good-looking although not the type I usually go for. We go back to his place and he behaves like a gentleman saying he will sleep on the floor. But I'm horny as hell and do fancy him so we sleep together. He is gentle, a little unsure, I can feel his lack of experience.

The sex is Ok but not like it is with Salime.

It's just straight fucking and while I was quite happy with this on this first night, I knew it was not something I would be satisfied with in the longer-term. Of course, Jake could get better and when we got to know each other properly we could talk about our needs and turn-ons. But throughout the sex, I just keep thinking, this is not Salime, this doesn't feel the same, doesn't feel as good. I even try to imagine it is Salime on top of me but my imagination cannot not make the sex any better or more exciting. Jake comes and asks me if I am near to coming. I tell him I already have. He smiles and seems pleased, as if he has passed some kind of test. Of course, if it was a test, he would not have passed it.

After the sex we just fall asleep, exhausted from the rave. The next day we make love again but again it doesn't feel right. He asks me for my number but I don't have one and I don't want him calling the bistro. I ask him if I can have a key to his place. I don't know why, I think that it is because I know he will allow me. I could also come here to read during the day when he was at work and get away from the pit in Clapham. I like his place, I feel safe there and I just need some kind of refuge. He gives me the key, he seems a bit surprised but doesn't ask any questions which I thought was incredibly naïve, but then that is down to his young age.

So that was Jake and I would use his place to escape, to read and do my writing. I tried to make sure he did not know I had been in. I did not want to see him again. I had a good rummage around the flat but otherwise I would just lie down and read and write. I was constantly nervous he would come back but knew he had a nine to five job and that he usually nipped to that dull as hell pub across the road for a few pints most evenings.

I am taking some dirty dishes to the kitchen in the restaurant and nearly drop them when the door opens and in he walks, Salime. We don't make eye contact and I am so shocked, or possibly scared, that I scurry with the plates to the kitchen and take my time placing them to be washed. Fuck. What is he doing back here?

I dawdle a bit in the kitchen but one of the other waitresses asks me to get a move on as the restaurant is busy. When I go out I see him look over. A smile spreads across his face. I go to his table, he needs serving.

At first I treat him like just a customer. I ask him if he is ready to order. He says he would like his usual glass of red wine but is not going to order any food.

As I turn he grabs my waist. I turn. He says, you look good Jean, after all this time.

I say, I think we need to talk.

I bring his wine. I say in a whisper, can we meet? We need to talk.

Jake is confused and starts flipping the pages backwards. There is no further mention of whether she meets Salime or not at

54

this point. But his disappointment is banished when he sees the next section is a chronicle of her time, thoughts and feelings while with him, Jake.

But this is probably where she plunges the knife and grinds it in. Should you read on, she is clearly infatuated by Salime? It can only be bad, really bad, truly bad, awful.

She writes: In Brighton he made a fuss about a kid who got knocked over. God, he's so serious. I suppose he's serious because of what happened with his mum. He told me she left him and his father when he was just 12.

His father was busy running the business and Jake was looked after by his aunt who resented his mother for being able to have a kid when she was told she would never be a mother. His aunt just provided the basics – food and looked after him in getting him to school and picking him up

Jake's mother had run off to Australia with another bloke. He had never really had a mum, I suppose like I had never had a father. I think this explains a lot about him. It affects you does your childhood. I have been reading a book by Carl Jung whose mother had a breakdown and spent a lot of time in hospital at a critical stage of his development. Jung later wrote that he felt mistrustful of the word love which he associated with women and felt he could never rely on them.

I feel sorry for Jake. He is a nice guy but introverted, he reads a lot and spends a lot of time alone, he doesn't seem to have many friends.

He only comes alive when he's taken an E at the raves, then he goes crazy, dancing madly as if he's shaking off all his demons, all his emotional shackles. And I know that feeling so well. The highs, the adrenaline shooting through you as the music shoots through you and everyone is a heaving mass.

But without the E Jake seems lost, deep, detached. He's boyish both physically and in temperament.

HE IS THE OPPOSITE OF SALIME!!!!!

Salime knows himself, he's seen how relationships work – or don't work – through his parents' marriage and Morocco.

Jake is not strong enough to deal with me in the longer-term, with me and all my hang-ups because he has too many of his own. Yet we have so much in common and that is the problem, I think.

I need a man, not a boy; I need someone who knows himself, who has experience, who has maturity and strength.

Jake's love-making is boring, there's no passion or adventure, he has no experience. I mean, what I do with Salime, what he wants me to do, well, it's almost….pornographic. But exciting.

I wish there was a future with this nice boy, he is kind, he does care.

But maybe he's not my future, he's my past. My future has to be with Salime and a new life in Paris with a man, a man who I know is old enough to be my father, but I think that's what I want.

I don't know whether Jake even wants a future with me anyway.

Though we are living together it doesn't feel like the real thing. And of course I cannot keep lying to him and going away all the time.

Today Salime is going back to Paris and wants me to join him in a couple of weeks, not months. He said he was sorry for keeping me hanging on before but he had a lot of work and he also had to be sure he was doing the right thing for himself as well as me.

"You've nothing to lose Jean, come to Paris and let's see how it can work out," he said to me.

I feel guilty, I feel a little bit, well, committed to Jake. I feel bad when he's been so good to me. He had been a breath of fresh air, someone in my life in London. But something is missing. I don't feel swept off my feet, Jake doesn't excite me. Even when we went to Brighton it was just so…I don't know. We kissed on the seafront with the moon shining and the stars twinkling and the sound of the sea crashing in but, though the setting was romantic, I just knew as I kissed him that this was not it. He was not going to fill this great void in my life, perhaps no-one ever can but I really don't think he can.

Salime. Salime is just the opposite of Jake. He fills me with energy, his demeanour, the way he speaks, this aura that surrounds him and permeates towards me. He's full of wisdom and knowledge and he makes me feel high, he's like taking an E. But he fills me with hope and comfort and security and nobody has ever made me feel like this before, ever.

It almost frightens me, but only because I cannot believe it is happening to me and I begin to wonder whether this is all real because it's a feeling I have never felt. I fear that even if this is not a dream, a mirage, even if it is real it will not last, he will go away, abandon me.

Because that's what people have always done to me.

I know I am risking getting hurt and it's a big risk because I am so fragile, I'm like a plate that has been dropped and badly cracked and if I am dropped again I will fall into thousands of pieces and nothing, or anyone, will be able to put me back together again.

But I have to take that risk, I have to take this risk if I am to find happiness. As Salime said, I have nothing to lose and I don't think he realised when he said it how literal this is. I have nothing and I have no-one to lose.

I hope Jake will still be my friend. He will never know how much I care for him and how happy I want him to be. He has been good to me, he came into my life at the right time and I don't regret ever meeting him or being with him. He is not the one for me but he showed me kindness and understanding when I thought there was no-one in the world willing or capable of that. He has helped me know myself better – to know what I want, what I don't want, to know what I need.

Jake was my summer love, my rave lover, my E buddy and I will never forget him. Even though he is not the one for me.

Her writing ends. Jake sips his pint slowly, lights another cigarette through misty eyes. He looks around, self-consciously expecting to see people looking at him. But the world is going about its business, the jukebox is playing Gene Pitney and Marc Almond's Something's Got A Hold Of My Heart and he wishes it wasn't.

He gets back to the flat, hastily packs, grabs his bank book. Has to get out before she comes back.

He gets to Brighton and finds a guest house. It's early evening so he hits the sea front bars. Boring in bed. Doesn't have the experience. What I do with Salime…pornographic.

CHAPTER TWELVE

HE SITS in a bar overlooking the seafront and through bleary eyes reads snaps of what she has written, what she feels. It is over, whatever we had, it is over.

He wonders, why did she not write any more about Salime when he came back to the café? Did he come back to the café or was she now making this up, as she had said, about writing how she hoped things would turn out with Salime? Why were the dates and entries so haphazard, why not specific dates – this is surely the whole point of writing a diary? It's a record, to be looked back on, remembered?

His head feels like a boulder, when he wakes up he can hardly lift it from the pillow. But he rouses himself and as he showers decides not to return to London today. He will stay here for the week, write her a letter, a nice letter, nothing bitter or angry, and ask that she leaves the flat by the weekend when he will return. He will also express how he feels, set her right about a few points she makes in her diaries.

He sits at the desk in the hotel room and starts to draft his letter. A few pieces of paper end up in the bin as he tries to write but then the words begin to flow.

Dear Jean

I have read the diaries and thank-you for letting me read them. They are obviously very personal but at least now I know how you truly feel and how you perceive me.

I cannot help what I am but please do not think I am some screwed up personality shaped, or rather misshaped, by what happened to me in my childhood and my mother abandoning me and dad when I was insanely young.

I think given what happened when I was a kid I have nevertheless grown up to be a pretty rounded and normal character.

I do not blame my mother for leaving. I knew for some time their marriage would not last. I remember being woken by their arguments.

I would sit at the top of the stairs and listen. I could pick out my father saying things like, I think you should just go if you feel that way.

And my mother would shout back that she will do, one day soon but when it suited her. Of course I didn't want them to split up but I saw how controlling my father was and how little interest and attention he gave my mother. He was always too busy. Too busy to be married I suppose.

That was the difference between my mother and Salime's. She was not willing to compromise, to go on sacrificing herself. Not even for me.

But I cannot help thinking you are comparing me to this man, Salime, who you have met. He sounds a great guy, but you must remember, he is double our ages and therefore has many years of experience on the clock. I like to think that at our ages, we are still developing. Maybe I´m not the complete personality I hope to become. But for now, this is who I am.

I met you and, yes, I fell in love with you, though I never really said it, never really expressed how I felt. I suppose I was afraid that I might scare you off.

It all happened very quickly between us. And then you kept going away and some of your behaviour was a bit mysterious. We never seemed to spend enough time together to really get to know each other.

It´s been a crazy summer. But I´ve had a great time with you, going to the raves, going to Brighton, sharing the flat together. They were nice times that I will always cherish.

Yes, you need someone stronger than me, in the longer-term at least. Salime, from what you have said, seems to be the one who can provide you with that strength and security.

You are special but I cannot find words to explain why. You just have something that got hold of me. But Jean, your feelings are clear and I think I am strong enough to accept that I cannot bring you the happiness you want.

I really do want you to be happy and I want you to stay in touch and let me know you are happy and for you to tell me about your life. I hope we can still have a special friendship and we don´t just forget each other and drift apart in the passing of time.

I´m not saying that what happens in childhood has no effect on how we grow up. It did affect me, I suppose it´s why I came to London.

My father and I did not get on as I grew older. Correction, it wasn´t so much that we didn´t get on, it was really that we just didn´t have any kind of relationship. He was, as always, busy running his business and he seemed to avoid me as much as possible, as he did with mum. It was as if I was a reminder of his loss of my mother. My father also started to become quite bitter about the world, always seemed irritable and on edge.

I looked at my father's life. He had few friends, stayed at home most nights with a decanter of whisky and the books from his business which he seemed to constantly pore over anxiously.

Our house was quite big and we could lose each other easily. We hardly ever ate together. I spent most of my time in my room reading.

When I finished college I realised that I had to get out, not just from my home, or rather my father's home because it didn't feel like home to me, but from Yorkshire.

I became obsessed with London, devoured every novel I could find that was set there, read every newspaper article that was about London.

One day I took the train to King's Cross. I came out of the station and walked straight ahead. I had no idea where I was going, I didn't even have a map.

But before I knew it I was in Oxford Street, then turned down a side street and found myself in Soho.

Its sleaziness excited me and made me curious. I walked its labyrinth of streets, took a few beers in some of the pubs. One of them, The Intrepid Fox amazed me. It was full of punks and Goths, the music was heavy and noisy. As you would expect.

In another pub, the Blue Posts I saw glamorous girls who, it turned out, worked in some of the peep shows and strip joints.

I found the Coach and Horses where I had read about the drinking exploits of Jeffrey Bernard and Keith Waterhouse who was then my favourite writer. And sure enough they were in the pub, drinking and holding court.

I saw the coffee shops and bars and the foreign girls on the streets, I felt the buzz of the place, the lights dazzled me and drew me in. I had planned to leave London early in the evening but as night started to fall on that November night, I realised I just didn't want to leave the streets. This is where I wanted to be.

I wanted to escape from Yorkshire, escape from my father, escape from an almost guaranteed life of drudgery and old-fashioned attitudes and, yes Jean, I wanted to escape from the past. This was the future. London.

I returned to Yorkshire late that night and tried to read on the train. But my mind, my heart, they were still on those London streets.

I decided I was destined for London. But how would my father take it?

Once I had found a job I realised it was going to happen. I was going to London and nothing was going to stop me.

The moment came to tell my father. I poured him a whisky after telling him I needed to talk to him. I handed him the drink, he looked at the glass, avoiding any eye contact, concentrated on the whisky, clinking the ice.

For courage, I poured myself one even though then I had hardly ever touched whisky. This prompted him to look up at last. His eyes were saying, but that's my whisky, what are you doing drinking my whisky and you don't even drink whisky?

I got straight to the point, told him my plans. He took a gulp of his drink, then placed it carefully on the side table next to his armchair and said, well, there's nothing to keep you here. Much more opportunity in London, I should think.

No drama, no histrionics, it was as if he was resigned to the fact I had grown up and would leave one day soon.

A week later I was in London, arriving on a bitterly cold February afternoon.

My first few weeks here were solitary but I didn't feel lonely. I felt excited, free, I could do what I wanted, no-one knew me here, no-one knew my past. I was not poor young Jake, the guy whose mother ran off to Australia with another man.

I had been to a few raves in Manchester and Leeds but my first rave in London was like no other. It was in a former jail in Clink Street near the Thames, just before Tower Bridge. I went on my own, knew no-one, yet once I immersed myself in the mass of pumped up bodies, I felt part of something, I felt the physical energy of all those people vibrating through me, I felt for the first time in my life that I had found where I belonged.

I thought when I met you we belonged together. I thought we were bonded by the need for some sort of togetherness. But I now know it is not going to work between us. For so many reasons but mainly because you want somebody I am not.

You say I am serious. Maybe, although the more I think about that the less I understand what you mean.

Anyway Jean, I want to stay friends, to stay in touch. I will always be there for you and I hope you feel the same.

I can't deal with goodbyes, well, not this one, anyway. It would be good if you could leave the flat by the weekend when I'm planning to return to London.

You have my address and my family address in Harrogate, please, please let me know how you are when you get to Paris and stay in touch.

I wish you every happiness in your life and I hope Salime takes care of you.

You will always be special to me and I shall never forget this summer.

With all my love

Jake.

He posts the letter to Nevern Place first class. She should get it the next day, Wednesday at the latest.

It feels so final, like jumping off a cliff, he thinks maybe this is what suicide feels like. Almost. No going back.

September is almost at an end, autumn is about to be ushered in, the summer of 1989 flickering precariously to its end.

He walks along the seafront. She has gone out of my life and I must start again, move on, to the next stage, down new roads and avenues, different routes, around different corners.

CHAPTER THIRTEEN

THERE IS no let-up in the searing hot weather and he is sweating as he emerges from Earls Court station.

He gets to Nevern Place, stops to look up at the flat and notices the sash window is slightly open. Music. Phil Collins, Something In The Air Tonight.

She is still here, still in the flat.

This isn't what he wants, what he had planned. In his head on the train journey back, the flat was empty of all her things. Long gone. Maybe a goodbye note, an address, a reply to his letter. But she was gone, long gone, in his head.

But the shock of her still being here is overtaken by elation. He will see her again. Just for one moment, just for one last time. For the very last time?

He unlocks and tentatively pushes open the door of the flat, the music is louder, she has it almost on full volume. He drops his rucksack and turns down the volume. Where is she?

He says her name, almost a shout, certainly audible wherever in the flat she might be but there is no answer.

Checks. The bedroom area, the kitchen, the bathroom. She is not there. The wardrobe. Her clothes are still hanging. He checks the bathroom again and her toiletries are all still in their place.

But she is not here right now.

He opens the window fully and sits on the ledge to light up.

Then his stomach jumps as he hears keys unlocking the door. He moves from the window and there she is with two bags of shopping. She is startled at first, but then her expression is that she has been expecting him. He had said in his letter he would be back at the weekend but maybe she thought it would be tomorrow, Sunday.

She puts the bags on the floor and walks towards him, puts her arms around him, pulls him tight to her. She puts her head onto his shoulder and he smells the just-washed aroma of her hair. Her hair always smelt so clean, so good. Smelt, not smells, past tenses running through his mind, what once was but is no longer.

They remain like this for a few minutes and as he holds her he knows how much he has missed, is going to miss, this.

To have and to hold her, despite all the words she had written, all the pain she has caused, all the hurt that he feels. He hears her sobs and tears come to his eyes. Why does it have to be like this?

She turns to face him, moves her face to his, their noses touch, their mouths open, her tongue finds his.

She makes the first move, the first move that says, we are going to bed, we are going to make love.

She tugs at his belt, pulls down his jeans. He reciprocates by undressing her and now they are on the bed. She is lying flat, he kisses her, licks her breasts sucks her nipples and spreads her legs. His tongue tentatively licks her, his first foray into oral sex.

Her moans give him encouragement to use his tongue more vigorously and to insert a finger. A few minutes later she climbs on top of him and works her way down his body with her tongue.

After a good five minutes, she begs him, please don't come Jake, I want you to fuck me. And he does. Boring in bed, no passion, not exciting. What I do with Salime is …almost…pornographic.

They sit with a bottle of wine and a pre-cooked lasagne, the light streams in from the fast-fading sunshine.

She serves the food but neither of them is hungry so they make do with the wine and cigarettes.

What to say now, who would speak first.

He lights her cigarette, then his, he smiles and she sends one back.

Jean gets up from the table and goes to a drawer and brings out an envelope, the envelope with the letter he had sent her from Brighton.

She places it carefully, half way between them, on the table, takes a sip of wine and looks at him with sad eyes.

He takes a sip of wine, a long, deep drag on his cigarette.

He says, so, what are we going to do?

He is confused, baffled by how she greeted him, the sex and her still being here after all she had written, after all he had written.

Jake, I'm sorry I wrote those things about you, I'm sorry you had to read them. They were my private thoughts at the time, some of them are just words, just writing, how I felt at the particular moment I wrote them.

Boring in bed?

Well, you weren't just now. You seemed uninhibited, whereas before, well, you just went for it now.

What about Salime?

Everything is just different with Salime. He's like someone, someone I have never met before.

But he's, well he's so much older than you, he could be your father. He's probably as old as your father, isn't he?

He regrets the tone of his voice, he regrets that it sounds like he's ridiculing her, that he sounds too incredulous.

She raises her voice, offended. I've no idea exactly how old my father is because I don't think about my father. My father has been out of my life for…well he's never been in my life. So what the fuck has that got to do with anything?

Another swig of wine then the slam of the glass on the table.

And the theory comes to him so quickly, so obviously, he hits back, his voice rises.

He says, because maybe, well maybe that's it, he's like a replacement, a replacement father, the father you didn't have.

She pours more wine, lights a cigarette and he sees tears welling in her eyes, he sees she's broken, sees the drink, sees the cigarette, sees the anxiety, confusion, emotion and he sees, completely, for the first time, how screwed up she is.

Her life will be this, frantic, chain smoking, drinking and the tears of her pain. Let her go, for fucking hell's sake, just let her go now, don't go in any deeper, just let her go.

Her sobs get louder, he goes to her. I'm sorry, I didn't mean to make you cry.

She holds her face in her hands, he backs off.

She dries her eyes, and looks at him. She gets up and goes to the shelf where Jake has a picture of his mother and father on their wedding day.

She puts it on the table. He's bemused.

Jake, have you heard of the Oedipus Complex?

Before he has time to answer, she explains, Freud believed that the mind keeps in the unconscious, via repression, that a child has a desire to have sex with the parent of the opposite sex. Girls with their fathers, boys with their mothers.

She picks the picture up and faces it to him.

Look at your mother. She's blonde. Who does she most resemble who you know, know right now?

He looks at the picture, frowns with bemusement.

He jumps when she shouts, she looks like fucking me, Jake, she looks like me and I look like her.

She calms down, takes her bag and pulls two photos from it and places them on the table.

One is of her father but he doesn't recognise the other.

She looks at him. He looks at the pictures, mainly to avoid eye contact.

This is my father, taken years ago.

She places the two photos next to each other and pushes them forward to him.

This is Salime. Pretty similar, eh? You see Jake, we subconsciously are drawn to people by how much they resemble our mothers and fathers. I've found the man I want because he closely resembles my father. You were drawn to me and got so serious about me because I remind you of your mother. That's what attracted you, the very first time we met at the rave.

He takes a sip of wine, nervously lights a cigarette. It is amateur psychology, he thinks, but natural that she should look to find an explanation.

But he dismisses it, you can take psychological theories and make them fit just how you want them to fit.

So why did you just make love to me when Salime is the one?

You know Carl Jung I mentioned in my diaries?

Another fucking psychologist, another fucking lecture.

He drags on his cigarette and looks to the ceiling.

Jung was unfaithful to his wife, he believed he couldn't rely on just one woman – with what happened to his mother. So he had a mistress.

He didn't want to rely on just one woman for fear she might also leave him, like his mother had abandoned him in his formative years. Well maybe it's the same for me Jake, I have strong feelings for you, you'll always be special and maybe that's why I'm still here and why we made love. And you will probably be the same. You say in your letter you want to stay in touch, that I'll always be special to you. You're saying that because, even when you meet another person, you want another woman, me, still in your life. In case that woman leaves you. Just like your mum did.

She lights yet another cigarette, takes a drag and says, anyway, what we did just now was just a fuck. That's all. It wasn't making love. I don't love you. I was happy to fuck you. That's all.

She has been indoctrinated by Salime. It could be Salime saying this. I can fuck you.

My mother, my mother, why do you go on and on about my mother?

She left you Jake. You never had a mother. Not when you most needed her. And this has made you who you are. Your mother was not there when you were changing from being a child into a man. Your formative years, the years when you were aware, when you had emotions, even beliefs. You can apply the theory to any point of your young life. She was not there Jake, she was not there when you needed her, she made a difference, she shaped you, her absence made you who you are, how you are.

Silence. Welcome silence though he can hear the distant traffic of the Earls Court Road and he wishes he was there, among the din of the traffic.

He sips some more wine but takes short, careful sips, he wants to keep his head, he doesn't want the alcohol to mix with the confusion that is already clumping around in his brain.

It's psychobabble, she's read too many books. She's complicated, she gets more complicated the more you know her. She's trying to justify herself. She's trying to make you feel tainted, make you feel that you have some defective gene or neuron. That you are damaged. She is trying to convince herself you are damaged. She is damaged, she is looking for a father, she has found him. You are not him. She is fucking with your head. You hardly know her, yet now you know so much about her, how she is. She is fucking crazy, fucking, fucking crazy. You need a beer, you need your books, you need an E. You do not need her. Get her fucking out of here. As kindly, as gently as you possibly can so you have no regrets over how you treated her. Why is she still here?

She refills her glass and tops up his and says, we need each other, Jake, even if we cannot be together, we will always need each other. I just needed to be here, to see you one last time, to make love to you. I want to stay in your life, Jake and I want you to stay in mine. I'm going to Paris early tomorrow morning. I've been honest with you Jake because bad things come from lying.

He gets up, goes to the kitchen and fills a glass with water. He looks out of the window at the Earls Court rooftops, sees the houses and flats opposite, some lit, some in darkness. He can make out people moving around, preparing meals or just sitting. Just normal. Normal lives, normal thoughts, normal love. It is almost midnight and tomorrow she will be gone.

He goes back into the lounge, she is sat on the sofa, staring at nothing, her familiar blank look, that sorrowful stare into nothingness.

Jakes goes to the window ledge, lights another cigarette and looks down onto Nevern Place. Tomorrow she will be gone.

He has his back to her but she starts to speak. As she does, he just stares out of the window but listens.

When I was about 14, a little girl went missing round our way. She had been missing for days.

Her words are spoken slowly, carefully, softly.

She pauses, sips, he hears her gulp the wine.

She continues, the cops were out searching, searching hour after hour, day…day after day. But nothing. It dominated the local news and then got into the nationals. The cops kept putting out appeals and releasing different photos of her. Pleading for information. Had anyone seen this girl? They got a lead saying she had been seen near the canal. They sent divers in to search for her. They searched the canal for days. But nothing. One day I was walking along the canal. I couldn't get the girl's image out of my head, her photo had been everywhere and it just stayed in my brain. All I could imagine was her body somewhere at the bottom of the canal. Dead. As I walked along after a bit I stopped and looked hard into the water and I thought I saw something. I thought I saw her, the missing girl.

I ran home as fast as I could to tell my mum. She called the cops and I took them to the spot on the canal where I thought I had seen her in the water. They sent divers in. They searched for hours but again, they didn't find her. They never did find her. She's still missing to this day. Ever since then, all these years later, I still don't know whether I really saw anything or whether it was the image in my head making me believe I really could see her in the water.

She pauses, sips more wine, Jake stares out of the window. Rooftops, a skyline, stars. The house opposite. In all the time he has lived here he has aspired to, one day, owning and living in a house like that. On the one side of Nevern Place, bedsits, studios, cheap. On the other, opulent homes owned by the well-off. This side, his side of the street, was where he was starting. One day he would be at the opposite side of this street.

She goes on, do we really see, Jake, or is what we see just what's in our heads, our unconscious conscious? Everything we see is based on what is past. What got into our head before, in the past and that's what makes us see what we see in the future?

He doesn't turn around, he just inhales even more deeply on the cigarette. He doesn't know how to respond, he doesn't want to respond because this is all just too deep, he doesn't want to plunge into this, in fact he doesn't want to even dip his feet there.

She gets up and begins to undress then says his name.

He turns around, she is naked. She comes to him with clenched fists then opens her hands and shows him two E pills

Shall we have these? And then go to bed?

They knock the pills back with the wine, he undresses, and they go to the bed.

He hears in his head the boom of rave music, he can't place what it is, which anthem, which beat but it's in his head and he begins to feel the effects of the pill and then he's flying, flying higher but holding on.

Then the music, the beats in his head, become recognisable. But he can't name the tune, it's just a familiar beat and soon it will stop, just stop, go away, leave his head and all the lights, the fixed lights, the strobe lights, in his world, will go out.

CHAPTER FOURTEEN

THE WAREHOUSE is just off the High Street in Wapping. There are a few hundred people here but it's small-scale compared to the raves over the summer. The scene seems to be contracting, becoming more surreptitious. It's fizzling out, it's being doused, stamped out, taken over by the drugs dealers and the gangsters. There's a more edgy feel now rather than one of unified love and having a good time. Summer has left 1989. He feels an anti-climax dancing here now in this drab warehouse that is neither in the city nor in the real East End.

Her name in Bronwyn, she has a stud in her lower lip and a small butterfly tattoo at the nape of her neck. Half her hair on the left side is deep purple, on the other side it is buzz-cut short. Her eyes are marble blue, her jeans are ripped and it's obvious as her tits sway as she dances, she is braless under her smiley face t-shirt. She tells him about an after-rave party there's going to be at her squat in Brixton, asks him to come along. Where's Brixton from here, he wonders? But the E is working, it's doing what it magically does and it seems time is on fast-forward because before he can even consider the invitation he is transported from this grim warehouse in Wapping to a large, multi-floored house in Brixton that is a fug of drug smoke and musical blare.

He wanders around, explores the massive squat, opens doors to bedrooms with mattresses on floors, people sitting around pulling deep on tokes, sipping from cans or plastic cups.

In another room a few writhing bodies, jeans around ankles, moans, giggles, highs.

Are you really seeing all this, are you really here? This is all slightly out of focus. Are you out of your mind?

He finds his way to the main room where there are around 20 people, some swaying to the music he does not recognise, others are just standing around talking, drinking, smoking, laughing.

He needs to find Bronwyn. He knows no-one here. He finds a plastic cup, takes a sip. It's obviously alcohol but he doesn't recognise the potent, bitter taste, but he keeps hold of it. Where is Bronwyn?

He puts his hand in his pocket to fish out his cigarettes. He puts a fag in his mouth and then tries to find his lighter. Fuck, where is it? Panic surges through him.

You need a cigarette. You need a light, you need it now. You will have to get out of here and find a shop and buy a lighter. You just have to light this cigarette.

Out of nowhere a lighter flicks into action and moves towards him, its flame illuminates a face that is Bronwyn's.

Cool place, yeah? she says as she lights the fag.

It's all a haze, he hears her voice but it's like he is submerging, deeper into a pool of water. He sees her gesture to follow her. She leads him up a creaking, carpet-less flight of stairs and then to a double room. He stands still, he can't see a thing. Then the flick of the lighter and Bronwyn lights a candle on a bedside table.

You want a little tequila?

Before he answers she lifts a bottle from the floor, opens it, and takes a swig then hands it to him.

He takes a small gulp and hands it back. She screws the cap on tightly and places it back on the floor.

She puts her arm around him, pulls her face to his, lips meet and their mouths open. It's a short kiss before she pulls away and says, you are so beautiful. You're such a beautiful guy.

He hardly knows her, they met just a few hours ago in the half jabbing light of the rave and now he is naked with her on a mattress, in a dim, candle-lit room in a squat in a part of London he does not know.

Boring in bed. What I do with Salime, well it's almost pornographic.

He is writhing with Bronwyn, he does not want to fuck her straight away. He is between her legs, hard, but does not penetrate. He moves off her, spreads her legs, puts his face there, feels her hairy mound and licks. She moans, yeah, fuck, oh yeah, fuck me, fucking fuck me.

Her words are almost a whine and they're turning him on, making him harder and more ready. He feels the power of giving pleasure which turns into the pleasure of giving pleasure. But as he enters her, as he kisses her mouth, as he licks her neck, as he feels her breath, as he thrusts deeper and as her moans get louder, he wonders, but where is the love?

And as he pulls out and then thrusts back in and as she pulls him in even deeper and as he comes, as she comes, he wonders again, where is the love?

CHAPTER FIFTEEN

A LETTER arrives for him at Nevern Place, his name and address hand-written in a scrawl he knows is not Jean's but his father's.

He picks it up from the table in the foyer and takes it upstairs.

He decides to pour a cold beer before he opens it then sits at his desk and looks out onto Earls Court. Christmas is slowly edging in, the shops are decorated, the way they are always decorated, nothing original about Christmas, he thinks.

He opens the letter and sees five sheets of A4 folded neatly three times to get them into the envelope.

He sips on his beer and reads.

Dear Jake

I have never written to you before. Well I mean fathers don't really write to their sons, do they? I'm writing to tell you Jake, and there's no easy way of putting this so I'll come straight to the point, I cannot continue. I am almost 65 and I am tired of life. I suppose I have been for a very long time, certainly since your mother left.

I know I have never handled things well as far as being a father to you is concerned. I needed to be stronger, to realise that as well as me being abandoned by my wife, you were abandoned by your mother.

But I was not strong, I palmed you off whenever I could, I buried myself in the business and thought that providing financially for you was the best thing for me to do. And I think I at least succeeded in doing that.

But in other ways, in emotional and loving ways, I was not there for you. I never got to know you, son and as a consequence you never got to know me. But I've no idea who the 'me' was, who it is you would have got to know if you had got to know me, if you see what I mean.

Your mother always used to say I was too reserved, too detached, even from her, although I loved her deeply. I just didn't know how to show it. I'm not sentimental or very emotional anyway.

I had been angry with both myself and her. Angry that I could not change into the person she wanted me to be, to give her the marriage and life she wanted. We married young. Too young. But then folk did in our day. You were on the shelf if you weren't married by your 20s, or else you were weird or even gay. Maggie, I

72

mean your mum, had a hard childhood. Your grandmother controlled her and her brother. Her brother was a good ten years older and went wayward. Got into trouble with the police, drank a lot, slept with older women and brought shame on the family. Then he went to London. This made Margaret, your gran, even more controlling of your mum. She was ridiculously strict with her and made her do the housework and shopping. Your grandad Clive was a tacit, laid-back bookish person, utterly henpecked by Margaret and had little say over how your mother was brought up or anything else for that matter.

Margaret used to constantly do your mother down. Constantly criticised her over the way she did things, shouted at her if she brought the wrong thing back from the shops. Told her she dressed like a tart. Boyfriends were out of the question and your mother never went out to discos or pubs apart from maybe once every few weeks.

It was on one of these rare occasions we met. I saw her in a pub, I was with a few mates, and I could not take my eyes off her. She was beautiful, blue eyes, luscious locks of blonde hair, petite and well, the most stunning girl I have ever seen. I got chatting to her and asked her out. A bold move from me. I had never asked a girl out.

She looked terrified when I asked, stammered and then made some excuse that she didn't go out a lot. I felt utterly rejected but thought no more of it until a few weeks later when I saw her in the same pub again. She kept looking over, which I found strange given that she had turned me down the last time.

Determination won and I decided to ask her if I could meet her during the day for a coffee. It turned out she lived only streets away. I found it strange when she said she would meet me in town but not locally and she said I must never acknowledge her in the street locally, especially if she was with her mother.

I could not understand this, she was 18, not a kid. Anyway, we met regularly in town but I wanted to take her out properly, for a meal and a drink on an evening. At first she said this would be impossible. She told me all about her mother and how much she controlled her and would never approve of her going out with blokes.

I was frustrated. I asked her if she liked me and she said yes. I said I would go to her house one night and pick her up and I would deal with her mother. I told her she could not go on like this,

73

she had to live and her mother had no right to control her in this way. The prospect of my turning up at the house had her in tears and she pleaded with me not to do so.

I calmed her down and promised I would not go to the house. We kept meeting during the day for a few more weeks. But as you can imagine, my frustration was really getting to me.

One night after work I decided I would have a few pints in the local near to where she lived and then I would go to the house. I would ask if Maggie was in and that I had come to take her out for a drink. You see I had to do something, I had to save your mum, she could not carry on like this.

So, with a few drinks inside me I went. Their house was a nice semi-detached house in a cul de sac. I opened the garden gate and strode down the path to the door. There was a beautiful brass door knocker in the shape of an eagle. I tapped it twice. I knew someone was in because although the lounge curtains were drawn, the light was on. I knocked.

The hallway light came on and I have to admit I almost decided to turn around and do a runner. I was relieved when the door opened and it was Clive. I said good evening and put out my hand as I said my name. He was a nice man and smiled and I asked if Maggie was in and that I had come to take her for a drink.

I could hear from inside her mother asking who it was. A friend, to see our Maggie, Clive shouted back. Margaret then came to the door. She was not the dragon I was expecting, but an almost older version of your mum. But as soon as she opened her mouth, she seemed suddenly very ugly.

What do you want with our Maggie? She asked. Clive looked nervous.

I told Margaret what I told Clive.

Margaret went back inside and I heard her calling Maggie who must have been upstairs. She came down and to the door. She looked terrified.

She said Hi. I asked her if she would like to come out for a drink, just to the local and that we would not be late and I would bring her home.

Her mother looked at her and Maggie at her mother.

To everyone's utter shock, Margaret said OK, so long as she was back in the house by ten.

That's really how we met. Before I asked her to marry me I had to ask her father first. Her father said, you'd be better off asking her fucking mother. The only time I ever heard him swear.

I did and again to everyone's surprise she agreed. I don't know why I am remembering all this, I suppose when the present isn't good to you, you go back to the past.

Our early married life was a struggle as I worked hard and long hours to set up the business. Maggie's relationship with her mother became more difficult as Margaret got older and Clive's life was something of a misery.

We had you and, though I am not in any way blaming you, your mum went into bad depressions. She complained about the drudgery of her life, being a housewife, mother, you know, the usual things. She had had such a life of drudgery in her late teens living at home, I think she expected so much more from marriage. I think she expected setting up the business and making money would be quick and easy and she would enjoy the fruits of it much sooner. But it was a slow, difficult and struggling process. At times I was making very little money and at one point I thought the business would go under. I really had to put in the hours and give it my all. Which of course meant your mum spending all her time with just you, a baby. But Jake, I had no choice.

Your mum started leaving you alone when you were five or six and we had rows about this. Blazing rows. She would go to a pub with old friends. Only up the road but I felt you were far too young to be left alone. I was at work by the way and had to work late. Then I would have a pint or two as a reward. Selfish, I know, but I was under a hell of a lot of pressure and I have to be honest the thought of going home to hear your mum whining and being depressed was just too much for me to cope with. Call me weak, call me anything you want to, but that is how it felt to me then. I have never been a strong person in that sense. Hard working, with stamina, yes. But emotional stuff, well, you know this anyway now.

I felt as you were growing up Maggie and me were growing further and further apart. And that was my fault because I was immersed in getting the business going. And eventually, after all the graft, it started to make money. Good money. I bought luxuries like a colour TV and gave your mum money to spend on clothes and make-up. But, well, it just wasn't enough.

I suspected she was seeing someone else for a few years. When you got into high school she left you alone for even longer and more regularly.

The early 1980s brought a recession and the business began to struggle. In fact the country was not a good place. Riots, a lot of social unrest. I felt I needed to work even harder to keep the business going. I felt shattered all the time and my drinking started to get heavy. I mean, I didn't drink during the day but I was getting through half a bottle of Scotch most nights and more on Friday nights.

One night I had an awful row with Maggie when she didn't come home until well after midnight. My anger was fuelled by the whisky and this, son, is when I realised I had to get a grip and also that your mother and me were never going to stay together. She came in and it was clear, even to me who had had more than enough, that she was sozzled. I asked her where she had been and she just kept saying, out, I've been out, can't I bloody go out if I want to?

I kept asking her, yes, but where have you been? After my asking repeatedly she got up from the sofa. I got up too and I grabbed her. She put her face very close to mine, I could smell the alcohol on her and she told me in words neither of us had ever uttered, fuck off and fucking let go of me.

I slapped her very hard on the face and threw her onto the sofa. I can still see myself doing it to this day. I can still hear her scream and her yelp. Every day I hear it. I hear that yelp, like a helpless animal. I had hit the woman I loved, the woman I had married. The woman I had neglected. Your mum, Jake, I did this to your mum. Fatigue, anger, the fuck word, which at that time was very strong and not often heard, and never said, least of all from a woman's lips. How times have changed. I blame television, but, well, I'm going off on a tangent.

Two weeks later I came home, she was sat in the lounge waiting, two suitcases beside her. She saw me looking at them and said, I'm going Peter. You may as well know that I am with someone else, Roger, and we are going abroad to Australia. I have been seeing him for months. I'm sorry, but I cannot be with you anymore. I want a divorce.

Within minutes, as I tried to take it in, the doorbell rang. She got up, picked up her suitcases and went. I watched out of the window as Roger carried her cases to his car. They got in, he started the engine and off they went. I hardly even clocked Roger, still don't know to this day how or where she met him, or what he did for a living.

Or why they went to Australia of all places.

When this sort of thing happens, you call upon coping mechanisms so that you can carry on, function, work, sleep, eat. Anger was my mechanism. And everything started to make me angry, I began to hate everything from politicians to television, to music, to everything. I started to ask, why am I still so angry? I had you, I had a son, the gift I made with your mother, a person, a legacy, another life that we had created together.

But it wasn't enough because every time I saw you, held you close, walked you to school or to your aunt's, I was angry because you were for the both of us. You should have had a dad and a mum. And I should have had a wife.

I'm sorry if my handwriting gets worse as this letter goes on. It's the whisky son, the whisky I'm drinking, the whisky I need to help me pour this out in a letter. And I don't mean to burden you, son but I can't go without at least explaining everything, why everything has been like it has been over the years, during your childhood.

I am a weak man, Jake and I will never be able to say how sorry I am.

I did take an interest in you, son. I did want you to do well, I did push you at school to work hard and make something of yourself.

I still took an interest in you before you left home. I wasn't snooping but I know you were taking this acid stuff or E or whatever. I found them in your bedroom. I got worried, the papers are full of young people going to these raves and taking too much and frazzling their brains.

But at least you took them for pleasure I suppose. Your pills I mean. Unlike me now. I'm not taking these sleeping pills for pleasure Jake, I'm taking them to, to erase myself, finish myself.

I'm ...sorry son.

I'll stop now because I need to get this in an envelope and post it before I get any worse. Then I'll come back and finish things off.

Find a good life Jake, and most importantly, find someone to love. And when you find her, hang on to her, never let her go, whoever she is, if you love her, cherish her, take care of her, hold her, kiss her, oh please hold her because that's what I miss, holding your mother, pulling her into me, feeling the warmth and love of her body before it all turned so bad.

Look to the future Jake, the future is the only hope.

I did love you Jake.

Love

Dad

He folds the pieces of paper as he, his father, had folded them and places them carefully back in the envelope.

His eyes are moist but tears won't come. He gulps the remains of a can of lager, gets up and goes to the shelf. He takes the picture of his mother and father on their wedding day and he takes the photo of him and Jean in Brighton, their backs to the sea on that balmy star-filled night in the summer, the summer of 89.

He places them on his desk and sits down. He looks closely at the wedding photograph. His father with slicked back hair, the fashion then, and his mother with long blonde hair and a fringe. A real 60s couple, married in the summer of 64. His mother was beautiful, he thought, a real beauty.

He takes the picture of him with Jean. With Jean in Brighton, not so long ago but it might as well have been a lifetime back.

And then the tears come, starting with a clench in the throat, it builds up, then bursts out in loud, yelping sobs. This was to cry. Hold her, kiss her, oh please hold her. Pulling her into me, feeling the warmth and the love of her body. Never let her go.

It hits him when he finally controls the sobbing. Maybe he didn't do it, maybe his dad hasn't killed himself. It's just a cry for help.

Jake runs to the phone downstairs and tries to phone home. It just rings and rings. He puts it down and tries again, for no reason other than he feels he just has to try.

Your uncle. Ring your uncle. He could get round there. Maybe stop him, call an ambulance, it might not be too late. But the letter is days old. But you have to try.

He runs back up to the flat to find his uncle's number in his Filofax, runs back to the phone when he gets it. He dials, nervously. It's years since he spoke to his uncle. It rings and rings and just as Jake is about to give up the line crackles into life and a man with a broad Yorkshire accent says hello.

Uncle, it's me, Jake in London.

Silence at the other end of the line. Then

Hello Jake.
Hello, look I've had a...
Yer dad died about a week ago.
So he did it. So he killed himself. So he is dead.
I'm sorry Jake. He was already dead when I went round there. The neighbours saw he hadn't taken in his milk or papers and called the police. They broke in and found him. No point in an ambulance, like, he was pronounced dead at the scene, as they say.
I'm coming up there. Can I meet you?
I, of course lad. I'm sorry I couldn't get hold of you but I couldn't find any number for you. I found your address amongst your father's stuff and I've sent you a letter, but there's no need for that now I suppose, now you know. Funeral's next week.
He hadn't seen his Uncle Jeff since he was a teenager even though he and his aunt had virtually brought him up. If that's what you could call it.
He was his father's younger brother who had never achieved nowhere like as much as his elder brother and Jake had always suspected some resentment about that, jealousy even.
Now he is in his father's house, the place that used to be his home that Uncle Jeff had cleared out and Jake has come up to help him finish off and take what he wants. He picked Jake up at the station and took him the short ride to the house. They had hugged when they first met but there had been no conversation in the car.
He remembered, Jeff was a man of few words, worn down by his childless marriage. Aunty Peggy was not easy to live with and deep, deep down resented her life with Jeff.
When they get to the house Jeff puts the kettle on and then sets to work packing more boxes. Jake brings him a mug of tea and then begins a tour of the house. The house that was once a home but had ceased to be for so many years as he was growing up.
He goes into what had been his parents' bedroom. The scene of the act, the act of suicide his father had executed. A bedroom where many years ago, his father shared a bed with the love of his life. His wife, Jake's mother. Man and wife, mother and father. Peter and Maggie, nee Shepherd.
The room is bare apart from the bed which has been stripped down to just a mattress. No sign of whisky bottles and pills, just an air of clammy depression.
He goes to his own room. He had taken most of his things to Nevern Place over the last year. There are just a few books and

carrier bags full of old magazines which he will dump here in Yorkshire. There are a few shirts and jackets, too but he will never wear them.

He searches the drawers and cupboards. He has no idea what he is looking for as he pulls doors open. Maybe he is looking for a childhood memento, a present his father had bought him when he was a kid, or a favourite teddy bear that had been abandoned years ago.

Just something to take, as a reminder, a reminder of better days. But there is nothing. Most of the presents Jake had received from his father were five and 20 pound notes put into envelopes. Money he had long ago spent and on what he could not recall. In this room, what was his room, there is nothing to remind him, because there is nothing to remember.

He looks out of the window. The tree he used to climb and once fell from there in the garden that his father took pride in tending. His only therapy apart from work. His mother would probably have sat out in this garden during the few summers she lived here, he thinks. Catching the sun while her baby slept indoors obliviously. This was their dream, a nice big house with a garden for their little boy to play in. It's what his father had achieved for his wife, for his son, for them, for his young little family. But it hadn't been enough. Love had never lived there.

At that moment, as he looks out of that window into that garden, for the first time in his life, he feels a swelling of pride building up inside him, pride in his father, pride that releases tears, the first tears he has ever shed for the man who he had never thought deeply about, had never known and whose unremitting pain he had never considered.

CHAPTER SIXTEEN

CHRISTMAS DAY. Soho is deserted. His first Christmas in London. He had planned to go home to be with his father but now there is nothing and no-one to go home to. There is nothing to go back to Yorkshire for ever again.

He soaks up the quietness and solitude of the Soho streets which he has never seen so deserted. Even the street-walking prostitutes are nowhere to be seen.

He crosses Wardour Street and sees a young woman, about his own age, sitting in a shop doorway smoking and swigging from a can.

He walks past her. She shouts, hey, and he turns around and goes back to the doorway.

He looks down at her. He expects her to ask for money. But she holds up her beer can and says, do you want some beer?

He tells her he doesn't then she asks him, you want to walk together?

They walk through Soho, up to Oxford Street and carry on for several miles. Her name is Agatha, she is Brazilian, from Sao Paulo and has been in London for just a few months.

They reach Notting Hill and she says she knows a Portuguese bar that will be open, even on Christmas Day, just off the Portobello Road.

As he sits opposite her at a table in Bar Porto he sees she is beautiful although with her brown hair cut short, she looks quite boyish. When she goes to the toilet he sees she has a sexy figure and the way she walks is more of sashay. She is very, very sexy, he thinks. She is also a good talker, she hadn´t stopped for most of their walk from Soho.

They talked about Sao Paulo and she told him about the favelas where she had lived and about the drugs and the gang warfare.

Her father is a doctor, her mother a teacher and he assumed she came from a middle class background.

He wonders where this is going and why she had asked him, a stranger, if he wanted a beer and to go for a walk. And what had she been doing sat in a shop doorway in Soho on Christmas Day?

As he lights a cigarette, he thinks how magical, how strange London is. Could you imagine this happening back in Yorkshire? A strange and beautiful girl sat in a shop doorway walks miles with you then you find yourself having a beer with her in a Portuguese bar – on Christmas fucking Day!

She comes back from the toilet and he buys two more bottles of beer. He notices she smokes like a chimney – and likes her beer.

As she settles back in her seat and takes a swig, he asks her why she is on her own, why she is in Soho? Why she had offered him her beer and the walk?

She lights another cigarette and then starts playing with and trying to pull off the label on the beer bottle.

When she looks up at him to speak, he sees a sadness in her face, as if talking to him has taken her away from something and now, his questions have taken her back to somewhere she does not want to be.

She explains. She had been in love with a boy since she was 17. His name was Lupas. He was four years older than her. His family had fallen on hard times and he had got caught up with the drugs gangs in the favelas.

Lupas had told her he was in serious trouble, he had shot dead a member of a rival gang and he had to get out of the favela. As far away as possible.

She says, I thought he was telling me because he was going to take me with him.

I thought he wanted to escape, for a better life, for us both. But he told me I was too young, that my father would never forgive him or me. I said to him, but if you are in love with me, if you love me, you will not want to be apart from me. He told me it was because he loved me that he didn´t want to take me with him. I cried, I begged him to at least tell me where he was going and that I would join him when I was old enough and we would have a life together, without any trouble, without any violence. He could get a job, I could get a job, take care of him.

Jake listens intently and holds her hand when tears begin to stream.

So you never found out what happened to him?

She lights another cigarette and takes another swig of beer.

He told me where he was going and I waited until I was 18. I waited all those years and then wrote to him and told him I was ready, ready to go to him, be with him. He told me to come and I packed my bags and went there. But when I got to the address, a neighbour said the apartment had been empty for weeks, nobody was living there.

She sighs and wipes her eyes. I waited all those years, never went out with any other guy. I waited for him, waited to be with him. I had also fallen out with my parents when I told them I was going to be with him. Now I was outside where I thought he lived, where he told me he lived, and he was not there. I don't know if he decided to move on because he did not want to be with me and just couldn't tell me or whether he got into more trouble and had to move on again. I went back home to my parents who were very supportive. But going back home was very difficult for me and the area just reminded me of Lupas and I wanted to just go far away.

He asks her, why London?

I was going to go to the US or even Cuba. But I have read so many books about London and everything seems to be happening here. I like the English ways, the culture and the literature. So I came here. I like the streets, I like to be on the streets. I live in a hostel in Queensway. It's Ok but during the days I like to walk and buy a beer and rest in a doorway, especially when it's cold.

I've only been here a few months, but I love this city. But I get sad. Sad about Lupas and wish he was here. I dream that when he had to escape from the favelas he decided to come here, to London, and I came with him and we found a little flat, maybe in Kensington, with a low light and a warm place and be together, safe in London, in our own little flat. And sometimes, I imagine maybe he is here, maybe he is somewhere in this city, maybe he came to London and he is here, not too far away from me and that we will see each other in the street, or in a bar or on Oxford Street. I dream too much, Jake, I imagine too much.

He should feel happy, he should feel pleased with himself as he lies in bed next to a gorgeous Brazilian girl who, and he still cannot quite believe this, he picked up in a shop doorway in Soho – on Christmas Day!

He listens to her soft breathing and she sleeps sweetly and he feels he is a protector, I've brought this beautiful girl in off the streets, into safety and warmth.

He had told her last night that he was inviting her back here for a beer and a talk and that he was not trying to seduce her, although he told her he liked her.

When they got back to the flat she was very forward and began kissing him immediately. Then bed, then sex. She was a passionate lover, knew what she liked and made him feel he was doing what she wanted and satisfying her. What I do with Salime is...

As he lays looking at the ceiling and listening to her soft breathing as she enjoys a deep sleep, the questions come. What next? Is there any future with Agatha?

Take it for what it probably is – a one-night stand, a newly-formed friendship with sex attached. She will probably get up, dress, drink some coffee and then leave. Arrangements might be made to see each other again. Casual dates, dates that might end up in bed. Two loners who met in a shop doorway in Soho on Christmas Day seeking companionship and solace until the right one comes along, the real love of your life. How do we know when the real one comes along?

How do we choose, how do they choose? Where are they? Where is the one for me, right now, if there is such a person? Is this her, this girl sleeping next to me, is she the one, is she here to stay?

A week later and Agatha has moved in. She had been telling him she was getting fed up with the noise at the hostel. He told her she could stay here.

That's kind Jake. And yes, I would love to. But only for a while. I don't really want to live with someone, I need a place of my own.

He told her he understood, but that was a lie. They had slept together, they got on, shared a mutual love of books and films, they seemed destined to try it out, being a couple.

Her things are still unpacked, she is out at work as a waitress in a restaurant near Kensington Gardens. He sips a beer and smokes. She only has a large rucksack and a small holdall. She said she wanted to sleep here in the lounge although he had offered her the bed.

Another girl moves in, another girl he does not know and another girl who confuses him.

Of course, it's the fact she's still in love with Lupas. She still thinks there is a future for her there even though she has no idea where he is or even if he is still alive. She wants to stay faithful, at least emotionally, fucking someone else may not be regarded as unfaithful in Brazil, in the favelas, maybe.

She dreams too much, she imagines too much. She said so herself.

And he can understand that. First love, real love? Possibly. And then she comes into his mind, just flutters in. Jean. It seems so long ago. He has not heard from her, no Christmas card or letter, nothing and he cannot get in touch with her because she had not, as promised, sent him her address.

That was 1989. The new decade is just days away. This is the time, this is the living moment. Jean is now a memory, a blurred vision in your mind from the summer of 1989. The future, not the past.

He takes himself out of the flat and goes for a few pints in Cromwells armed with a notebook and pencil.

You have to move on, you have to stop standing still.

He starts to write a list, a kind of manifesto of how he is going to be and what he is going to do.

The ideas scattergun in his head and he can hardly write them down quickly enough.

Move on, look to the future

Be more outgoing and not so intense.

Stop expecting too much when you meet someone – having sex is not them signing up to your life for the rest of theirs.

Read more books

Be calmer

Reduce cigarette intake

Reduce alcohol intake

Be more happy-go-lucky

Take life in my stride

Get a new job and meet new people

Go up to strangers and start a conversation

Be chatty with barmaids

The next and last bullet point comes after he has read the list so far.

And the next lines he writes shakily:

Forget about Jean Ridley. Completely forget about Jean Ridley.

Days later he finds an envelope on his desk when he gets back to the flat.

Dear Jake

Just a note to say goodbye. I just want to explain why I did not wait to say goodbye to you properly. Well, the reason is I probably could not have done and you might have tried to persuade me to stay and I would probably have succumbed because, well I think I may have been falling in love with you.

I do not want my emotions to run away with me. I still believe my future is with Lupas, I will go on with this positive feeling until life is over and there is no possibility of us ever being together, or if I have confirmation that something fatal has happened to him.

I loved our short time together, you and me. I think you are a very special person and I would not want to break your heart. Or you to break mine.

Also Jake, I think, from what you said about Jean, when we talked the other night of previous lovers, I think you are still in love with her. I have no proof, it was just the way you spoke about her. It was very obvious that you miss her terribly.

So what an odd couple we would have made. Both missing other people dreadfully, both really in love with other people. So it could not have worked.

I think you should not give up on Jean. I think you should pursue the person you love. And I think she probably really is still in love with you. What she has with this older man is a compulsive infatuation with someone she sees as a father figure.

As she gets older she will not want such a figure. She will want someone like you Jake and I think you have to be patient and allow this to happen. Even make it happen.

Enough advice from me. Thank-you for our lovely time together. I hope 1990 and the new decade bring you peace, love and happiness and I hope you find long-term love in your life. You deserve it.

Agatha.

CHAPTER SEVENTEEN

1990

IF A strip pub off Old Street is the way to change your life's direction then so be it. At least it was opening his eyes to reality. Life isn't just about looking for love, finding the right one.

You are 23, it's time to live a little even if that means experiencing the sleazy side of this place, London. The girl onstage now is blonde, topless and is slowly peeling off her knickers. Ronnie's grin becomes wider as she finally tosses them to one side and is now naked.

He looks around the room and realises, none of the men are smiling like Ronnie. They are looking, nervously sipping their pints and taking long, slow drags on their cigarettes, but for the most part their faces are blank, sad even. He looks back at Ronnie, who looks at him and holds his empty glass and gestures to ask if Jake is ready for another.

He nods yes and then looks around the pub at those faces again. There are a few young blokes but mostly it's a middle age and slightly older crowd. It hits him, almost winds him, the thought that this is all there might be, a few pints at lunchtime and the closest thing to anything sexual is watching a girl you don't know take her clothes off in a grotty pub on a drizzly January lunchtime. Is this how I could end up? he asks himself.

The blokes wait for the next performer who is going round the pub with an empty pint glass which the punters are dropping change into. Tips. Ronnie returns from the bar and the girl, black and stunning, comes over to them for a donation. Ronnie fishes a fiver from his top pocket and puts it in her glass, his face beaming and his eyes making direct contact with the girl. She says, why thank-you generous sir.

Jake reluctantly puts a quid in and, to his surprise, she smiles and winks, looking him up and down before moving off.

Hey, you're in there Jake boy, the look she gave you, Ronnie pants.

He's embarrassed but before he can respond, thankfully, the black girl starts her performance and is dancing to Tina Turner's Private Dancer. Ridiculous. It's either a terrible corny cliched choice or she's taking the piss but he is not sure.

Ronnie Blythe is his colleague at his new job with a PR agency in Soho. It's a small company set up by a guy called

Richard Sutcliffe-Robinson. He is dapper, self-made and is building up the business into a success he could not have imagined when he started it. Ronnie is one of the agency's senior copywriters, he weaves words and sentences into powerful messages that get clients business. The power of words. Richard wears Saville Row suits, only sips the odd half pint at lunchtimes and is said to be extremely self-disciplined and a workaholic.

Now Ronnie, well he has the gift of words but he's completely the opposite. He bashes out copy with a fag in his mouth and a large mug of black coffee beside his computer. Ronnie is from Glasgow and although he has a gift for writing, it's a struggle to make out what he is saying when he speaks in his treacle-thick Glaswegian.

Ronnie has a wife, he's in his 40s and neither his marital status or age stops him constantly being on the look-out, ready for the chase.

I lurv filth Jake, sex, beer and fags, that's what I live for, although, yeknow, I do like a bit a culture.

He tells Jake this as they hit another pub that is not a strip joint. It's a nice, slightly trendy, but traditional boozer in Farringdon and this is their first proper lunchtime pint together. He will be working closely with Ronnie and Richard says he will learn a lot from him. Ronnie is to be his mentor.

Now, what yee got on on Saturday?

Not a lot, why?

Two birds I know are having a house-warming party. Hillo and Hello – Hilary and Helen. Both fuckin horny, it'll be a scream. Hillo has a bit of a party piece and..ah…before yer ask, I'm not telling yers. Yers have to come on Saturday to find oot.

He can only imagine but tells Ronnie yes, he will come along.

Ronnie is propping up the bar and chatting to a busty barmaid in the Old Sergeant, his local in Wandsworth. The house-warming is just down the road but Ronnie wants to 'oil the works' before they get there.

He gets Jake a pint and they sit at a table.

Ye all set then, Jake. Tis going to be one fucken good party, it's in ma bones, it's in ma cock. You'll love Hillo and Hello, lovely wee girls.

What do they do, how do you know them?

Hello is an air hostess and Hillo is a nurse up at Charing Cross Hospital. Ah met them both in Magaluf a year ago.

Did you, you know?

Shag ém? No, oh no, no such luck. Áve been working on those two for the whole year. Hillo told me she quite fancied a three-in-a bed situ, with Hello. Ah think she has what they call bisexual tendencies. Ah tell ye what Jake, when ye see them, first thought will be, would love to see those wee lassies in action together. Ha.

Ronnie orders more pints 'before we enter the lair' and then he asks Jake about his sex life. It comes from nowhere, just like he's asking if he has read any good books lately.

So, have yer been getting any humping in of late?

It's not a question he has ever been asked, ever. He goes for the macho, matey answer and hates himself for it.

Yeah, always plenty of opportunity, especially in Earl's Court, lots of foreigners and travellers going through.

He hates this answer, he hates the way he has answered this crude question.

Ah, so you like yer Foreign lassies, do yer Jake? Can't say as have had many er them, tend to go for the busty blonde south London types, barmaid types, yer know, the girls who are always on the lookout for some fun. Mind you, I'm not really in your age bracket anymore. When yer get to your fortis, yer take whatever's on offer, wherever. Y'll get there Jake, enjoy the younger totty while yer canae.

He rolls a cigarette as he says this, his eyes on the task in hand. He looks up.

So, what der yer goo for, are yer into the dark Latino types, or the Swedish blonde sort?

Whatever moves, he says, getting into the full swing of this anodyne conversation.

Ha, Jake, yer wee buggar. Don't blame yer, yer young, enjoy whatever young flesh happens to come yer way. Yer only live once – yer only live once so yer should shag as much as possible. Live once, shag millions. Ha.

Ronnie goes on to regale him with his latest exploits, graphically detailing whether they gave head or liked being 'gone down on with a good 'tonguing'.

At last they drain their pints and Ronnie says, let's go to see what shenanigans are on offer at the party.

The furniture has been moved out of the living room to create an open space for dancing and hanging around. The party is in full swing with about 20 people dancing in candlelight.

Jake stands out of the way with a can of lager and a cigarette. Ronnie has disappeared into the melee, saying he's going to seek out Hillo and Hello. He surveys the smoke-filled room but it's too dark to see much. He notices two orange flashing roadwork lights placed on a shelf to create a disco effect.

A fat shaven-headed guy elbows him gently and asks if he wants to score an E, for a fiver. He pays, takes the tab and puts it into his pocket for later.

Awkwardness grips him, he knows no-one, everyone seems loud, shouty, slightly aggressive, keyed up, drugged up, edgy.

You need to loosen up, you need to shake off this depression and inhibition that seems to have locked you into a zombie-like state. But this party is crap, full of crap people, Ronnie's kind of people, sleazy, on the lookout for whatever.

Apart from the E man, no-one is mixing, it seems like everyone else already knows each other and they stick together in clusters.

He puts the pill on his tongue and swallows, washing it down with the now luke-warm and quite strong lager. He smokes a cigarette and then sees Ronnie pushing through the crowd with two girls in tow.

Ronnie brings them over and shouts their names to Jake as an introduction. Jake shakes hands with each of them but can only make out that one is blonde, the tall one, but the other he cannot see very well but she's much smaller, possibly even petite.

Ronnie mouths some sort of comment then beams that cheeky grin and the girls laugh loudly. Jake tries to force a smile but has no idea what's so funny.

Ronnie beckons Jake and the girls and they make their way through the party throng, leaving the main room.

Jake is behind Hello who he can now see more clearly from the hallway light. She has a great ass, long mousey hair. They climb some stairs and end up in a bedroom that is bathed in candlelight. They perch on a bed and Hillo goes to a set of drawers and brings out a bottle of vodka and a bag of white powder.

Ah, that's fucken better, away from that din. Ah see yer have the wee goodies, says Ronnie, nodding at the vodka and bag.

Yer never leet us doon Hello, nah, she never leets us doon, Ronnie says turning to Jake.

Hillo opens the vodka, takes a swig and hands it to Ronnie who gulps it back thirstily.

Hillo takes some of the powder on her finger and snorts it. She passes the bag to Ronnie, who does the same after passing the vodka bottle to Hello.

The bottle finally comes to Jake and he takes a small swig. Then the bag of coke comes to him and he just holds it and stares, frozen, not knowing whether he should snort some or not.

You are mixing a potentially lethal cocktail of drugs and alcohol. What are you doing in this place, what is this all about?

The others stare at him as he stares at the bag. Finally, he says, I don't do coke guys, thanks, but no thanks.

Ah, Ronnie says rolling another cigarette. Do yer not do coke or ave yer never done coke, Jake?

Never tried it. The E's enough for me, and the booze, of course.

They laugh in unison with Ronnie, letting out a loud roar of contemptuous laughter which annoys the fuck out of him.

Yer cannae take a decision like that unless yer tried it. If yer try it and it doesnae agree with yer, yer can take the decision, I don't do coke because I tried it and it doesnae do for us. But what yer sayin Jake is yer've never tried it, that's different, that's not a wee subtle difference, that makes a huge fucken difference. Ha, don't knock it till yer've tried it as the ald sayin' goes.

Hillo gets up and takes the bottle and the bag from Jake and puts it on a bedside table.

She says, I think he needs relaxing, needs easing, what do you say Ronaldo?

Her accent is very South London. During his time in London he has heard so few Londoners.

I can feel it, that not so wee vibe, that vibe that tells me it's showtime, time for Hillo's infamous party-piece, says Ronnie.

Hello swigs from the bottle and laughs. He has not heard her speak yet.

Hillo takes another swig of vodka and then comes over to Jake perched on the edge of the bed. She straddles him and his face is just inches from her enormous tits.

She pulls his head into them, moves them up and down his face.

Ah, fuckin´hell, ha, ha, ha, what a fuckin show, Ronnie laughs as he beckons Hello to come and sit on his lap.

Hillo removes her t-shirt and her large bare tits are now right in his face and she says, suck ém baby, suck ém. Mummy says suck my tits, baby, suck my tits.

The three of them laugh and then give a round of applause. Jake tries to get up, he just has to get out of here even if it means pushing her. He has to get out of this mad fucking place because he feels like he is going fucking mad.

On the street he speed-walks down Garrett Lane towards Wandsworth High Street and sees a few drunks shouting obscenities and coming his way. He crosses the street to avoid them and in panic doesn't see the car which screeches to a stop, missing him by inches. The driver winds down his window. Stupid cunt, are you trying to get killed or wha?

He ignores this and is relieved when he hears him drive off as he walks on the opposite side of the road, safe on the pavement.

He walks up towards Putney and sees signs for Fulham, relieved he is going in the right direction to get home. He keeps going, walking at a pace, his head swirling, the bitter cold biting his ears as he he buttons his coat to the top.

Tonight was not you, this is not you.

In Putney he reaches the high street and keeps going, keeps going, moving, moving away, as far away as possible, just keep moving, keep walking.

As he reaches Putney Bridge and stops to catch his breath he looks over into the river, illuminated by lights from the buildings on the river bank. It looks inviting in there but cold. It looks like in that river you could just get washed away, to somewhere else, the river just moving you, floating you along, just you, buoyed by the water, bobbing along the river in the dead of night to be taken somewhere where there is light, where there is warmth, to somewhere you do not at this time know but a place where, once you get there, all will be fine, all will be warm, all will be light.

He looks at the river and tears from the cold blur his vision, he is coming down from the E. And in the river she is there, waving her arms, she is shouting for help, his help, she needs him. In the cold River Thames, she is shouting for him, shouting for his help.

Jake, Jake, Jake, help me, please. Help me Jake.

Her voice echoes into the night.

And he shouts, shouts with all the power he can muster: Jean, Jean, I'm here. I'm here. It's gonna be OK, I'm here...It's gonna be....it's gonna be OK. It will, I'll make sure it's OK, I promise. Jean.....CAN YOU HEAR ME, CAN YOU SEE ME? I'm here, I'm coming, I'm coming to get you, I'm coming, coming to save you, to rescue you.

CHAPTER EIGHTEEN

IT'S MONDAY morning and the daily meeting with Richard where everyone outlines what projects they are working on and the progress they are making. Richard writes it all down in a leather-bound notebook with a Mont Blanc fountain pen.

The boss looks fresh from the weekend, his silver hair slightly damp from the shower he took after his early morning workout. Richard will not have spent his weekend getting pissed and taking drugs and going to horrendous parties in rundown areas of south London, thinks Jake, watching him intently.

Richard will have been reading up on the latest PR trends, devouring PR Week and spending time with his wife and children, going on country walks, sipping half pints of local ale in a cosy country pub warmed by a real log fire.

A Sunday lunch will have been cooked, they will have sat down at a large dining room table, just the family or perhaps a few close friends round with their children who get on spectacularly well with his kids.

Jan is her name, the wife. He has a picture of her with the kids on a table next to his desk. Jan is blonde and from where he is sat Jake thinks she looks beautiful. Beautiful with her beautiful kids. Richard's beautiful wife and beautiful kids. A proud father, a hard-working and successful husband. His own business, his own boss, somebody else's boss and he hadn't even turned 50 yet.

Compare and contrast with Ronnie who is now, in his usual convoluted fashion, explaining what he's working on. Ronnie's tie is skew-whiff, his hair dishevelled, he keeps biting his nails. And we know how Ronnie spent his weekend. As he likes it, belly full of booze, nose full of powder, wanton women, a wife at home he neglects.

Talented Ronnie, kept on by Richard because his words are winning, they persuade, they sell they have effect. If only his life was as well composed as his sentences, if only his life flowed just like his words.

Ronnie finishes his amble, Richard nods, thanks everyone and closes the meeting.

Back at his keyboard, Ronnie begins hammering away – he has lied about the progress of a project, has told Richard he will have it finished by this lunchtime so he is hacking away to meet the deadline.

A cigarette is burning in the ashtray on his desk. Ronnie picks it up, sees it's burned down to the end, stubs it out and lights another and takes long, deep drags sending clouds of Benson and Hedges into the air, before he continues bashing out more words.

Lunchtime arrives, Ronnie is by the printing machine as Jake walks past to go to the toilet.

Hey Jake, fancy a wee lunchtime snifter?

Yeah, OK. One-ish?

Aye, ahll be through with this fucken shite by then, nay bother.

Jake sits at a table as Ronnie goes to the bar. Should he ask him about Saturday night, should he tell him how humiliated he felt? Should he ask him what the fuck that was all about?

He returns with two pints of bitter. Jake had asked for his usual lager.

What's this?

That my dear, dear Jake is a proper pint, none a that pissy-puffy lager shite yer normally throw dooon yer neck. Go on, try it, yéll thank me for introducing yer to the nectar of a man's drink, a drinker's drink.

This pisses him off, Saturday night is needling the back of his mind and everything about Ronnie today is seen in a fug of anger, resentment. His lecture about coke-taking at the party, in that room, is still echoing like Ronnie said it just a second ago.

Yer cannae say yer don't do it if yer havenae tried it.

I'm not drinking this, I drink lager.

He pushes the drink away and gets up, goes to the bar and gets his lager.

Ronnie looks up at him when he gets back to the table and sits down, concern is expressed as a frown.

Hey, what's goat into yer Jake. Ah just thought yer might like to try something different for a wee change. Ah'd have got yer the lager masel if yer really didnae want the ale.

Jake takes a sip of his lager then says, you're assuming I'm so young and naïve that I've never tried real ale. Just because I've never tried cocaine doesn't mean I've never tried other things and decided I didn't like them.

Saturday night. There, it's on the table, there to be taken, there to be discussed.

Woha, hey Jake, ah was making no assumptions. I just thought yer might fancy a pint of the amber-nectar. That's all. Look, ave ah done something to piss yers oaf? What's up, tell yer uncle Ronaldo.

He doesn't want to go into Saturday night, yet to not confront it now will make it more difficult any time later.

So, he sips his drink and then out it comes.

Saturday night, what the fuck was that all about?

A grin, the familiar grin, spreads across Ronnie's face.

It was a bit a fun Jake, a bit a drugged up fun. Yer tellin mee yer didnae enjoy Hillo's juicy big tits in yer mush? Hello and me were getting on fine. Yer should have just gone for it. She liked yer, fancied the pants off yer. Ahm sorry if it wasnae yer scene Jake, there was never any intention of making a fool a yer or making yer feel uncomfortable.

It infuriates him that Ronnie seems to think life is just one, long never-ending joke, prank, jape. It's his conceit, too. Like he's having a party that no-one else has been invited to because they don't know how to enjoy themselves the way he does, drink the way he does, shag around the way he does, takes coke the way he does.

You don't want to be like him, he's no good, it's not the way to live. Is he really happy, does he know what happiness is? Do you? You don't seem so sure. You seem to envy the way he is, his happy-go-lucky take on life, his ability to get what he wants. Is that really you, is this what you really, underneath it all, think you should be doing, is this the way you think you should be living?

Ronnie wipes beer froth from his lips and flicks ash into the ashtray. He looks up at Jake, a smile, but not the usual grimacing smile. This is warm, considered, even contrite.

In a soft, low voice, Ronnie says, ah know what yer think a me Jake, ah know what the likes a Richard really think. There's plenty a folk who laugh at me, laugh with me but they don't, deep, deep down, approve of ma lifestyle, the drinking, the drugs, the shagging. Ok, the sleaze of it all.

He pauses, takes a sip and a drag and continues.

Ah come from Glasgow as yer know. The Blythes were a poor family and ma mother and father had to graft, fucken graft, for what little they had, what little they could give to us. Oh no, am not gonna give yer a long sob story about what a shite childhood ah had. But it does affect yer, Jake, yer upbringing, where yer from, it shapes who yer are. Ah used to look at ma Ma and Pa and think, fuck, is that all there is, grafting away and for what? Ah grew up angry with ma father for being a failure, ah used him as an opposite role model. Ah would be anyone ah wanted, so long as that person bore absolutely no resemblance to ma Pa. Ah hated his failure, ah hated the way he'd surrendered his life to drudgery and poverty, ah asked masel, why Pa if you're so useless did yer bring us into the world to share yer shitty life? To give yer something that ye'd achieved, to be able to say, ah may not have a lot but ah have kids? Ah did a pact with masel Jake and that pact was, don't live a life of deprivation and poverty. Find something yer good at, earn the brass and have all that yer want, all that's on offer, fill yer fucken boots.

 He stubs out his cigarette which is down to the end and lights anther. Jake sips, Ronnie continues.

 Ah came down to London in 1979. Thatcher had just got in after the winter of discontent and all that stuff. Change was on the way and ah was just 20. London calling. Ah settled in London easily and got a writing job and realised ma writing could sell ice to Eskimos. There's money in tha kind, of writing Jake, forget novels and journalism. That's for the holier than thou brigade. Anyways, there's young gun Ronnie on the loose in London. So, ah meets a lassie, Irish lassie of all lassies, started seeing her, shagging her senselessly, fell for her and her for me.

 He smiles as he recounts this, recounts someone loving him. A sip of beer, a long slow drag of his fag and Ronnie's story unravels.

 Ah was 20 Jake, and here ah was shacked up with a lassie, Kathy. Then she goes and ruins it all. Am pregnant she says, smile beaming from her beautiful fucken face. We're gonna have a baby, Ronnie, she says. Well, ah felt like I'd just been kicked in the knackers and punched in the stomach all at the same time. Cut a long story short ah told her she would have to get rid a it, have a termination. Ah told her ah didnae love her enough to have a bambino with her.

 Ronnie sighs, it comes from deep within, like something is always there that he cannot get rid of, too deep to mine.

 Ah broke her fucken heart Jake, ah broke that wee lassie's heart. Too fucken selfish, too fucken full a masel.

 Too young, says Jake.

Ah, not really, not back then, people had to grow up quicker than they do these days. But anyways, ah was just out for masel. To avoid becoming like ma father. Anyways, and here's the rub. Kathy says she's going back to Dublin. We broke up and ah never knew whether she had an abortion. Anyways, two years later she writes to me and tells me she had a son – ah have a son. So ah ignores the letter, ah don't write back and then moved to other addresses and never had them forwarded them on. So, Jake, ah have a son who ah have never met, who's never met me his da. It's been with me all those years but one day, a long time ago, ah decided, I wasnae gonna brood, wasnae gonna let it stop me living ma life. After all, that's why ah abandoned Kathy, because ah wanted to be free, wanted ma life to be free so ah thought, Ronnie, go out there and live the life yer craved, live the life yer sacrificed a good woman and child for otherwise the whole fucken thing will have been for fuck all.

Jake isn't sure what to say.

Ronnie goes to get more beer and as he returns and sits down with the drinks, he says, June, ma current missus wanted kids and we tried. Tried and tried, but to no avail. We had all the tests, yer know, to see if it was her, or me firing blanks, then we started the IVF, spent thousands of dosh on that but…well, zilch, nothing, sweet FA. I saw it tearing her apart for many, many long years and if ahm honest it tore us, me and her, apart. Things have never been the same. We're still together but only because of the hoose, yer know, the mortgage but we're practically strangers to one another. She has a fair idea what ah get up to and just seems to accept it. Except a course there's one thing she doesn't know. That ah am actually a father. Ma dirty big secret Jake and they don't come much bigger. The secret that ah don't really share her pain of not having a child, the secret that ah had a kid with another woman but couldnae have one with her, the secret that somewhere out in this cruel fucken world Ronnie Blythe has a bairn, a son, a child.

Ronnie takes a big gulp of Guinness, lights another fag. Jake looks at this man, this man with all his secrets, with all his regrets.

I'm sorry, Ronnie, is all he can think of to say.

Ronnie's tone changes, it's not as quiet, it's perkier

Anyway Jake, ave decided. Am goana try to find Kathy. Ah only have the one address from years ago in Dublin. But it's worth a try.

But what if she's moved?

It's worth a try, maybe ah can do some detective work, turn maself into Taggart. Hey, Jake, how d'yer fancy joining us. In Dublin, thee and me. Both of us let loose in Dublin fair city?

Friday night, Temple Bar, Dublin, the heaving centre of the city. Jake and Ronnie are in a bar, it's noisy, raucous even, it's not Jake's scene but Ronnie is impressed by the 'local talent'. There are girls who are drunk wearing very little, inhibitions drowned by alcohol. They are two pints in already and Jake suggests moving on to another bar.

They head away from the city, cross the Liffey Bridge and Jake spots a bar on the riverfront that looks more sedate. When they go inside, Jake is delighted, it's a traditional pub, oak-panelled with photographs of yesteryear Dublin adoring the walls. The punters are a mix of ages, not too many youngsters, and a few old men nursing pints while reading the evening paper.

Bit fucken quiet, a bit deed in here, says Ronnie.

We can go somewhere else if you like.

Ha, you old fogey, anyone would think it was me that was 20 years younger. No, this'll do us, says Ronnie as he clocks a woman sat at the other end of the bar on her own.

Wonder if she fancies some company.

Go ahead, go over, don't let me cramp your style.

Nah, not in the mood for chatting up totty tonight.

Something on your mind?

Ah, was just thinking as we walked here, coming to Dublin to find Kathy's probably a bad idea. Too many years have gone by now. Ah havnae been in their lives, they're probably getting on just fine withoot us.

But can you live with that, not ever knowing, not ever meeting your own son?

Ah've lived with it all these years, ah just think it's too late. And then there's the missus to consider. Ah've told her enough lies over the years withoot scurrying arooond behind her back getting involved in ma past. Let sleeping dogs lie and all that.

They find a table and Ronnie goes to the bar. Jake watches him. Watches a man who has made a mess of his life yet tonight the real Ronnie has been revealed. The sleaze-chasing older Ronnie who doesn't take life seriously, is really a very serious man, a hurt man, a man with a history whose past has dominated his mind, the mistakes he's made, the hurt he has caused, the woman he spurned, the son he has never known. Ronnie never knew where he was going, what he was looking for and, Jake concludes, he still doesn't. So you get to his age and you still haven't worked out life. You get to his age and you're still chasing ass, still looking for the highs, still trying to make the past disappear so you can try to get on with the future, any kind of future. What a mess he's made. Yet after tonight, Jake feels warmth towards Ronnie, sympathy, sadness. And he hopes when he gets to Ronnie's age no-one has to feel sorry for him like he feels sorry for Ronnie right now.

It's emerging, you will find out who you are when you know the person you are not. You are learning, learning from the mistakes of people you are meeting, you are realising that what seems like pleasure and happiness is often a charade, a cloak that hides the pain of a not too distant past.

Ronnie returns with the drinks

So, young Jake, what's the big plan?

We can have these and then go back into the centre if you're looking for something more lively. I must...

Ah, no, no no, ahm note talking aboot tonight Jake. Ah mean the plan for yer life, the rest a yer life.

Jake takes a sip of Guinness and says, haven't really thought about it. Take it as it comes, I suppose.

Kids, family, are yer wanting to settle doon?

Probably, eventually, if it happens, if I meet the right person. But I'm no clairvoyant Ronnie, who knows what will happen in my life.

Ronnie goes silent, a shadow of perplexity comes over his face, he begins to speak, hesitantly.

Can ah make an observation Jake? And tell me to mind ma own business if yer thinking am talking shite.

No, go on

Yer seem a little reluctant aboot stuff.

Reluctant?

Ah mean reluctant to let yerself go, let yer hair doon, get involved with women.

Are you saying I'm gay?

Ah, no, fuck no Jake. What ah mean is, it's like there's something, or someone, hanging over yers, in the background all the time. Something or someone, yer won't let go of or it or they won't let go a yeez. Like yer saving yerself for someone. Ok, that's ma observation. Tell me to fuck off and shut the fuck up.

Jake takes a gulp, lights a fag. Ronnie's perception floors him for a second but Jake knows Ronnie is right. Her face and her voice come into his mind, as vividly as if she had just stepped in front him right now in this pub in Dublin.

Not really, I mean there is nobody. Well there was but I read too much into it, thought it meant more than it did. It didn't last long…but…

But yer havenae moved on, havenae got over it? Over her, I mean.

I think I have, I'm not thinking about it, about her as much as I was. And I am up for meeting other women.

But she's still in there – Ronnie points to his heart – and in here – Ronnie points to his head.

Jake tells Ronnie. Tells Ronnie the story of Jean. Ronnie is a good listener, his attention is total and Jake feels, as he tells him, that he's unloading it all, the valve is being released, what has built up over the months is coming out. He is telling himself the truth he has tried to deny. He was in love with Jean and he still is and talking about her now is what he's been needing to do, for so long.

In his stride, after telling Ronnie about the summer of 1989, Jake tells Ronnie, I see people like Richard and I think, that is who I want to be, to be successful, to be happy to share my life with someone. But then I don't really know whether that's me and I think at the age of 23 I ought to have some sort of idea of who I am, where I am going. I look at other guys my age who are confident, they have a swagger, they move from one woman to the next. I look at the city types, the yuppies and I think, look at all the money they've got. all the parties they go to and they're as young as me, some of them are younger. But when I look at them again, I think how shallow it all is and I think, hope I am different, I don't want to be greedy or shallow. But then what do I want to be? What's the point of me if I don't know who or what I am? Jake stops, takes a sip. Sorry Ron, I'm going on a bit.

Hey, Jake, don't apologise. Sounds like yer needed to get that off yer wee chest and am flattered yer felt yer could talk to me aboot it. But can ah say ma piece? We're all searching for oursels, we're all looking for something and we think that something is what others have got. No yer don't want to be a yuppie tosser. Yer have to have something in yer heart, something more tangible than loads a money, so much money yer don't know what to do with it is sick. Am pushing 50 Jake and well, yer would have thought ah would have learned aboot life by now with all the mistakes ah have made. And the older yer get, it doesnae mean to say yer get any wiser. It's why what happened with Kathy happened. Ah was looking for something else and ah have yet to find it Jake. In all honesty, ah have yet to find it, whatever IT might be.

Do you think you could have been happy with Kathy and the kid?

Ah don't know Jake. Probably not because ah don't think ah ave ever met happiness or shaken its hand. Ah think life is just a series of highs and lows and alls yer can do is hope there are more highs than lows. But there isnae a Promised Land. Yer are who yer are Jake, yer can pick yer mates, yer can pick yer wife, but yer only have one choice with yersel and whatever yer are or whoever yer are, well that's what yer stuck with. But ah will tell yer something Jake. This lassie Jean. Go with yer head, go with yer heart. For someone to stay in yer head for this long, well, there's something in it.

I should go to Paris and find her?

Am not doling oot advice, did yer hear what ah said, go with yer own heart, yer own head. Yours, your head, your heart, not mine nor any fucker else's. Never be afraid, Jake, to make a fucken arse of yersel. Yer only learn by fucking things up. The bigger the fuck-up, the bigger the lesson learnt. It's what this fucken life is all aboot. Dealing with fucking up. But nobody ever found happiness by being afraid of fucking up.

They head back to the hotel, back into the centre of Dublin.

Ronnie says, there's a disco back at the hotel. Der yer fancy it?

Might join you later. Want to go back to the room and freshen up.

Jake stands on the balcony of his room on the top floor of the hotel with panoramic views of the city. The moon is out, stars twinkle in a freezing sky. He smokes a cigarette and quaffs from a tumbler filled with whisky from the hotel minibar. It's edging towards midnight, the streets below pound to noise and music, the music of a Friday night.

He thinks of going down to join Ronnie in the disco, feeling guilty about leaving him on his own.

He goes downstairs to the disco but Ronnie is nowhere to be seen in a sea of bodies dancing to Abba's Dancing Queen. He goes to the small saloon bar further down the corridor and there he is, stooped over his drink, surrounded by cigarette smoke, eyes staring into nothing.

Didn't fancy the disco then?

Nah mate, not my scene tonight. Never was one for discos.

Jake gets them drinks. While he's been at the bar, Ronnie has decided to pucker up, lighten his tone.

So, Jake, do yer think ye'll stay working for Richard? How yer finding it?

I don't know Ron. I'm not sure commercial copywriting is where I want to be.

Ah know what yer mean. Not sure it's ever been for me really. But, from what ah have seen a yer work, yer have talent Jake. And Richard certainly thinks so.

Really?

Yep. And he's not easy to please isn't Randy Richard.

Randy?

Ronnie nearly chokes on his beer with laughter.

Ah, yer don't know aboot the clean-living Mr Successful smoothie do yer? The man behind the executive clean-cut image.

What about him?

Ah shouldnae burst the bubble of admiration yer have for the boss-man Jake, but he isn't what he seems. Let's say this, he has needs ootside the wee marital confines. Shame really because his wife is one sexy woman. Never banged a posh lassie afore, but, well…

Go on, spill the beans.

Ricardo has a penchant, as they say, a penchant for the ladyboys. The chicks with dicks.

Nah, Richard? How do you know that?

Saw him take a card doon, yer know, the tart cards in the phone boxes. Ah was coming back from seeing a client and saw him in the phone box across the road from the office. He didnae see me. Had the card in his hands, made the phone call, then left. He put the card on the phonebook shelf. Ah goes into the phone box and picks up the card. Hot transsexual, tight butt, big cock. Bayswater. So ah follows him. To a flat just off Queensway, Moscow Road. Ah watch him being buzzed in. Followed him a few times, to the same address. He can't keep away from the place.

Fuck. Have you told anyone else in the office?

No Jake, and ah don't intend to. Am telling you cos, well, yer a mate and ah don't like yer thinking he's such a hero, someone to aspire to. He's not. He's the same as everyone else, he has weaknesses. It's his secret, no-one is getting hurt, the wife, hopefully will never find oot. It's something he has to live with, his secret, and we all have them, eventually. Secrets, they're the life raft of life, they carry you thorough the choppy wee waters, they stop yer going under, providing they stay a secret.

Poor woman. Imagine if she found out. And the kids.

Well she won't find out unless he's clumsy. Anyways, there yer have it. The boss's little indulgences. Good luck to him ah say. Dread to think what he does with a chick with a dick mind. Urrgh. Not ma fuckin cup a tea, tell yer the truth. I'm a fanny man, always will be. Ah well, each to his own, ah suppose.

I'll never be able to look at him again in the same light. Jesus, who would have thought it.

CHAPTER NINETEEN

IT'S ALL changed, wrecked, the opposite of what it was all meant to be, full of love, full of hope, full of hedonistic innocence where time and money and trouble were not welcome; free, without rules, anyone's rules and now it had been hijacked, commercialised, brutalised, beyond recognition. Even the music had changed from the sunny, smiley, happy boom-boom beat to something more aggressive, something simmering with tension, edges to it, ragged edges, edgy, that's what he thinks it is now, edgy.

Guys with flick knives, anger etched on their faces, girls out of their minds on nothing but drink and dodgy drugs, tarted up like drag queens, sporadic punch-ups here and there, police in the background, waiting and ready. Raves are entering a new phase now, he observes, and they are no longer his thing. It's not so much that he has outgrown them, more they have outgrown him and many others like him who went every red hot summer weekend in those summers of love for the spirit, the freedom, the life. Now, it's just hate and lives that amount to nothing more than human waste, wasted lives. A new generation, the new degeneration.

The rave is at the venue where he met Jean at the back of Kings Cross.

He leaves and walks down Caledonia Road. It's 11pm and he could get the Tube and be back in Earls Court in 20 minutes. But he's in no mood to get on a Saturday night train full of Saturday night drunken mayhem. He walks in the direction of Bloomsbury. These streets are quieter, with their big mansion houses and garden squares. He's not sure why he's chosen to come in this direction. But if he gets to the West End he can either pick up the Tube there or walk on, through Piccadilly, on to Hyde Park Corner, through to Knightsbridge and South Kensington and he will be home.

Soho throbs, screams, shouts, is drunk, is high. Fliers invite punters to clubs, bars and restaurants, he can smell onions frying in the dodgy looking pans of the hot dog vendors plying their food to those who need to line their stomachs in preparation for a night of hard liquor drinking. Couples are arm-in-arm wrapped up against the February cold, girls walk in groups laughing, having fun, Saturday night fun. It's what you're supposed to do when you're young. Supposed to do especially in this London melting pot.

What is it, what's the matter with you?

CHAPTER TWENTY

THE TRAIN crawls through the south London suburbs, places he has yet to see, Balham, Crystal Palace, Purley which reminds him of the Mr Angry character on Steve Weight In The Afternoon. Mr Angry from Purley and the memory makes him smile. It's only a brief smile because Jake is not, as psychologists say, in a good place. His mind is cloudy, the weekend in Dublin confused him. Ronnie is not the happy go lucky cheeky chappy he plays on a daily basis. And there is the shock of Richard, a real role model, a tangible person to look up to, be inspired by. But if what Ronnie told him was true, and he believed him, Richard is just a charade. He is not the strength, the perfection he is looking for. Can no one just be successful, normal, strong? Just give me someone to believe in and I can be that person.

He's on his way to meet the marketing manager of Trundles brewery, one of the company's main clients. Jake is encouraged that he is trusted to go to the meeting by himself to discuss what writing projects are coming up during the next few months and what they want the company to work on.

He tells the receptionist his name and his company and that he is here to see Biendiva Buckley, senior marketing executive. It's a difficult name to remember how to pronounce but he memorised and practised saying it on the train.

The receptionist makes a phone call. Yes, certainly I will. Thank you. She puts the phone down gently. Ms Buckley will come and meet you in a few minutes. In the meantime if you would like to take a seat. Can I get you a tea or coffee or some water?

Jake declines the offer and sits down in one of the leather chairs in the reception. The walls are covered with photos chronicling the history of the Trundles Brewery which started in a small canal-side warehouse in Wandsworth in 1870. Dray horses pull barrels of ale, in other pictures the beer is being brewed and tasted by men in flat caps and grey uniforms. In the middle of the reception is a giant barrel with the Trundles Real Ale trademark.

It surprises him that he can't smell even the slightest whiff of beer. Instead it's a corporate smell, air freshener clean, insipid.

The lift arrives and out steps a woman in the tightest pencil skirt and top he has ever seen. She begins to walk towards him and he realises, with a Christ almighty feeling in his stomach, this is

Biendiva Buckley. She greets him with a wide smile and guesses that's how she meets everyone, she's in marketing for fuck's sake.

She puts out her left hand and he stands up quickly and nervously to shake. It's not a firm handshake he notes. Nice to meet you Jake. Nice to put a face to a voice on the end of the phone.

Likewise.

He has spoken to her numerous times on the phone when she has called to make amendments to copy but he imagined two things which he had been utterly wrong about. One, he thought she would be much older. Two, he did not imagine her to be this stunningly, irrefutably, unfucking-deniably gorgeous.

They go through what's coming up. He writes it down as she sits opposite him at her desk. He tries to scribble away while maintaining eye contact, a technique recommended by Richard on account that it makes the client feel like they have your undivided attention.

He is tense, he is nervous, he's not really listening to what she is saying and his writing is a scribble which will prove a problem when it comes to working out what they have agreed needs to be done. As well as her, he is also distracted by her own note taking which she does with a large fountain pen and a leather-bound binder which looks like a giant Filofax.

He wonders how old she is exactly. He notices she is not wearing a wedding or engagement ring, just a very expensive, ultra-feminine gold watch which is a diamond shape illuminated by the sparkle of what he imagines are actually diamonds. Her accent is posh but her voice carries a sexy huskiness. While he knows he has had carnal thoughts about women he hardly knows, even strangers, he has never known his imagination to be so febrile when it comes to imagining being in bed with Biendiva.

So that's the next three months covered, I think.

His thoughts and fantasies are interrupted by her formality, it is like he has spent the last few minutes - or however long it has been, he does not know - in a trance, as if he had just come round from being put to sleep at the dentist.

He impresses himself when he responds, ok some really good projects for us to get on with and hopefully we can get quite a bit of media exposure. I think we have some good material to work with.

You sound pretentious, utterly and ridiculously pretentious.

Do you Jake? You see I'm not so sure, I think we have quite a weak programme for the second quarter of the year which is a time we ought to exploit to the full.

This floors him for a few seconds but he picks himself up, fires off another round of bullshit.

Well we have had weaker programmes to work with from other clients. Perhaps I could suggest we have a brainstorm with you, myself and Richard and maybe someone else from your department where we could thrash out other opportunities and look at how we could strengthen the programme.

Oh Jake, what a brilliant idea. I think that's exactly what we need, fresh impetus.

And then she gives him his get-out-of-jail card with regards to his illegible notes which could cause him problems back at the office when Richard wants a report of the meeting.

Scrap the notes you made Jake. I want to start with a blank canvas. I'll give Richard a call and tell him this was just a brainstorm rather than a formal scheduling meeting and I'll arrange to have the meeting you have so cleverly suggested. He will want you to be involved, be at the meeting I mean, Richard?

Well I think so.

Well it was your idea and I'll make a point of saying that I want you to be there. Anyway Jake, I've another meeting now. So lovely to meet you at last and I'm looking forward to us working more closely in the future.

She stands up, straightens that tight skirt, waves back her mousey long hair and puts her hand out. He smiles, with confidence, and they shake hands. He follows her to reception, or rather he follows that curvaceous figure, eyes her all the way until they smile their goodbyes and he's back out into the sharp winds of Reading in February. A snap in the air. Strength in his stride. On the train back to London he replays the meeting, tries to picture himself saying what he said, did he come across naturally, was his nervousness too obvious?

Did she fancy him?

The signs. The only sign that is tangible to him now is she wanted another meeting and would tell Richard she wanted him. Wanted him at the meeting. Was that code for just wanting him?

You are reading too much into it. She is in marketing, she admitted her programme was not very strong. She just wants some help, from you and Richard, to improve her programme. She is ambitious, she is sexy, she is a package, a formula for success because that is how marketing in particular and the world in general works.

The euphoria he felt as he left the meeting is ebbing away now.

Back in Earls Court, the real world, his world. A pint in Cromwells is a necessity, maybe a few.

A week has gone by since his meeting with Biendiva and Richard comes to his desk and tells him she is coming to the office on Thursday for the brainstorm and to keep his diary clear.

She's coming for eleven so we can have the meeting and then go for some lunch, says Richard.

Great

Richard smiles and walks back to his office

Ronnie is at the desk in front of Jake's and has heard arrangements being made. He turns around grinning. Lunch with the lovely Biendiva Buckley hey? We are coming up in the world. So, would yer?

Would I what?

Spread her legs and lick her puss-puss

Well she is very attractive... I...

She's also out of yer league and mine young Jake. A Dadda's Girl. Only interested in her own breed. D'yer play golf per chance?

Golf? No, why?

No fucken chance then. You keep Biendiva Buckley only in yer wee head, to be brought oot in the mind's eye for the surreptitious wank when there's no other tarts to fantasise aboot.

With that Ronnie turns back to his computer screen, swigs a mouthful of black coffee and resumes bashing away at his keyboard.

Thanks for the guidance, Jake mumbles.

The meeting goes well, Richard comes up with some new ideas for Biendiva's campaign, Jake is in awe of the man's creative thinking, he's full of ideas, knows the business inside out and communicates with eloquence and brevity. His deep voice is his icing of the cake.

Biendiva and Jake scribble away as Richard speaks. They cover a lot of ground and Jake's workload has been multiplied by about ten but he is encouraged as Richard tells Biendiva Jake will be able to handle all this. Then the bombshell is dropped. Richard says, listen I'm really sorry chaps but I'm not going to be able to make lunch. But you two go along, a chance for you both to flesh out how what we've discussed can work and we'll need a timetable.

It's Jake and Biendiva in an upmarket Italian restaurant Richard has had booked in Belgravia. Jake can't help thinking about what Ronnie had told him and whether Richard had ducked out of lunch to go to his chick with a dick's place. The restaurant is cosy and ostentatious. The waiters wear penguin suits, music is some classical piano number and the ambience makes Jake even more nervous than he was when they left the office. There are a few diners in already. Mainly business types and a few couples.

Jake watches Biendiva take off her coat. She is wearing a white lacy top and grey pencil skirt, as if this is the staple uniform of marketing girls. A waiter immediately comes over, offers an aperitif and Biendiva goes for a spritzer and Jake decides he'll have the same.

Biendiva breaks the ice as he is about to do the same but she beats him to it.

So how long have you been working for Richard?

Oh, just a few months.

He questions her about her career and it's all small talk for a while, she is clearly ambitious, has plans to set up her own marketing consultancy eventually. When she asks Jake about his future plans he knows his answer is vague and muddled and the only conclusion she could possibly come to, to his consternation, is the awful truth that he has no plans, he doesn't know what he is going to do.

He takes out his cigarettes and offers her one but she's a non-smoker. Not a good sign. He notices she sips her spritzer slowly, he's already halfway through his. Then, to steal some ground, he asks her if she reads. It comes from nowhere and he realizes what a ridiculous question it is. It's like asking someone if they eat Hobnobs.

Not a big reader, no, I prefer magazines rather than literature or novels.

But you must have read a novel, at some time, and liked it.

Patronising, that was patronising.

Years ago at school and at college I had to read a lot of marketing books. I take it you're a bit of a bookworm?

Sure am. Every moment I have spare goes on reading.

Novels, literature or non-fiction?

Anything. I usually have a few books on the go and divide my time reading them. A novel, history book or other factual book.

So you never go out or go to the movies or dinner parties?

Oh yeah, I like to take a book to the pub. I also go to a few raves, though not so much now.

Raves, why have you mentioned raves? Raves will not be her Prada bag.

Oh, do you know what, I've heard so much about raves. They sound fantastic fun.

Jake is surprised by this and says, would you like to go to one? There's a big event happening in west London next weekend.

Wow Jake, yes, I'd love to.

Ok, I'll get the details. But look, the rave scene has changed from what it used to be. Some of them can be a bit, well, edgy. I started going in the eighties but they have changed. But, well, if you fancy trying something new.

Details?

Yeah. It's all done surreptitiously, no-one knows the venue until right up until the rave is going to start. Cops would try to stop it if they got wind of it.

How exciting.

So you definitely want to come with me next week?

Yes, that's if you want me to.

The conversation becomes easier as the wine flows and he detects she is being increasingly flirty. They wrap it all up and part company with a handshake and Jake promises to call her next week at work.

How easy was that, getting a date? What would Ronnie say? Maybe better not to tell Ronnie or Richard. Biendiva is a client. Maybe Richard would frown upon it.

In Cromwells that night Jake has his book and a pint on his usual table by the window. The book remains untouched as he stares out the window and weighs up in his mind this woman, Biendiva.

It's only a rave, she's just curious about the rave. And any flirting, well that's her job. And the wine. Don't read too much into it. She's in a different class to you anyway. Remember what Ronnie said.

He sips his pint and lights a cigarette. And imagines Biendiva naked. Then imagines kissing her.

It's a rave, she's agreed to go to a rave with you. She's out of mine and your league Jake. Best to save Biendiva for a surreptitious wank when there's no other tart to fantasise over.

He puts her out of his mind, watches the Earls Court Road, the traffic, the travellers, the locals passing through the neon-lit corridor that is the Earls Court Road.

Who is out there, who will come into my life in the days, weeks, months and years ahead?

And like a shadow emerging from the darkness, the darkness of his thoughts, Jean is back, as she always is, back in his thoughts. Brighton, sunshine, stars, smiles, kisses. Last year, the summer of 1989.

Why won't she go away, why won't you let her go?

He arranges to meet Biendiva in a pub off the Portobello Road. He knows the rave is in the area but will have to make a call to get the exact location an hour before it starts. That's how it works.

She is not in the pub when he arrives but he is a good few minutes early so isn't worried and orders himself a pint of lime juice and soda with lots of ice. He feels the inside of the pocket on his denim jacket to check the plastic bag with the E tabs is still there. He has no idea whether he will offer her one, has no idea what her attitude to drugs is. It may well be negative since she doesn't smoke and appears, from what he saw in the restaurant, to be a slow and moderate drinker. But maybe she goes for it at weekends, he ponders.

He has not been sitting at a table with his drink long before he sees her coming into the pub. She looks around for him and quickly spots where he is and beams a smile as she walks over. It is a pretty smile, a sexy smile, an encouraging smile. He makes her smile.

Smiles melt hearts. Smiles frazzle senses, Smiles give false impressions, smiles can be misinterpreted. Never read too much into a smile. You have seen that smile before. Remember? And that smile haunts you, embeds itself into your mind. It always does.

What can I get you to drink?
What's that you're drinking?
Lime and soda

No alcohol?

It's not good to drink alcohol, the rave will be very hot and the dancing...the alcohol dehydrates.

I'll have the same then, but just half a pint.

He ponders what she is wearing as he goes to the bar. She's in jeans and big brown boots and a blouse. A blouse for a rave!

She looks like she's going for a country walk on a Sunday afternoon. But the jeans and blouse are tight and even in casual clothes she looks stunning.

Back at the table they chat about the previous raves he's been to and he explains how the rave phenomenon began. She listens with what appears to be a genuine interest.

He remembers he has to make a call to find the venue and goes to a phone at the far end of the bar.

There has been a change of location. The rave will not take place in W11 he is told. He is given an address in Wapping and his heart sinks. It's the other side of the city and he has no appetite for trying to get there. He is going to have to disappoint Biendiva. Well, at least he can start on the beer if he's not going to be raving.

When he tells her she says they can get a cab

It's not that far. Come on let's go.

The cab glides down Ladbroke Grove and onto Holland Park, hits traffic at Shepherds Bush but gains momentum once they reach Chelsea Embankment. And he can't believe he is racing through the streets of London with this beautiful woman in a black cab on his way to a rave.

Soon the cab is in Aldgate and then takes a sharp right where a sign points to Wapping.

They go past the massive News International building where The Sun is written and printed and he remembers seeing the industrial unrest on the news when Murdoch had moved his newspaper operation here. Past there the cab takes them to the street Jake was told on the phone. They get out, Biendiva pays the cab which speeds off into the night for its next excursion.

They look down the street which, even though it is dark, they can see is full of rundown houses. A few blocks of flats and boarded up properties. So where the fuck is the rave, he wonders?

He motions for them to follow the road eastwards as he sees what looks like a crowd of people at the end. As they walk he can hear music. Yes, this is it. The rest of the road is clear of rundown buildings and gives way to empty brownfield land and he can see the warehouse now about 500 yards away. People are making their way, coming in all directions, the pounding music gets louder.

They are in the warehouse now, strobe lights zigzag across the space, the music booms and Biendiva covers her ears. He laughs and shouts that she will get used to it.

He pulls her into the crowds and begins dancing. She joins in but seems self-conscious. He thinks he has the solution. He guides her to another quieter less crowded part of the venue and takes out the bag of E from his pocket. He puts one into the palm of his hand and holds it out to her. She looks at the pill and nods no, emphatically no and he realises it was a bad idea.

He pops a pill when they get back into the crowd and she cannot see him. He needs it, he feels too tense and her revulsion towards the E makes him want to blot out the fact he stupidly offered it to her.

After a few minutes he feels more relaxed and less inhibited. But as he dances, the music doesn't feel right, it's more edgy, darker, violent, it's just a noise and an almost antagonistic, angry noise. He sees about ten hooded men running through the dance area.

As they dance, he can feel pushing from behind. At first he thinks it's just overcrowding but there is a sudden violent surge as people behind seem to be falling, others are trying to get away from the melee. Something is happening as he moves forward himself. He looks for Biendiva and panic hits him as he realises she is no longer next to him. He tries to look behind him but is pushed out of the way as revellers move forward. There are screams as the pushing and movement of the crowd gains more momentum. More people are falling over, this is turning bad, he thinks, where is she? A tall guy wearing a t-shirt with the smiley emblem on it barges past him. There is no smile on his face, just fear.

He moves out of the way as several people rush forward. He frantically looks in all directions for Biendiva in her tall boots and tight white blouse. She cannot be too difficult to spot in her obtrusive clothing. A tall skinhead stands in front of him. Jake only comes up to his stomach, a beer gut stomach. His t-shirt has the smiley emblem on it except it is not the usual yellow, it is black and it is not smiling, a drop of red blood comes out of its mouth. He begins to shake, a feeling of wanting to be sick envelops him and he's not sure whether it's the panic or the E taking effect. A bad E.

He looks to his left, there are girls on the ground being trampled on as the crowd continues to move forward, as people move away from whatever danger has struck. And one of the bodies is Biendiva. He sees the white blouse and pushes against the people coming forward. The skinhead is still standing defiantly in front of him but he dodges past him. He gets to Biendiva and pulls her up by the arm, her hair is all over the place, her blouse blotched with blood. He holds her as she takes support from his shoulders and he makes his way forward.

You just have to get out of here.

As they reach the open air there are sirens and he sees cops jump out of vans in riot gear. A dog handler runs forward followed by about ten other coppers.

Everything has to end and the genuine rave scene and all that it meant is now finished. The days of the second summer of love, 1989, have come down from that heavy ecstatic high and there's nothing left but the vision of the yellow smiley face that is now black, that is no longer smiling and has a tear trickling from its eyes and blood dribbling from its mouth.

They hitch a cab and Biendiva tells him on the way back to her place that he should stop apologising. It was not his fault, how was he to know it was going to turn nasty? And anyway he had probably saved her life.

They are on their way to her place in Wimbledon where the taxi will drop her off and take Jake back to Earls Court.

Let's do something more tranquil next time we go out, she says as the cab reaches her place.

He is taken aback. 'Next time we go out'. He chooses not to make anything of it in front of her.

Then she surprises him again.

I know a nice place near my flat where we could get a nice drink and relax. Why don't you get out here?

Jake is taken a back but she insists. He pays the cab driver and he walks with her into Wimbledon High Street.

The bar is in the basement, they enter via a spiral staircase. The tinkling of a piano gets louder as they descend the stairs.

When they get in he observes this is more like a private members' club. The besuited man at the door knows Biendiva and says how wonderful it is to see her. She asks if it is ok for them to come in with what they are wearing. The doorman says it would not be normally but since it's quiet and quite late, it will be fine.

They go into the bar which is more like a hotel bar, Jake thinks, an upmarket hotel. They find a table and Biendiva takes a seat. Jake remains standing to go to the bar and asks what she wants.

Oh no, sit down, they will come to us, it's table service here.

Jake takes a seat and feels naive and foolish - and out of place. It's true there are only a few people in, it is dimly lit but he can make out the clientele is well to do with many tables holding champagne bottles and the punters are dressed up as if they have been to some swell do somewhere in town. A man plays the piano in the far corner of the room but Jake does not recognise the tune.

Ah, this is nice and relaxing, says Biendiva as she stretches out. Jake is not relaxed, he feels tense and unsure what his next move should be.

The waiter comes over and Biendiva orders a spritzer. Jake could murder a beer and asks what they have. A few Spanish lagers and Bud. He goes for a Spanish beer and assumes it will not be coming in a pint glass.

So how did you know about this place, is this one of your usual haunts?

Daddy's best friend owns it so he knows me well. I also come here with friends and clients. It's just a very relaxing place to come and unwind or chat.

She goes on to tell him daddy is a solicitor with his own practice in Mayfair. In fact it's more than a practice, it's a law firm. Daddy had been disappointed that she had not followed him into the legal profession but now accepted that marketing was a legitimate profession even though it perhaps didn't stretch her as much as law would have done.

Mummy is also a solicitor who works in legal aid for poor people whereas daddy specialises in commercial law. Biendiva is an only child and it seems to Jake this is absolutely all they have in common.

Out of our league, Jake, out of our league.

Back in Nevern Place he pours himself a beer and gets through ten cigarettes after refraining from smoking all night for fear of being frowned upon by Biendiva. The cigarettes taste good, the beer even better as he looks out onto the Earls Court night and feels an emptiness, a deep emptiness.

He is busy bashing away at the work that resulted from the meeting with Richard when one of the PAs shouts across to Jake, Biendiva. Putting her through.

His fingers freeze at the keyboard. Ronnie stops his typing and swivels round, a knowing, accusing smirk on his face, fag protruding from the corner of his mouth. His phone buzzes and Jake picks up.

Hi Biendiva. How are you?

Five days have elapsed since he had seen her at the weekend. Five days during which he had decided he was going to keep his relationship with Biendiva on a strictly professional basis, five days he had spent deciding he was going to wait for something else, someone else to come along into his life. He was not expecting this after the disaster that was Saturday night.

Hi Jake, just a quick one, not work-related. I was wondering, are you free next Friday evening? I'm having a little dinner party with a few friends, nothing massive. I wondered if you would like to come.

It's out of the blue, the murky blue and he has horrendous visions of sitting at a table with people he does not know making forced conversation.

Sure, yeah, would love to.

Brilliant. Around eight o'clock?

Look forward to it.

He decides to wear chinos and a blue shirt, guessing Biendiva's friends will be fairly conservative dressers. He hates the chinos and shirt look but doesn't want to feel out of place.

He takes the District Line to Wimbledon and tries to read his book but his mind is on the dinner party and he realises he has never been to one before. Doubts about agreeing to go plagued him all week and now he is on his way the doubts become stronger. He could get off at the next stop and phone her, tell her he had come down with something.

But the train stops at West Brompton and starts again and he stays on the train.

Just go, do the right thing, you have nothing to lose.

As he gets off at Wimbledon he thinks, it's not too late, even now, I can find a phone box and tell her I'm not coming and get the train back home. A pint or two in Cromwells, a good read, maybe meet someone, meet a girl. A girl in my own league.

The night could be so different. You don't have to put yourself through this.

He's in her road and sees her flat. It's on the third floor of a row of Victorian buildings. He sees lights on, dimmed, cosy. He checks the time. Too early, about ten minutes too early. He walks past her flat, keeps walking, killing time hoping no-one on their way to her place sees him. But it's dark, his collar is up, his head down. A cigarette. *Have a cigarette and when that's finished start walking back to her flat.*

A gust of wind blows out his lighter as he tries to light the fag. He flicks it again and cups his hand around the flame. Lit. He takes a drag and carries on walking. He's conscious of walking too far. He doesn't want to be late, to walk in to be looked at by everyone, a grand entrance. The fag burns down, helped by the wind, he tosses it into the gutter, checks his watch, just a minute before eight, time to turn around and walk back.

He reaches her door and presses the buzzer. Within seconds her voice comes over the intercom.

She buzzes him in and he walks up the stairs. The building is well-lit, decorated in all white and the smell is of new paint. It's so unlike the smell of his place where you have to keep pressing the lights on as you climb the stairs. This is posh.

He reaches the third floor and her door is open. He hears Kylie's Tears On My Pillow playing at a low volume and taps on the door and shouts hello. Biendiva's voice comes back, come on through. Voices, conversation and he sees three other people apart from Biendiva, two guys and a blonde girl sipping wine.

The introductions are done and Jake gets chatting to a woman called Margot who is in PR. She is heavily made up, blonde and slightly older than the others. The conversation is anodyne and he hopes the other people are going to be more interesting. He is relieved, to get away from this woman when Biendiva announces dinner is to be served and they are to take their seats at the table.

The starters arrive and it's a guy called Jeremy who is dominating the conversation which revolves around him and his business. He is telling how a client refused to take his advice on crisis management so he ditched the client but months later the client begged him to provide his services again and they offered him a higher rate.

This Jeremy guy says, I always insist to new clients from now on that I must have carte blanch to make all their communications decisions. That they are wasting their time and money if they do not take my expert advice.

Others nod in what Jake takes to be sycophantic agreement, Margot says, 'absolutely, it's the only way you can work'. In fact over the course of the evening, Margot says 'absolutely' constantly.

Jake looks around the table, watches as the rest of the party latches onto Jeremy's every word. He is talking so much hardly any food has left his plate.

Biendiva offers to top up everyone's wine and they all accept, except for Jeremy who raises a hand to say no, I'm fine then continues to impart his oh so fascinating wisdom.

Jake is bored and irritated. Irritated that everyone seems so fascinated by this irritating twat, this know-all, this life and soul of this fucking soulless dinner party. Two things cross his mind that he would like to do right now. One, throw a glass of wine in Jeremy's face and tell him what an arrogant mother-fucking twat he is and, two, have a pint in Cromwells far away from this crap, among normal people, people not up their own arses.

Jeremy finally shuts the fuck up and there is an awkward silence as he concentrates on eating his food. Everyone else has just about finished.

Hmm delicious lasagne Biendiva, says Jeremy between mouthfuls.

Her face lights up. Oh, thanks, I'm glad you like it.

Everyone nods their approval of the food served up and Margot says Biendiva must give her the recipe as she is a hopeless cook. An 'absolutely' hopeless cook. Everyone giggles, Jake forces a smile, a polite smile, just to be civil, Jeremy wolfs down his food to catch up and then sips on his wine. He puts the glass down after a tiny, hardly-any-point-having-it sip and suddenly he looks directly at Jake and Jake can feel his eyes burrowing into him and he knows, somehow he knows, what is coming next as Jeremy says, so Jake, Biendiva tells me you are a copywriter, you write all her company's material.

Jake takes a gulp of wine, he is feeling tipsy, it is warm in this room, he feels out of place, the whole situation, this dinner party situation, seems contrived, it's claustrophobic and now this twat wants to put him on the spot, question him.

Jake knows that the tone he is about to use will come across as, oh please, I can't be bothered to explain what I do and how could it possibly match the fascination levels of what you have been chuntering on about for Christ knows how long.

And so it comes out.

Yes, I do mostly copy, not that interesting really.

Jeremy responds, oh come, our whole industry is about words. It's, well it's the currency of communication. Of course it's interesting.

The currency of communication?

Jake cannot resist.

Currency of communication. Well not really. It's just putting words together to make sentences so that we can get the message across. Whatever that might be. And it's better not to use jargon or gobbledygook or catchphrases like currency of communication because it means nothing to most people.

Jeremy frowns, takes a slightly larger sip of wine. Biendiva takes a sip too. Margot and some sappy bloke called Phil look at their plates. Finally, Biendiva says, what Jake is saying is that simple messages are more effective. Economy of words and all that. Of course I don't need to tell you that Jeremy, you will probably forget more about this business than I will ever know.

Every ounce of respect he had for her has just been flushed away by what she has just said. The temptation to say, why don't you just give him a blow job right here, right now, is so overwhelming that he breaks the rule he made before he came here; that he will refrain from smoking tonight, just in case anyone objects and he will only light up if someone else does.

But now he does not give a fuck and reaches into his pockets, slams down the lighter on the table, finds his fags and lights up, billowing a cloud of smoke across the table after he has taken his first long, deep, angry drag.

He can feel the stares, daggers of disapproval and picks up the fags again and says, oh, how terribly rude of me, would anyone like a cigarette?

No, I don't smoke, but thanks, squeaks Margot.

Phil nods a no, Biendiva says nothing but gets up and starts taking the plates away and Jeremy, fucking Jeremy says, I'd love one, thanks Jake.

Jake passes him the packet. At least he has a weakness, maybe he is human after all.

Margot excuses herself to go to the toilet, probably to escape the fag smoke, Phil is folding and unfolding a napkin. Jeremy lights up, passes the packet and lighter back to Jake.

So Phil, how's business with you? Any new clients? Jeremy bores on.

Margot comes back from the toilet but joins Biendiva in the kitchen.

Silence between the men is interrupted by, who else, but Jeremy.

So Jake, what's it like working with or rather for Biendiva?

What do you mean, what is it like working with Biendiva?

Well, I mean she's a pretty hot chick. Oh, good at her job, of course, but I mean, well, must give you a bit of a buzz in the old trousers to be working with somebody so utterly fuckable.

Phil looks up and smiles, it's the first time he has changed his expression all night.

Jake stares at Jeremy whose grin is the type to induce violence.

I hardly know her and I only know her on a professional basis.

I wouldn't call being invited to one of her dinner parties purely professional. She must really like you, Jake. Jeremy blows out cigarette smoke.

He has no idea where this jerk is coming from, let alone where he's going with this conversation, if that is what you can call it.

Then he starts again, she is very friendly is our Biendiva and if she likes someone, there is no stopping her.

What does he mean, why is he saying this, what is he driving at?

Tell you what, though, Jake, I'm not sure you are her type. She goes out with guys who have a few bob, guys with ambition, self-starters who have something to say for themselves. Don't think you tick any of those boxes. No offence, Jake. I mean you are young, just starting out in the business. I'm sure that one day you will be very successful.

It's the slowness of his speech, his accent, the patronising bastard. He is reeling, he hated this twat the moment he opened his mouth, who the fuck does he think he is?

You mean guys like you Jeremy? Do you tick all the boxes? Hey don't answer, it's a rhetorical question. We know you're the great successful man, the go-getting businessman, the maestro of communications, I mean we should know because you've spent the entire fucking evening so far boring the fuck out of everyone telling them. Well we can't all be like you Jeremy and I wouldn't want to be like you anyway. You're a cliché, a walking, talking windbag of clichés, soundbites and bullshit.

He gulps what's left of his wine and takes another cigarette.

Jake, really, there's no need for such an outburst. You've taken me all wrong.

Biendiva and Margot hear the raised voices and tentatively come back into the lounge.

Biendiva smiles, but it's a nervous smile that says, what's going on here?

Everything OK, anyone for a brandy, or more wine?

I seem to have upset Jake, Jeremy says in mocking weary.

You haven't upset me. You're just a gobby arrogant twat, but you have not upset me.

Jake, please, calm down, says Biendiva.

Look, it's best I go, this isn't me, poncy dinner parties and talking business and shit.

Jake puts his coat on and makes for the door, all eyes on him, burning on him.

Out into the night air, the Wimbledon night air, a biting wind cuts through as his body readjusts from the heat of the flat to the cold of the street. He buttons up his coat to the top, lights a cigarette and walks. On the high street the pubs are beginning to chuck out, people queue for kebabs and burgers, police sirens wail, shouts, shouting, drunkenness, the anthem of the end of a Friday night in suburbia.

He walks further up the high street and he can hear it, it is not too far away, he is getting closer to the sound. Ride On Time.

How he got back to Nevern Place is a blur, who he met and who he spoke to in the nightclub in Wimbledon is, at this moment, impossible to recall as he waits for the kettle to boil and spoons filter coffee into a mug.

Sunshine beams through the windows and with his coffee he goes to the window and opens it. It's around 10am and he sees Earls Court wide awake. Normality after the night before.

It's only Saturday, he thinks, at least last night was a Friday, it's only Saturday and he has the bulk of the weekend to enjoy, to do what he pleases, to go where he wants and that feeling of absolute freedom awakens him fully and he feels refreshed and excited by the day ahead even though he has no plans.

Fragments of last night begin to fall together, Jeremy, Biendiva, the dinner party, all the things that were said, all the things he had said. They were not his kind of people, he had rejected them, rejected their dinner party lifestyle, their ego trips. I don't know who I am, what I am, but I am not them, not those people.

He walks down the Earls Court Road, to Brompton Road round to South Kensington and does a full circle before he is back in Brompton Road. As he walks, he thinks about last night and then about his dad and then about last summer, the summer of 1989 and then he thinks about her. Jean Ridley. She comes back into his mind, he sees her face, hears her voice, as vivid as if he had only seen her last night. Where is she now, who is she with, is she ok, does she remember me?

In the Old Brompton Road he feels the cold and needs a hot drink. He goes to The Troubadour and orders coffee. He takes out his book and begins reading, relaxing, escaping.

The waitress is a gorgeous French girl in tight faded jeans and a white shirt. He looks at her and she catches his glance and smiles. He returns a shy smile then reads.

CHAPTER TWENTY-ONE

IT'S SATURDAY night and he cannot believe he is in the flat of the waitress with her friend sipping wine and eating bread, cheese and olives. Her name is Sylvie and they eventually got chatting in The Troubadour. She invited him to meet her friend and drink some wine. Her friend is Karim, also French, taller and busty.

He finds conversation with them easy, their English is excellent and they love books. Karim loves Henry Miller.

I love all the sex and the fact is all just happens so naturally, so liberally, she says.

When the conversation pauses Sylvie tells Karim to put on some music. It's a compilation tape of recent chart-toppers and the first track is Sidney Youngblood's If Only I Could.

The girls start dancing, Jake smiles and smokes but they pull him from his seat to join in. Karim stops dancing to light a spliff, which she passes around.

The wine and the weed fuse to make him feel heady but inhibited as he goes on dancing with the girls. When Ride On Times comes on he remembers he was doing this dance to this song only hours ago in Wimbledon but it sounds better now, feels and sounds like it used to and the girls love the song and dance until they sweat.

Here I am getting off my fucking face with two gorgeous French women I have only just met, sipping wine, smoking, dancing.

Jeremy, you twat, you fucking pompous twat with your ambitions and your fucking money and your fucking business in fucking communications. Biendiva, you uptight bitch, sucking up to him, marketing, fucking marketing, what is it anyway? Bollocks, bullshit. You must give me the recipe for the lasagne. It's just meat, tomato and fucking pasta. You just mix it all up and shove it. Shove it in the oven. Or just shove it, shove it like you can all do with your fucking lives and your careers and your dinner parties.

If Ronnie could see me now, all Ronnie's fantasies, two gorgeous girls.

Now Bruce Springsteen is on, Dancing In The Dark. Off my fucking face. Just me, no-one else, no-one is competing with me, I am here because I met one of them in a café and she brought me to her place and I am dancing and I am off my face, off my fucking head. I am me, only me, this is me, no pretence, no acting, no pretending. This is me, whoever me is, whoever I am.

Monday morning and he wakes early and puts the kettle on, lights a fag. He is in a foul mood, brought on by the thought of going in to work, facing Ronnie's questions about Friday night and dreading the phone going in case it is Biendiva.

It hits him that this is not the job for him. Writing crappy copy for a stupid brewery, dealing with the ego that is Biendiva, having to constantly make amendments to copy he has written. What's the point of employing a writer if you're just going to change everything they write. And she is a marketing person for Christ's sake, not a writer.

The job is not you, that world, the PR world is not you with its egotists and pretentiousness. It is not real writing.

In the office there's a Monday morning air about the place as people stroll in and ask each other how their weekends were. It's the usual answers – good, quiet, over with too quickly. Can't wait for Friday. Drudgery. Why do we do it? There's got to be a better way of living.

Jake taps away at his computer on a press release that is due to go out by the end of the week. Biendiva will have to have it by the end of the day so she can 'sign it off'. Sign if off, what a fucking joke, it's a press release about something no journalist will write about because there's no story.

Ronnie walks in yawning and carrying his mug of black coffee trying to tame the beast of yet another hangover no doubt. And Jake mentally prepares himself for interrogation about Friday night.

To his surprise, Ronnie just mumbles good morning then sits at his desk with his head in his hands waiting for his computer to crank up. It isn't like Ronnie who has this infuriating habit of being lively and jolly in the mornings, no matter how much he's knocked back the previous night. Which is usually more than the medical fraternity would recommend.

Heavy weekend? Jake asks, concerned.

Ronnie rubs his eyes and turns to face Jake. His eyes are wet and bloodshot.

Ah, heavy life, more like. Listen, d,yer fancy a snifter at lunchtime? Ah could do with getting a few things oaf ma chest.

Yeah, sure, got to have this shit done though by the end of the day, says Jake pointing at his screen.

Ah, fuck that. Ah can give yer a hand wi that this afters if you're not finished. What is it, Biendiva shite? Pub gets decorated and she thinks that's news and some tawt'll print it.

Something like that. Well, yeah, exactly that. I'll get it bashed out by lunch then I don't have to worry about it.

Ronnie sighs and swivels round in his chair to face his computer, a man who clearly had other things to face over the weekend.

In the pub Ronnie goes to the bar, Jake waits for him at a table. Ronnie's mood has not changed since this morning. He really looks in a bad way.

Ronnie places the drinks on the table and sits down heavily, with a long, pained sigh. He stares at his beer glass, picks it up and takes a sip.

Come on then big man, what's up?

Ronnie looks up from his pint, but not at Jake. Jake cannot see what he is looking at but Ronnie's eyes are those of a man lost, deflated, deeply troubled. Finally, he looks Jake in the eye and Jake wonders what happened to the old Ronnie, where is he? This is not the Ronnie I know.

Ronnie takes out a fag, his hands shaking, he lights it, takes a long pull on it and exhales, a man in need of his tobacco.

Jake, have yer ever thought, what's the point of it all? Yer know, grafting, making pots a money for some other fucker and then all you do is go out the weekend and pollute yerself, blot the monotony of it all out, kid yerself yer having the time of yer life when alls yer doing
is making it all go away, making it all a blur, making it all just feel that tad better? Well maybe youse don't, yer still a pup compared to me. Ah've been at this game now, the PR shite, for almost three fuckin decades. And what have ah to show for it? Round and round ah go on the great hamster wheel a life.

He pauses, Jake lights a fag and sips his beer. Ronnie picks up where he left off.

Well ah have been feeling that way for a not so wee while now, or ah had been until ah met this bird. Ah havenae mentioned her before because I didnae know how deep it might go, whether it would last. And with ma recooord, it was never likely to.

Anyways, a coupla weeks ago she asked me to go live with her. She's 20 years younger than maself, a beauty, Catriona. Lives on a farm in Newbury, on her Jack Jones. Mother and father killed in a car crash, she was orphaned at 18 then inherited the farm. Does a bit of this and that in marketing but generally employs a few hands to run the farm and lives oaf the fat a the land.

He breaks to suck on his fag and take a sip of his pint.

She wants you to live with her on the farm?

Wants me to run it for her, with her like, give up the grind of ma life and make something wi her. Farm's beautiful, five-minute walk from a cosy village pub so ah wouldnae go short in that department.

Fuck, Ronnie, so what are you going to do? It's a no-brainer if you really are sick of the job and everything. But, what, are you going to leave the wife?

That would have been the plan. Leastways it was until the wife, June, dropped a bombshell. Ah told her ah had met someone else and ah was leaving her. I just decided, after a bit a pressure from Catriona, it was time to bite the bullet. So you won't be able to look after us, is her only response. Ah thought she meant money-wise and ah assured her ah wouldnae see her go short. Then she just came out with it. Ah don't mean look after me in that sense, she says. Ah mean look after me as someone who has terminal cancer.

He takes a large gulp of his pint and asks Jake if he wants another. He nods and Ronnie goes to the bar, Jake watches him, his posture is different, gone is the swagger, the look of a man who is in an endless pursuit of fun and naughtiness. He is broken.

It is bombshell news to Jake on two fronts, one that Ronnie had had enough of his job and the even more shocking news that June has cancer. What to say to him when he gets back from the bar? What do you say to someone in this dreadful predicament, this awful, life-changing situation? And Ronnie of all people. Can he really leave June now when she most needs him? And at a time when Ronnie is on the cusp of finding real love, happiness and substance in his life? Jake lights a cigarette and Ronnie comes back with the drinks, he sits down with another agonised sigh.

So bet yer didnae expect this news from your uncle Ron.

I'm so sorry Ronnie. Don't really know what to say.

Ah shouldnae have told yer. Too young to have to listen to some middle aged man's problems. Ah just needed to tell someone. Havenae spoken to a soul aboot it all weekend. Just thinking and drinking and feeling sad for her, sad that it's come to this. Ah cheated on her, the marriage was empty, ah wasnae ever there for her and now the poor cow gets cancer. Hardly a fucking blessed life she's had is it?

He takes a sip of his pint.

Why did she get lumbered with Ronnie fucking Blythe? The great hard-drinking hedonist whose only role in life is drinking and shagging, Ronnie says shaking his head.

You shouldn't be so hard on yourself. You didn't cause her to get cancer.

No but ah added to the general misery of her life. Truth is Jake ah knew maself, I knew maself years ago and ah should have left her but ah just didnae ever have the heart to do it. Didnae have the balls. I wasnae getting any younger, it wasnae like it was with Kathy when I was so young. Biggest surprise was that she never left me. Maybe that's what ah was waiting for. For her to make the move. Ah thought ah could just keep getting away with it and just keep things as they are, at least she has a home, food on the table, we have the occasional meal or drink together. Even had a couple a holidays abroad together. But even then ah would go off and do ma own thing, usually search for filth and drugs and drink. Ah ended it with Kathy all those years ago when I was young without much angst. As ah got older I tried to tell masel that one day ah would stop all the shite and me and June would stick together and be a proper couple and we could rekindle how it was when we first met. I kept her as an insurance policy, someone to be there when ah got older and in case ah changed ma ways. And now, just when ah think ah have the guts to change things, to do the right thing for once, for maself and for her, this happens. And this changes everything. Ah was ready to go and make a new life with Catriona, to be brave and end it with June and see that she was ok, you know, she could have had the house, ah would have made sure she was ok financially. But how d'yer walk out on someone who you've been with all this time and now she needs yer, is asking for something for the first time after never asking for anything from me. Asking me now to look after her because she's frightened, frightened of the Big C, of what's coming to her and now she needs me, needs me. Though who the fuck would ever need me?

The tears, his regrets, his grief, make Ronnie look 20 years older right now. And Jake has no idea what to say or do, what can you say or do to a man who has totally fucked up his life?

Both their glasses are empty, Ronnie looks as though he's about to suggest having another one but turns around to look at the pub clock and says they had better be getting back to the office.

They stroll the short walk back to work in silence, subdued by their lunchtime conversation, both feeling awkward with each other and Jake realises how much he wants to get away from this job, from these people, from this period in his life. The feeling is so strong that he feels nauseous, anxious, made worse by the beer and the fags and no food inside him.

You don't want to end up like Ronnie, you don't want to spend your life chasing after everything and ending up with nothing.

In the office Jake bashes away at the press release, churning out almost anything that comes into his head. He just wants to get it finished and yearns for the working day to end. Ronnie's phone rings and he answers it with a sigh. OK, Richard, I'll pop in.

Ronnie heaves himself from his seat, stubbing out a fag. He looks at Jake and says, Ricardo wants to see me. What the fuck does he want? Can't be doing with any shite todays.

Jake watches Ronnie cross the office and go into Richard's office. Richard beckons for him to close the door which is unusual as the boss usually keeps his door open, even for meetings.

A few minutes later Jake's phone rings. At first he fears it's Biendiva but then twigs the call is internal. It's Richard. Jake, can you pop into my office?

Richard is scribbling away with his fountain pen and doesn't look up as he tells Jake to take a seat. Ronnie is staring at the floor picking his fingernails and looks nervous.

Richard looks up. Seriously. Earnestly, bad news to deliver.

Look, I'll come straight to the point Jake. Biendiva Buckley from the brewery has called and says she does not want you to work on their account with us. She says she feels there is a clash of personalities.

Jake feels himself turning red as Richard continues, I don't want you to tell me what happened, I'm sure it's nothing you've done wrong. Clients often ask for different people to handle their account, unfortunately for us it's their prerogative.

Ronnie, mumbles, ah yes, the clients, the fucking clients.

Richard ignores him and goes on, but what it does mean is that I'm going to have to hire another writer which means, I'm afraid, there isn't an account for you to work on. Apart from that the company isn't in a position to hire another writer and keep you on, too. So I'm really sorry Jake, but I'm going to have to let you go.

You're sacking me?

No, I'm making you redundant. I'm going to pay you up to the end of this month and give you three months' pay. And I might add Jake, it is not my choice, I think you have great potential in this business and somewhere down the line I would be happy for you to come back and work with any new clients we might acquire.

Jake struggles to stop a smile, stop a cheer, the relief, the sheer relief and a few quid to keep him going as well.

I understand. Thanks Richard. And, well do you want me to leave now, or should I work some notice?

Richard just keeps on giving.

No, Jake, you may as well clear your desk at the end of today. See

Helen in accounts before you go, she'll have your money and P45.

Richard stands up and shakes his hand with a warm and genuine smile, but then he is in PR so he's used to it. As he walks back to his desk, he remembers Ronnie's predicament, he cannot be celebratory.

Ronnie comes back and puts an arm around Jake. Listen, ah have to nip oot. Let's go celebrate yer good news. Meet us in the Bell and Crown in aboot an hour.

Jake nods as Ronnie goes back to his desk, puts on his jacket and leaves the office.

Jake has nothing to pack away, the only personal item in the office is his own jacket draped on the back of his chair. He puts it on and walks out of the room, down to accounts, collects his money and leaves.

He walks out of the building for good and mixes into the West End crowds, hoping he doesn't bump into Ronnie. His mission is to get away from all those people he hates in this job and even the ones he doesn't hate such as Ronnie. Ronnie's story is so dreadful, so imperceptible, that it makes Jake clench his body at the thought, the thought of ending up like that. Jake had never really liked or approved of Ronnie's life and now he sees it as a prototype of failure, a lesson in how not to live your life.

In the past few weeks in the job, he had learned more about who he is and who he is not than at any time of his life. But as he sits with a solitary, celebratory pint in Cromwells – at four in the afternoon, what freedom, what bliss – he knows that while he may have found what he doesn't want, finding what he does want is a search he has barely begun.

You sip your celebratory pint and look around, around the pub and through the window. Lost. Do they know what they want, all these people you see? Does the guy there, in the jeans, brown leather jacket and leather briefcase trying to hail a cab, has he found it, what he's looking for? Still looking or, as they say, sorted? The old man sat over there in the pub, with his book and his pint of stout, reading and sucking on a pipe, did he find it, did he find it and lose it a long, long time ago? Or is he still looking, even at his age? It's so hard to even begin to look when you have no idea what it is you're looking for. And you have no idea whether there is any point in looking at all.

PART TWO
CHAPTER TWENTY-TWO

SPRING 1990 has arrived and Jake is still looking for work but is only a few weeks into the pay-off from Richard. There's also the money from the sale of his father's house which was left to Jake. But he doesn't want to touch that. Her may need money like that later in life.

He wants to take his time in looking for something else and is enjoying days reading, running and just hanging out in Earls Court. The year has not been a good one so far but he is determined to move his life on in the next few months and start to enjoy London again.

He has been much happier since leaving the job, happier until the letter arrived, the letter he never expected after all this time.

He has devoured the shocking detail of Jean's letter over and over again, he can hear her voice, her desperate terrified voice coming from the words on the pages. Jean's voice. It is these words that cause him most concern:

I would love to see you, no need to see you, maybe I need rescuing.

But why can't she just leave him? She says she loves him, but is frightened of him. *And the bigger question. She's out of your life now, why get involved again? After all this time?*

Why not pretend you had never received the letter, she would probably guess that you had left Nevern Place and had not got the letter. Would she have ever dreamed of contacting you again if life with Salime had been the utopia she believed it was going to be? A cry for help, not a cry for you to have her back. A woman you met months ago, a woman with problems, a vulnerable beautiful woman you fell for but she told you it was not the same for her. Why should you help her? She is a stranger now and in fact always was. You met her, you fell for her, you tried to give her love but she turned it down, found someone she thought was better in every way, she made you feel inadequate, triggered doubts about who you are, who you should be. She sent you packing, down a path of loneliness and rejection. Why should you help her now? To become her hero? To make her fall in love with you? She's a fragment, a fragment of your life that you should just set free so you can free yourself.

But she is so different to everyone and everything. We have so much in common; shattered childhoods, loveless parents, loneliness. We are soulmates pulled together by a bond that exists because everything else - love, family - never existed in either of our lives. No love in all the world, apart from the love we could give each other. And maybe she's my only chance, the only chance of love, a love that can grow, be nurtured, watered, cultivated. We could make it grow. A chance to change two lives, a chance to fight for something difficult but not impossible. Why give up on the only happiness you ever remember, the happiness with her in the summer of 1989?

This is the stuff of fantasy. You cannot make someone love you because, like you, they had a bad childhood. There has to be chemistry, inextricable chemistry that has nothing to do with the past, yours or hers. Perhaps that is the problem, she's not attracted to you because you are one of the same. She is looking for someone she never had, a father. Why else take up with an older, much older man? The fact he may be proving to be a psychopath does not suddenly elevate you to be that father. And why do you want her, why this woman? This woman with her past? Why not a woman who has no emotional baggage, a normal woman who can love you and make you happy? A woman you love because you love her and not a woman who you think you love because she had the same loveless life that you endured as a child? How can Jean show you love when she has never experienced it? How could she write those things in her diary? About you?

The inner voice, contradicting itself, whirring around his head. But her voice and face and memories refuse to subside and he thinks of the months without her, since she left, and how shitty they've been, how generally lost and unhappy he has felt. How the summer of 89 had held so much promise and then disappeared, replaced by long cold, dark nights, dark days, dark thoughts. A voices in his head, telling him different things, the rata-tat-tat of so many questions machine gun-fire in his mind. I make up my mind and then the other voice has to have its say, shoot its questions. Who is it, where is it coming from? Is it mine? Is one of voices my mother, or my father, or both of them? Where is my voice, where is me?

He reads her letter over and over again, disseminating it, looking for the tone, trying to detect hidden meanings, searching for clues in the hand-written scrawl of her mind. But he doesn't know what he is trying to ascertain. Her words swirl around his head creating pictures, moving pictures, of Salime's rage-ravaged face, of Jean's terror, fear. Tears. As if she hasn't been through enough in her life. Oh Jean, the love I could give, I would never frighten you, I would make you so safe, so loved.

He takes a deep breath, tries to clear his mind. After an hour re-reading her letter he decides he has read enough. He needs to put it to one side and just relax, to clear his mind and the only way he can do this is to read his book, finish a glass of wine and have no more, then go to bed and sleep and then see what he thinks in the morning. The voices do not argue with this and within a few minutes he is absorbed in his book, in the writing, another story, he escapes from the now and the world he is in.

He stops reading after a few hours and is pleased he has read so much without losing his concentration, without being distracted. He looks at the glass of wine. He has been so absorbed he has hardly touched it. He closes the book and opens the window, lights a cigarette and sips the wine. A gentle voice in his head says, *think, give yourself time to think things through. Time will help you, time will give everything a perspective and that's what you need. Time to finish that cigarette, time to sip away that wine, time to sleep.*

The streets, the Earls Court streets, are emptying, the bars and restaurants will be closing, there is virtually no traffic now going down the Earls Court Road.

He looks up at the sky and sees the moon but a cloud moves in as if it has spotted him looking and wants to protect the moon's privacy. He sips the last drop of wine, stubs out his cigarette, closes the window, strips off for bed and as his head hits the pillow he sees the moon appear again.

And he says, in a whisper, good night, darling. Goodnight Jean.

CHAPTER TWENTY-THREE

JAKE ARRIVES at Charles de Gaulle airport on an early flight. He is due to meet Jean in the early evening in a bar just outside the Latin Quarter.

He knows he can cancel meeting her, ignore everything and go back to Earls Court and continue with his life, such as it is. But his mind is restful, he enjoys the thrill of travel, of coming to another country and he has read so much about Paris's bohemian culture. He is looking forward to exploring this city in the hours he has before he will have to decide whether he is going to go through with meeting Jean or just book into a hotel and then return to London tomorrow, Sunday and ignore all her subsequent letters and never explain why he failed to show up.

He puts making that decision out of his mind as he lugs his rucksack and makes his way to the metro bound for central Paris. The day is mild, the sun is getting stronger and he takes in the usual sights, the Eiffel Tower, the Seine. He sips a beer in a pavement café down a side street.

The French women remind him of Sylvie and Karim, stylish, sassy and sexy and as he sips his beer he vows he will come back here to Paris for longer than just a day or two. He even thinks it would be a place he could live, maybe learn French and find a job and live the bohemian life. Maybe in a few years, though, he is still in love with London and isn't fully acquainted with his own capital city yet. London still has more to offer he thinks. But Paris, well one day, yes, he can see himself here.

He walks along the banks of the Seine and checks his watch. He has just a few hours left before he has to decide whether to meet Jean and a cloud begins to descend on his mind and with it the voice, the voice telling him he is mad to be coming here to get involved with Jean again.

The question will not go away: why can't she just leave Salime? Has he really got such an emotional hold on her? She hardly knows him.

He walks and walks and the time gets nearer, he has worked out where the bar he is due to meet Jean in is and he is making his way there, knowing he can still turn around and not go through with it. He could even stand across the road and watch her go in, see her again, fleetingly, but abandon any plans to actually speak to her, to get involved. Just see her, get some rudimentary idea of how she looks after all this time. He could wait and watch her eventually leave the bar when she gives up and realises he is not turning up. He would be able to see her facial reaction as she left the bar. He could even follow her back to where she lived, stake out the place, watch for Salime arriving or leaving. He could do all this from afar without any involvement, without any participation. He could just be an anonymous spy. Covert, an observer, uninvolved without any commitment.

Then he imagines, what if he saw them together, what if he saw Salime shouting at her, abusing her on the street? Could he really just watch and walk by? Could he really do that when even the letters made him rage?

They planned to meet at six, it is now fifteen minutes to as he sips a beer in the bar and he keeps looking at the door. Maybe she will be early, she could come through the door at any time now. He lights a cigarette, his hand shakes, he is nervous.

You can go now, go now before she arrives, get well away from the area. It could be difficult. How will she be? She may want to come back to London. Come back tonight.

There are a few people in the café bar, a man smoking a large cigar and reading a newspaper, a middle-aged couple of women talking rapidly in French and a girl who is obviously a student as she is reading and taking notes. It is a bar to come and sit, to chill out in, read your newspaper or book or just sit and relax. Just about everybody is smoking. The décor is all polished wood, he can even smell the polish. Piles of newspapers and magazines are scattered around. At the far side is a bookshelf with old hardback books. The place has a bohemian air about it, the sort of place where writers and artists might come to sip beer or drink coffee or hold court. It is softly lit, not too bright, not too dark. What was its name again? He cannot remember, his mind has started racing again.

At the other side is the window looking out onto the street and he can see it is getting slightly darker. He looks at his watch again and sees the big hand is about to reach the hour, the eighteenth hour of the day, the time they have arranged to meet. She should be here now, in just seconds if she is to be on time and he is sure she will be. Maybe she is outside, in another street, smoking a cigarette. Maybe she is as nervous as he is. After all this time, this is it, he is going to see her again. Jean.

He can't imagine she has changed that much, but who knows, after everything, everything that has been happening to her in Paris with Salime.

The door opens and a blonde woman comes in, he cannot see her face clearly but it is not Jean, she is much too tall to be Jean. He knows if he sees her coming through the door he will know it is her and this woman is not. He drags on his cigarette and drains his glass. He imagines going to the bar and while his back is turned Jean will place a hand on his shoulder and say hello and he will ask her what she wants to drink. That's how it will happen, that is how they will be reunited again. So he goes to the bar, trying to make the scenario happen. He orders the same again and the waitress tells him she will bring it over to his table. He forgets that in France you call the waitress, you don't go to the bar.

He returns to his table, his eyes zoom in on the door but nobody is coming or going. The waitress brings over his beer, sets it down on the table and smiles. He says thank-you in French and she smiles warmly.

He takes a nervous sip of the beer and thinks about looking at his watch but tells himself not to, calm down, try to be cool, relax, enjoy the bar, enjoy the beer, get yourself in a relaxed state of mind for when she finally arrives.

His imagination fires up. He imagines her turning up here now with her bags packed, asking him to take her back to London, to Nevern Place where she can put her Paris nightmare behind her and she can have learned her lesson, put it all down to being young, naïve. What if Salime sees them, what if he's guessed and races to the airport and there is a massive confrontation?

Where is she? He is nearing the bottom of his glass, his second beer. He does not want to be tipsy when she arrives, he needs a clear head. But the glasses here are not pints, he reassures himself he has only had the equivalent of one pint, which is nothing to what he can get through back in London and still be in possession of his senses. He looks at his watch. It's just a few minutes past six. She could be just delayed on the metro.

Or maybe she isn't coming. Maybe she just won't show up. Has had second thoughts. Afraid of what would happen if Salime found out. He has no telephone number for her, only the address on her letters which he knows is far away because he looked it up on the map. She lives in the suburbs, this is central Paris, it is more than possible she has got delayed on the transport system.

It's only a few minutes, maybe she said 'around six' and meant that it could be any time around six, not dead on six.

So how long will he give her? Of course, he will give her at least an hour, that's reasonable. People can be an hour late. Or even two hours. Three, he thinks, would be pushing it. Anyway, it's only a few minutes past six. He looks at his watch. It is only minutes, but it's now fifteen minutes.

She will be full of remorse when she arrives, she will hug and kiss him and apologise for her lack of punctuality, she will say she was waiting for Salime to go out or something. Whatever, she will be here and she will have a perfectly plausible reason for being so late. So late? *It's only fifteen minutes.*

To smoke a cigarette and then to order another beer or order another beer and then smoke? The waitress passes him and without another second's thought he asks if he can have the same again. She says oui and her smile is even warmer. Maybe she thinks he is staying in the café because of her. He wishes he had brought his book, why the hell hadn't he brought his book, or bought a newspaper? He had thought there would be too much to do and see, he didn't want his head buried in a book when there was the wonder of Paris to take in and he did not want to miss anything, even while sitting in a café with nothing to do.

The café door opens again and a couple come in. He looks slightly older with flecks of grey on an otherwise black head of hair. Jake guesses he is in his 50s or even older, she is slightly younger but not much. She is blonde with high heels and tight denim jeans. He is dark, swarthy, wearing an ocean blue cotton shirt open to reveal his hairy chest and his height is accentuated by a pair of thick-heeled cowboy boots. As he sits down and picks up a menu, Jake notices he is wearing a gleaming silver watch that looks extremely expensive. The young woman is stunning, a perfect figure, a wide smile, she could be a model.

The waitress attends to them. Jake does not hear what they order but the waitress comes back with two bowls of salad and two glasses of what looks like sparking water with ice and lemon.

Jake cannot help watching them as they sip their drinks and eat their salad. The guy eats slowly, carefully wrapping lettuce around his fork and gently stabbing at the sliced tomato. He chews thoroughly before swallowing and then takes his fork to collect his next mouthful.

The woman is also a slow eater and he notices she puts her fork down between each mouthful as she chews. These people are the height of sophistication, they are a perfect couple, they treat their bodies with respect, they eat healthily, they do not down beers and smoke endless cigarettes. They are both tanned, they look as though they have money. The way they look at each other attentively when the other speaks, the love and respect for each other. He speculates they have a good sex life, live in a tall-ceilinged apartment overlooking the Seine. He pictures her getting out of bed naked and drawing the curtains, the man awaking to the beautiful and sexy sight of his gorgeous wife's derriere. They are perfect in every way, with a perfect life, a life they live to the full. Together and in love. Just like I could be, just like we, Jean and me, could be.

Jake is so engrossed in the couple his new beer remains untouched. The guy looks over, can feel Jake is watching them. Jake quickly averts his eyes and looks down to light a cigarette. He looks towards the window to his side. He is brought crashing back to his reality, the now, here in Paris. And he looks at his watch and it is now seven o'clock.

The couple are long-gone, even the waitress who served him has finished her shift, the café is now busy with drinkers, and as Jake sips on his fifth beer, he looks at his watch and sees it is after nine o'clock. She is not coming, that is clear, for whatever reason, she is not coming. He has been jilted, blown out, call it what you will. The lights in the café are turned down even lower, a new atmosphere pervades the place and he feels slightly disorientated, though he convinces himself he is not tipsy and certainly not drunk. He has just taken another beer. He really should not wait any longer, he should go back to the hotel, read to take his mind off everything and then sleep so he can get up early tomorrow and explore Paris in the morning before returning to London.

Right now he wishes he was in Cromwells with a pint, and regrets begin to sear through his mind. And the inner voice starts up, it always does.

It was crazy to come here, crazy to waste money on a flight here, what were you expecting? She is bad news, you know she is, she has never been anything else. You have got to get her out of your mind, forever, you have really got to move on, there is someone better out there, someone not so complicated. She is wasting your life. If she wants to be with a psychopath, or now does not want to be, it is up to her. Why does she stay with him? She has probably decided that she loves him after all and is staying with him and meeting you might complicate that decision. It is time to move on, stop being so desperate for a woman who can never be with you. She will never be yours.

He begins to think of how he will get back to the hotel. The metro is about a five-minute walk away and it is just two stops. The hotel is around the corner from the station. It will be OK. He can have another beer, drown his sorrows, stay here in the café bar a little while longer.

Who knows, she may still turn up even at this hour. He takes out the paper from his wallet that he had written the bar and its address on. Yes, he is in the right place. She had described the bar, its bookcases, the papers. This is the place.

A waiter walks by and he asks for another beer. He lights a cigarette while he waits for his drink to come and looks over to the far side of the bar and sees a man drinking alone. He cannot make out his features, but he is convinced the man is looking over, watching him. Maybe it's just the light, maybe he is looking at something or someone else.

The waiter returns with his beer. Jake checks the time, it is now 10.30, she is more than four and a half hours late. How would she explain that, if she were to turn up now?

He decides he will finish this beer and then return to his hotel, maybe find a bar closer to where he is staying and have a couple of nightcaps, maybe a whisky. He tries to calculate how much he has drunk and concludes he has had the equivalent of five pints, which isn't too bad.

He does not feel tipsy, he feels angry and aware of the situation, of the harsh reality that she has failed to turn up. Failed to meet him even though he has come all this way from London to Paris to see her and she cannot even show up.

Out of nowhere, Sylvie comes into his thoughts and he decides that when he returns to London, he will ask her out, he will suggest they date as a couple, see how things go. He has not seen her or her friend for a while so he will go around and reacquaint himself and ask Sylvie if she wants to go out, for a drink, maybe dinner and he hopes things will develop from there. He will shred all Jean's letters, maybe even burn them, banish her forever and if she writes to him again he will read the first letter just to see if she offers any reason for not turning up but after that he will ignore them. He may even write to her and tell her he has moved, giving a false address so he never receives any correspondence from her again. There will be no connection, no trace, he will throw her addresses – Liverpool and Paris – away so he cannot write to her.

But why has she not turned up? He castigates himself for playing the victim. Maybe she couldn't come, maybe Salime found out about their arrangement and stopped her from coming. Maybe he has locked her in their apartment, maybe she is crying, screaming to be let out, screaming to see him, to be with Jake. He sees her in a dark room, hands and legs tied, wriggling to try set herself free.

He fishes in his wallet for her Paris address. How far is that from here, could he get there, bang on the door, demand to be let in, or call the police to say a madman was holding a woman against her will? Could he rescue her, does he need to rescue her? I would like to see you, no, need to see you. The scenarios race through his mind, his imagination pelts irrationality against the inside of his head.

And the inner voice speaks. It always does.

All this is unlikely, there will be a simpler explanation and that explanation is she decided seeing you was a bad idea, that her love for Salime is too strong and if she is in trouble you are not the man to save her. She has always thought you were weak, in every sense. What I do with Salime is almost pornographic.

They could have made up, he might have apologised, saying he didn't mean the cruel things he has said, the awful things he has done. He may have opened a bottle of expensive French wine, played soft, kind music, like If You Don't Know Me By Now, he may have seduced her, he may be licking her body, going down on her then fucking her passionately. Pornographically.

Right now, while you wait here, like some loser, Salime could be fucking her until she screams in ecstasy, while you drink your beers and wait, wait for nobody to show up, wait for nothing to happen. Like you always do, like you go on doing. Like it's still 1989 when anything was possible, when you first met her, before you knew her, properly knew her.

He takes out his wallet, beckons the waiter to bring him his bill and just as he is about to place the francs on the table, a hand slaps down a French note. The man says in a strong French accent, I will get this.

Jake looks up at a smiling stranger, a stranger wearing an ocean blue shirt and as he looks down at the arm that has placed the money on the table he sees an expensive silver watch. A watch, and a shirt, he has seen before, not so long ago. The hand reaches to him for a handshake.

You must be Jake. I am Salime Douali. Pleased to meet you.

He shakes Salime's hand. And wonders whether he has completely underestimated how much he has had to drink. Is French beer stronger than English?

Before he has any time to think, Salime says, I know, you were expecting Jean. I understand this is a very confusing situation for you. Look, I know a quieter place, not far, just around the corner, in fact. It's not a bar, it is a place, an apartment I use. I have some nice whisky, let us go there and talk, Jake. Let me explain everything.

Your head is whoozy, you have been drinking for several hours, you even popped an E. Yes, you forgot, didn't you? You broke all the rules of E – no alcohol, just water. They do not mix. And now here he is, Salime Douali. The same man you saw with that blonde, the same man who was part of the couple you so aspired to. Shit, maybe that was Jean. You don't know, your mind is squiffy, a concoction of alcohol, the E and the confusion of being in a different country, here in Paris, a place you do not know.

And the voice goes on, it starts up again, rapidly in the short time he has to acknowledge Salime and decide whether he will go with him to this place. This place with the whisky where all will be explained. The voice is louder now, deafening.

You should never have come here, you should have cut her off, moved on, lived on, you should not have put yourself in this situation. Where the fuck is she and what is he doing here rather than her? How did he find out you were meeting her? Why was he here earlier? Who was the woman he was with? It could have been her but you would not know because of the state you are in, the situation you are in. Tell him to fuck off and run to the metro and go back to the hotel and take the flight tomorrow and go back to London, to Earls Court, to Nevern Place, to Cromwells. Go back to the place and the people you know.

For fuck's sake go.

So this is Salime Douali. What I do with Salime is almost pornographic. And what he does to you is fuck with your head, he bullies, he shouts, he threatens, he makes you afraid, he makes you live the life you do not want. He frightens you so much, this bastard, this twat, this…. I can fuck you, but it is not love.

They turn a corner off the main street, Salime's probably expensive shoes click-clop on the pavement.

In a rage that strikes Jake like an electric shock, he grabs Salime, pushes him, stumbles at first but regains inertia and pushes Salime Douali against a wall.

What the fuck are you doing to her, what the fuck are you doing to her you bastard? Where the fuck is she, where is Jean?

A sardonic grin spreads across Salime's face. The older, handsome man. The Daddy.

Jake, let go of me and calm down. There is no need for this. If you want to know everything, I will tell you, but let's be civilised. Now take your hands off me. Take your hands off me, let's go to the apartment, have a nice drink and I will tell you everything, the whole truth. I promise you this.

The 'place' is just around the corner. They enter the building which has a concierge who Salime exchanges what Jake assumes are pleasantries, and then he beckons Jake around a corner where there is a metal shuttered lift. Salime presses a button that opens the door and he allows Jake to step inside first.

He does not look at Salime as the lift rattles upwards quickly.

Then they are inside the apartment, tall ceilings, wooden floors, everything minimalistic, tidy, a potent smell of polish, professionally and thoroughly cleaned.

The walls are white, sepia poster-like paintings adorn the walls. There are no bookshelves, he notices. There are two armchairs and a sofa and a large glass coffee table in the middle.

Please, take a seat. You drink whisky?

Yes, please, with water.

Salime disappears to the kitchen and he can hear glasses being taken out of a cupboard, hears the whisky bottle being opened and the clink of ice.

What the fuck am I doing here, what is happening? He looks around the room for traces of Jean, a discarded cardigan, a picture. There is nothing. No sign, no trace.

Salime returns with two tumblers generously filled with whisky and, he hopes, as requested, plenty of water. The glasses are placed on the coffee table, Salime has rolled up the sleeves of the blue cotton shirt and, he notices, has taken off the silver watch.

His arms are tanned, his finger nails very short, his hands look soft, they look like they have never been troubled by hard, physical work. Not even washing up, certainly not cleaning. He has not cleaned this flat himself.

Salime sits back and stretches out his legs and takes a small sip from the glass. He looks around the room as if he has never set foot in it before. Then he looks directly at Jake who takes his first sip and asks if it is ok for him to smoke.

Oh yes, let me get you an ashtray.

Salime disappears again but within seconds comes back with a large, bowl-like glass ashtray which he places on the table then takes out a small cigar from the pocket of his jeans and lights up. Not quite the health nut he had appeared when eating his salad and drinking his mineral water in the café bar.

The whisky OK?

Fine.

It's a good one, given to me as a gift. But I only partake occasionally, special occasions or if a little stressed.

Jake nods and nervously puffs on his cigarette before taking a small, tentative sip of the whisky.

It could be spiked, maybe he has spiked the drink. He prepared it in the kitchen. This might not be whisky and water. It may be, it may be contaminated. You may be dead within minutes. Where the hell is she, where is Jean?

So Jake, welcome to Paris.

He holds his whisky out and says cheers in French, Jake reluctantly clinks glasses but does not say cheers. Salime reclines in his seat and crosses his legs.

So I expect you want to know why I am here and not Jean.

How did you find out we were meeting?

Oh, Jean is very easy to read. She rarely goes out and when she said she was coming here and might be a few hours I became worried.

Worried?

I don't know how much you know about Jean's problems, psychological problems. I am treating Jean for a variety of personality and behavioural disorders. It is why she is in Paris. When her mother knew I was leaving London to go back to Paris, she was distraught and concerned that it would be difficult to find another psychiatrist that Jean could get on with. So I offered to provide Jean with accommodation and allow her to live in Paris while I treat her and get her better.

Salime's English is perfect, his voice is deep, his words are delivered carefully, every sentence as if they have been carefully and diligently composed and edited before being released from his mouth. Just as Jean had described his speech.

Jake feels nauseous and confused and wonders whether he is fully understanding what Salime is saying.

Jake says, but Jean hasn't been in contact with her mother for months. They've never got on, after what happened to her, her mother, when her father left.

Salime smiles, a bless-you-for-being-so-stupid smile, takes a sip of his whisky and drops his voice down about two decibels.

Jake, Jean has probably told you all sorts of things, aspects of her life, her past, her childhood. Obviously I don't know what she has told you but most of it will not be true. Jean makes up stories to suit any given situation. She wants to be a writer but instead of writing a book she is trying to write a life. A better life than the one she has had. She told me about your terrible childhood, your mother. It could be that in order for her to assimilate with you, she had to become a victim herself, to put her, how do you say in English, on an equal footing. It's all part of the victimhood.

Where is she now?

I persuaded her not to come and meet you and she is in the apartment I arranged for her, where she lives most of the time. I'm sorry, I only found out about the meeting a day or so ago, otherwise I would have written to you or tried to telephone to explain everything so that you would not have a wasted journey.

I don't understand, why would seeing me be such a big deal? I'm a good friend, she wanted to see me.

It is important that Jean does not confuse anything or anyone from her past as she undergoes her therapy. In time, she will be able to see you again, when she gets better and is able to handle situations. It is very important she does not deviate from the treatment or do anything that might set her back. I'm sure nothing bad would happen if she saw you but her state of mind is fragile, meeting someone she has not seen for a very long time could confuse her.

He does not know whether he should say this, but he cannot leave Paris having not put this to Salime.

She says you are lovers, that you were lovers in London and that you wanted her to come to Paris to be with you. Now she says she is frightened of you.

Salime gets up from his seat, glass in hand and walks over to the tall windows and looks out into the Paris night, contemplating, considering what he will say next. He turns around and walks back to the centre of the room but stays standing. Suppose this has riled him, what if he lashes out, throws the glass, kicks the table?

Jake, did you not listen to what I have been saying?

There is silence, Jake believes it to be a rhetorical question.

Jake, I asked you a question. Did you listen to what I have just been saying?

His voice is not raised which makes his question all the more intimidating.

Jake says, look, I'm not saying you are lying, it's just that this condition you say Jean has, it contradicts everything I have ever known about her. It contradicts the letters which sounded desperate. And I've never met you before. Look at it from my point of view, I am due to meet Jean, you turn up, she is nowhere to be seen and you tell me I cannot see her.

A-ha, yes, I can see your point of view. Hmm. Ok let us go through each of your points. All you know about me is what Jean has told you. OK, you say I am not lying. So therefore Jean is lying and as I have just told you, Jean is being treated for a psychiatric condition of compulsive lying. She is a pathological liar, she makes things up. Not because she is evil but because she is ill. So what Jean has told you in the letters is unreliable. She is what in legal terms is defined as an unreliable witness. Yes, you were expecting to see Jean and then I turned up. Who you have never met. If I was Jean's lover and I was stopping her from seeing you, why would I go to the trouble of finding out where you were due to meet her and then turn up here to explain the situation? I would just have stopped her from going to meet you. If I was so cruel and mistreating her.

He pauses to take a sip of his drink. Realising both their glasses are almost empty he asks Jake if he wants a top-up. He disappears to the kitchen and brings the bottle of of whisky and a tray of ice.

Jake watches him pour generous measures of whisky and taps two ice cubes into each glass. Everything he is saying is plausible. And in a way he is relieved because now he thinks he can justify completely, to himself, getting her out of his life. She is not who I thought she was.

She was always strange but now she is a complete stranger. She is, he considers with sadness, sick.

Salime continues, Jake, you are very young, Jean is a very complex character. I cannot and would never stop you trying to see her or writing to her or being in any way emotionally involved with her. But in my opinion, you would do better to move on with your life. Jean will always be psychologically susceptible. She told me she only knew you for a few months, it is not as though you had a long-term relationship. She's really just a girl you met.

Jake nervously takes a sip of his drink and lights another cigarette. Salime is looking at him, weighing him up, analysing him. Part of being a psychiatrist he supposes, studying other people.

I know, I know it was not a long time but Jean just, well, just seems so...

You fell in love with her. But you fell in love with the Jean she told you she was. The real Jean is an entirely other person. You have fallen in love with a fictional person, a product of her own warped imagination and psychological state of mind. Even Jean does not know who she is. Jake, you have to look to the future, the future, not the past.

Will she ever get better?

Oh yes, in time she will get better, she will live a normal enough life once her treatment has been completed. But once that happens, Jean will not be the person she is now. She will not recognise herself, she will have to come to terms with her new self. Her past will be completely re-remembered.

Re-remembered?

She genuinely thinks the things she told you about her childhood were real, true, happened. When she is better, she will not remember this false past.

Will she remember me, London?

Not when I've finished with her...rather when the treatment is complete it is unlikely she will remember, or that thoughts of this time will just randomly come into her head. While she will not completely remember everything about this time in her life, she will recall parts of it but only if reminded, if her brain is prompted.

Jake's head is pounding, he is not sure whether he really understands all of this and fears he may understand even less by tomorrow. He needs to get out of here, he has had enough of the whisky and though Salime is softly-spoken and amiable, he is erudite and patronising and Jake doesn't want to hear this anymore. This is not how he wants to think of Jean.

He gets up and says, well, erm, thanks for the whisky. I had better be getting back to the hotel. I fly back to London tomorrow.

Salime gets up and goes to shake Jake's hand.

It has been good to meet you Jake and I'm so sorry that this trip did not turn out the way you had hoped. Think about what I have said. Remember, Jean is getting the best possible care she needs. I will take care of her. But think about what I said about you. About how you can go forward now.

I will, thanks.

He keeps his voice at a tone that he hopes tells Salime not to think he has completely convinced him. He doesn't want to make it so easy for him. If Salime is lying, he wants to leave the impression that he is not being fobbed off, that he will consider what he has said and decide for himself whether he believes it.

Of course, he has no idea what he will do if he if he concludes Salime is lying. His head is a jumble of confusion, frustration and alcohol, here in this city he does not know, being told things he could never have imagined, everything fuzzy, everything complicated, everything wrong.

Out on the street the Paris night air is clammy but he is glad to be outdoors again, a chance to try to clear his head, to attempt to take in what Salime has said.

It should have been so different, this Paris trip. It was about coming here to see her again, to rekindle if not their romance, then at least their friendship, for him to help her out of the terrible situation she is in.

Terrible situation? But she isn't in a terrible situation. She is in treatment. She is in care. All the things she said, all the things she told you, they were not true. You have never met the real Jean, only the made up one. You never really knew her, not really and now all that you thought he knew was wrong. Normally you meet someone, you get to know them, their thoughts, their personality, their history and they learn about you and then you both decide whether there is any chance of compatibility, any chance of making each other happy. And you make the rational assumption that everything, or at least more or less everything, they tell you resembles some sort of truth. As Salime said, even Jean does not know who she is.

The metro rattles along, he looks at the other passengers. Who are they, what are their lives, what are their secrets, do they know who they are?

As the plane takes off he is overcome by this sickening, empty feeling, a feeling he has abandoned her, that Salime could have been lying, that she is in danger. He has no way of knowing. But right now he has to put all this out of his mind. He opens his book and tries to escape.

CHAPTER TWENTY-FOUR

BACK IN Earls Court he drops his luggage off at the flat and looks at the mail. There is nothing from her, he had never expected there to be, but he looks, just in case.

He goes to Cromwells with her letter, the letter that sent him on the pointless mission to Paris and orders his beer.

This time last night he was in that Paris bar waiting for her. And right now, had things turned out so differently, he might have been sitting here, in Cromwells, opposite her. Saved. He might have saved her and in doing so, saved himself.

But as usual he is, as it were, back, empty-handed, on his own with only a beer, her letter and nagging doubts that she is really safe, that Salime was telling the truth.

A beer and her letter, a head just a whirlpool of confusion and regret. On it goes, the story of Jean, whatever story that really is.

So now to forensically examine, piece by piece, what Salime had told him. He wishes he could have written it all down, or better still, tape-recorded it so he could be absolutely certain rather than rely on his emotion-sodden memory of what was an alcohol-soaked, not to say surreal evening in Paris. There are flashes in his mind that ask, did I really go to Paris, did Salime really turn up? Flashgun images of her being abused, beaten and held against her will explode periodically in his head. Had I been there, had I looked for you, had I found you. Maybe I need rescuing. What if he had irretrievably let her down, left her in danger? But how will he ever know?

On his third beer, Jake's mind sprints to the conclusion: Salime is a psychopathic liar. One phrase in his diatribe screams in his brain; She will not remember her past when I have finished with her…when her treatment is complete.

It's a killer line, he should have picked up on it there and then. When I have finished with her. Would a psychiatrist, a doctor, use such phraseology? When I have finished with her.

You stupid, fucking arsehole, you should have grabbed hold of him, pinned him to the wall and beat the fuck out of him until he explained what, exactly, he meant. Until he had told you where she was and what he had done to her. You should have said, Salime, 'when I've finished with her' is hardly a medical term is it? What the fuck do you mean? You mean when you have indoctrinated her, fucked up her brain until it believes your doctrines, your psycho-crap, until she believes the abuse is there for her own good, until you can completely control her. The things you should have said, the things you should have done and the one person in your life, the only person in your miserable fucking life that you cared about you have abandoned.

Screwball, arsehole, the voice pelts him with vituperation, it's so violent it's like he's having a migraine.

He leaves the pub, abandoning half his pint. He goes to the end of Penywern Road, just a few streets up the Earls Court Road from Nevern Place. He knows the guy who is always standing at the end of Penywern deals crack, coke or whatever. Surely he will have a spare E for sale.

He needs it now, he needs lifting out of himself.

I can get you some in about an hour, says the dealer.

An hour, why an hour?

It's a rave drug, most of my clientele want coke, But I can go to the phone box opposite the station and get my supplier to get it here. But you'll have to give me time man and it's gonna cost.

Fuck the cost. I'll come back then at about ten. Yeah? And you'll have it?

Yeah man, take it easy, no probs brother. But I need a ten quid deposit – in case you don't turn up and leave me with gear there's no call for on the streets.

Jake pulls out a tenner and hands it over.

I'll see you at ten.

An hour to kill, what to do? Only one thing for it. Another beer.

The dealer is true to his word, Jake gets his E and goes back to Nevern Place. He has a few beers in the fridge just to top himself up until the effects of the E take hold.

Breaking all the old rules again. Only water with E.

He sticks the tape on, he knows that within a few minutes the E will take effect.

He turns the cassette player to full volume and the anthem of 1989 blasts into the room and he waves his arms, he dances, he gyrates his body, almost contorts, you're such a, you're such a… Ride On Time. Her face, her hair, her eyes, her everything come back into his mind. They always do. An E, a narcotic high, a few lines from a summertime tune – his summertime and right now, he just wants to blow it all away.

CHAPTER TWENTY-FIVE

HE HASN'T run for a while and decides exercising again could be good for him. He tears up Earls Court Road and into Holland Park, he does a few laps and then runs up to Holland Park Avenue, up to Notting Hill then Bayswater. He stops for a rest and notices a telephone box.

It is wallpapered with cards, some of them for raves but others for prostitutes offering their services. Buxom beauty, stunning, Thai massage, Black Angel, Spanish beauty, English rose. They all claim to be just a few minutes away. This is where Richard found and visited his chick with a dick.

He surreptitiously goes into the phone box, picks up the receiver and pretends to be talking into it while he surveys the cards. He takes a few down, folds them crudely and stuffs them into the pocket of his shorts.

As he runs back to Earls Court through Kensington Gardens, he tries to remember the last time he had sex. It is a few months ago and he feels the urge, feels horny. But to pay for it, well that is something else. It isn't that he cannot afford it but thinks he would be proving how far he has fallen if he pays for sex. And what if the girls are exploited, what if they are forced to do this work?

He runs back to Nevern Place and hopes he will have put prostitutes out of his mind once he's had a cooling shower.

It doesn't work, he feels horny as hell and studies the calling cards, has them spread out over his desk. There are no prices. He could just call a few numbers and see what the going rate is.

You should not need to do this, even think about paying for sex. It's what sad, fat middle-aged men do who can't find a woman willing to fuck them. You are a young man, you have had a few lovers, it has never been a problem. Talk to a girl at the bar, and what about seeing Sylvie?

Sylvie. He remembers the plan he had in Paris when Jean had not turned up. To reacquaint himself with Sylvie and take their friendship to a romantic level. She is a sexy girl, seems normal, is fun, likes what he likes – reading, music, E. Maybe they could go to a rave together, he is sure she would love it.

Sylvie will be at work now, she works at the Cumberland Hotel in Marble Arch. He can go round to her place tonight.

He looks at the calling cards. He is curious but the raw horny feeling that gripped him on his run has dissipated. He tears the cards up and throws them away.

The morning hatches into afternoon and he decides he will spend it reading, being calm, use his time constructively, stop reading Jean's letter and try to feel and think normally.

He is into his book and concentrates for a good hour before deciding to put the kettle on and make tea. As he waits for the kettle to boil he leans out of the window and smokes. Although he still has plenty of money, he thinks he should decide what he is going to do next for a job, for a career. He will get a few media magazines when he goes out and check the jobs pages.

As he pulls on his cigarette, he is pleased that he is reading again and making plans, that thoughts of Jean and Salime are being ousted from his mind by more practical everyday considerations. His run has done him good, cleared his mind, relaxed his body, in all he feels more positive.

The feeling lasts an hour or two as he carries on reading but then, out of nowhere, the voice returns.

So you are just going to pretend Paris did not happen. You are not going to think about what Salime said and decide whether it is true or a pack of lies? She might be in trouble, she might really need you. Rescue me.

He slams the book on the coffee table and lights another cigarette. It's as if he has now pressed the play button on a video recorder as his mind whirrs into life and rewinds the events in Paris.

It's a simple question: who is lying, Jean or Salime? Is it conceivable she or anyone could make up her entire life? Why would she? Because she is sick, psychologically sick. Salime's words, his prognosis, his story.

But why would he make up this story about her? Jake is no threat, if Jean really wants to stay with him she will. What I do with Salime is, well, almost pornographic.

If Jean is sick, why is she writing to Jake? Why does she want to maintain the connection?

He skips the tea and opens a can of beer. *It's the wrong thing to do, it clouds your thoughts, it tangles your thinking. Alcohol.*

He goes to the window and lights another cigarette. For no reason that he can fathom he thinks back to the years before he came to London. Living with his dad all those years, often with little or no communication between them.

The days and weeks spent with his aunt and uncle were long, lonely days. He had sought solace in his books, his books were his friends, they were the only ones to speak to him, to tell him things, to take him to places, places outside that childhood world, and out of himself.

He had not been an unhappy kid. He had got used to his own company, making his own entertainment. But he was not good at school, had few friends and shyness crippled his progress.

His school reports always said, Jake must try to make a bigger contribution to class activity, he must ask questions and seek help when he doesn't understand. He needs to interact with his fellow pupils.

His father would read the reports with a glass of whisky in his hand. He would say nothing, just a sigh, as if he knew why Jake was like he was at school but words failed to enter his head, or failed to exit through his mouth in the form of wise, fatherly, parental advice.

Later in his school career he buckled down and turned his reading to academic subjects. At only 15 he knew he wanted to be a success at something and having qualifications was the route to this.

An advert played on the TV for the Halifax Building Society advertising cashpoint debit cards. It featured a young, good-looking man waking up in his loft apartment, presumably somewhere in London, making coffee and realising he was out of milk. His grey and black cat stared up at him mournfully. They look at each other and both their faces say: there's none for either of us.

To the soundtrack of Easy Like A Sunday Morning, the guy goes down to the street and puts the debit card in the machine. He gets his cash, gets the milk and returns to his apartment, makes his coffee with milk and gives the cat its morning drink. Their only problem of the day, but it's sorted. Easy like a Sunday morning. An advert that lasted no more than a few seconds but it had stayed with him all these years.

And now it has come back to him. And he asks, why now, why am I thinking of this advert?

Because it is simple, it's about the guy being independent and having access to cash and solving the milk problem and taking care of the cat who is dependent on him and will be his for as long as it lives, so long as he takes care of it, solves its problems, provides what it needs.

And that is how he wanted his life to be and how he wants his life to be. To take care of someone, someone special, someone who only wants what you can offer, what you have to give and no more.

Me and just one person.

Dear Jean

I hope you are well. I am sorry we did not get to meet in Paris. As you probably know by now, I met Salime and he told me of your problems.

I am so sorry. I had no idea you had this condition. I hope what Salime told me is true. I only have his word so I don't know. He seemed plausible.

Well, I hope the treatment goes well. I just wanted to let you know I am thinking about you and wishing that all your problems – the condition – rights itself and that maybe one day, if you still remember me, we can meet again.

Maybe you can write to me and keep me up to date on how it is going and how you are feeling.

But don't feel obliged. In fact, maybe it is best, as part of your recovery, that you forget about me and concentrate on the future.

Maybe ask Salime what he thinks.

Anyway, I wish you well Jean, I really do wish you well.

Love and kisses

Jake.

He posts the letter the next day.

You have just told her you believe Salime. You have told her that you have bought everything he has said. If it is not true, she is going to think you are weak, gullible, that you don't challenge anything.

But she already thinks this. This much you know.

Nausea grips him, but it is immediately replaced with an idea that kick-starts an adrenaline rush that is so strong he wants to run, run fast to think it through.

He changes into his running gear and runs up the Earls Court Road and into Holland Park.

To go to Paris again, to find the address she had put on her letter. He thinks ....to spy, to see if he can see Jean, watch them, see if she emerges, watch Salime's behaviour towards her.

He is running faster, as if running faster will generate substance to this idea, give it plausibility.

And what if Salime spots you, in the street, what if he realises this is what you're doing, spying on them, on him?

I cannot just swallow everything Salime has said without seeing for myself, without satisfying myself. Otherwise I am abandoning her. What if it's all lies, what if she is telling the truth in her letters and that Salime is a pathological liar who is really controlling her under some psychological spell.

He runs up Notting Hill and back through Kensington Gardens and when he gets back to the flat, sweat-soaked and exhausted, he flakes out in his chair. He still doesn't know whether going back to Paris and finding her is a good idea.

In Cromwells with a pint he goes over her letter again. He stares at the address at the top.

189 Boulevard de Clichy. In a district called Pigalle.

So you find this address. Then what? You stand outside watching. Maybe there will be a café opposite you can go in and watch from there? If someone comes out of the flat – it could be a house – are you going to follow them?

Jake says, fuck, out loud. The inner voice tells him this is a crazy idea, this will not work. *They might not even be there, they might have gone away. How many days is he going to stay? What a waste of time and money.*

You should move on, it is not, she is not, your problem.

He orders another pint, sits down and takes the letter from his jacket pocket again. He looks at it folded up, sighs and puts it back in his pocket.

Have the beer, sleep on it.

He gets back to Nevern Place and he hears the communal telephone ringing.

He rushes downstairs, picks it up and answers. The line is crackly like hundreds of fireworks are being let off simultaneously in the distance. That's all he hears at first. He repeats hello, hello, hello into the receiver.

Then a voice

Jake, Jake, is that you, can you hear me?

Her voice is shouting, the line is bad.
Yes, yes, it's Jake here.
Jake, it's Jean, listen, please, please you have to....
The line goes dead, the high-pitch humming that says the call is finished stays in his ears. He knows the line is dead, he knows she has gone but says, Jean, yes, I'm here, I'm here.

He puts the phone down quickly realising it's possible she might call back. He waits a few minutes. Nothing.

A man comes out of one of the flats. An Aussie guy, tall and lean wearing shorts and t-shirt. He sees Jake by the phone.

Hey mate, you finished with the phone?
Yeah, yeah, it's all yours.

He goes up to the flat, an image of her crying into the phone, desperate to be saved from some heinous crime committed by Salime is all he can see.

The pleading in her voice. The tone of it, the 'please, please' stabs like shards of glass in his ears.

He takes the whisky bottle and pours himself a large one. It's getting late, the traffic on the Earls Court Road is an intermittent hum interspersed by the sound of her, her voice. Her voice on the phone, far, far away. And, just now and again, he thinks he can hear the phone. He goes to the top of the stairs but it is not ringing. Only her desperate, pleading voice is ringing, in his ears, and all night and for much longer after that.

Why has she never rung before? Maybe she has, but he's not been here to pick it up. She wouldn't ask anyone to give him a message. Why was the line so bad?

This is agony. What is happening to her? Why doesn't she ring back?

His imagination leaps away like a dog out of a trap at the races.

He's holding her against her will. He's caught her phoning him and has dragged her off the phone.

He has thrown her on the bed and is raining down blows on her body in an uncontrollable psychopathic rage.

She is screaming, crying, blood oozing from her nose, from her head, bruises disfiguring her beautiful face. Her luscious hair is being pulled, a tooth is knocked out.

She fights back but the more she does, the more potent his fury and he strikes her harder.

If she screams loud enough, will someone hear, call the cops, come to her? Rescue me.

She pleads with him to stop as she curls her body into a ball, laying on the floor.

And now maybe he has calmed down and gone for a drink and she is in the bathroom, wiping blood off her face, surveying the damage, wincing in pain or writhing on the floor in agony with broken bones.

The police must be on their way, maybe she has called them, and an ambulance.

Blue flashing lights illuminate the street, neighbours watch as she is carted off on a stretcher.

A drip to her mouth, a medic giving her oxygen as the ambulance speeds away, its sirens blaring, disturbing the late night Paris air.

Jean, what is happening to you, what is he doing to you?

And in his mind, she is sobbing and calling out for him.

He has to slow down his mind, his emotions, his imagination. He needs to escape from it. He rummages in a drawer, finds the E and slugs it down with whisky.

It goes against the rules. Water only.

But he needs the alcohol and drug cocktail, he needs to kill off the neurons that carpet bomb his brain with these vile, images, he has to stop the inner voice before it even starts up. The E kicks in and he feels as though he is falling, falling off something high, down below is a void, a dark void. He goes to the bed and lies down, holding onto the sheets as the room begins to spin.

CHAPTER TWENTY-SIX

JAKE HAD not bothered to consult the Lonely Planet books to find out about this place, Pigalle. He had meant to but changed his mind. He preferred to have no preconceptions about places he had never visited. It was all part of the adventure, the thrill of travelling. He decided he would do much more travelling and he would follow this policy of not boning up on places for as long as his travelling career lasted.

As Jake comes out of the metro, he sees the neon lights, he sees the sleaze, he sees the frontages to venues offering all kinds of physical and visual pleasures. Boulevard de Clichy is like Soho but all in one, very long street. There's the famous Moulin Rouge which is much smaller than he imagined. There are the sex shops called SeXy Store, Pussy's, Sexodrome, All-in Live Shows. One sex establishment after another, interspersed by the occasional bar or doorway leading to apartments above. It's mid-afternoon and he just walks and walks along the Boulevard, mesmerised by this corridor of smut. He wonders about the live shows and what they constitute. Would people spend money and time watching other people having sex? Of course they would, of course they do, he says to himself, that's what porn is all about. And there are plenty of people going into the live shows, couples, single men, older, younger.

He takes note of the door numbers. He is only at 65 so he has some way to go before he reaches 189. But he wants to find it, take a look, be near to where she is and then take stock, decide how he is going to play this out.

All a bad idea, you should have a beer, explore Pigalle, maybe even go to a live show. Anything but see her, see Jean, possibly see both of them, possibly, if not probably, land you, land her in trouble. A live show. You might even like it, get turned on.

Past a bar that is blaring out Back To Life (however do you want me). The bar's name, according to the purple neon sign is just Bar, like nobody could be bothered to give it a name, like, say Cromwells. Jake smiles as he thinks they should have called it the Dildo Inn given its surrounds.

He feels like stopping for a beer but decides to carry on walking until he finds the flat. Then maybe he can stop at a bar nearer. He needs to find out how far on this street of smut the flat is. The street seems like it will never end.

Past more bars, past more sex shows, the door numbers are increasing and now he is at 180. He walks, 182, 183, then a shop, then a bar, 185, 186, then the numbers change to 190. Shit, he's gone past it, he's missed 189. The numbers continue to go up, 191, 192. He needs to go back on himself. How could he have missed 189?

Easily as it turns out. It is not on the street, the door to 189 is on the side of the building in an alleyway. He sees the buzzer for 189. Just one press. That's all it might take to see her again. Answering that door. Face to face. After all this time.

Nerves begin grip him. *Press it now, get it over with. Unlock the mystery.*

No, he cannot do it right now, he needs a drink, a needs a smoke, he needs to think.

What are you doing here, what are you going to do?

He decided to come here because he knows, after the phone call, this is the right thing to do. This is what he tells himself whenever the inner voice questions him. Someone he cares about, or cared about, is in trouble and despite what Salime had told him, he owed it to her to check it out, to find out. And what he is going to do here is not spy on them, or walk past their place in the hope that one or both will come out.

He is going to press that buzzer and he is going to announce himself. He is going to see for himself, he is going to talk to one or both, he is going to say what he should have said the last time he was here: show me the proof that what you told me in that Paris apartment is true.

And he wants to see Jean, to satisfy himself that she is OK, that she has not been harmed, that she does not live in fear. They may put up a show of solidarity, they may both lie, Jean may have to lie because the consequences will be terrible if she doesn't. But it will allow him to use his judgement, to take a reading of the situation and, importantly, show her that he really does care about her even if they have no future.

He will go to a bar, he will order a few glasses of wine. He will not get drunk, but he will loosen himself up, unlock any tension that might become a barrier to him doing what he planned. What he wants to do, what he needs to do, once and for all.

In a bar, several doors down from 189, a smiley waitress comes to his table and takes his order. He asks for house wine. He takes out a cigarette and smokes. Between each drag he takes deep breaths. This is the right thing to do, not just for her, but for me, too.

The inner critical voice has its say, as it always does, but he finds the voice is not so loud today. It's as though it is allowing him to go through with this, that there is no point in telling him how inevitably futile this whole exercise may prove to be. It's as if it is saying, go on then, go and do it. But you'll see.

Jake is calm as he sips his red wine and smokes. He tells himself that soon he will know and then soon he can move on, the right thing done. This may not end with any final conclusion, it may dig up more questions, more dilemmas. But it seems now the logical thing to do.

It is a few days since he received her call, or her attempted call. Maybe she is in the apartment now penning him another letter. He imagines she will be shocked when he buzzes the door, assuming she answers it of course.

He orders another glass of wine. He's been in the bar for almost an hour and has sipped his drink slowly. After he finishes the next glass, he will do what he has come here to do. Nerves make his hand shake as he lifts the wine glass to his mouth but he keeps a firm grip on the stem. Keep a grip. Hold on, just hold on.

Outside 189, he looks up. A small light, a table lamp, is on, it makes the place look warm and inviting. An appearance, and that is surely all it is, of warm embers burning inside. Romantic, intimate, safe.

Just like you always wanted, just like you wish it was with you, with her. In a room, in a room bathed in love, even for just one moment, one day, one night, one week, one month, but better a lifetime.

They, or one of them, is home. Both could be snuggled up together, in the warmth, in the glow of the light. Is he really going to walk up to press this buzzer? A stranger to them both, interfering in lives he does not really know. To leave, to turn right round, to go back to where he came, where his place is, and stay there is a thought that gusts through his mind. Just for one moment. But he looks left and then right, he walks up to the door, the door now in front of him, the only barrier between him and whoever is behind it. He's come such a long way, both emotionally and in miles. He touches the buzzer but does not press it. Apartment 189. Where she lives, where they live. Jean and Salime. Salime and Jean. A couple.

His head is slightly woozy from the wine, adrenaline should power him, but instead he feels paralysed, he cannot move his hand, his eyes glisten with moisture. What shall I do? But the voices are silent, as if watching, waiting, as anxious as him. And then the sound of the phone call, the pitch of her voice, the dead sound when the line had disconnected. His name, Jake, from her mouth, her voice. He presses the buzzer, long and hard. He waits.

Light is thrown onto the steps from the glass of the door. The hallway light. Through the corrugated glass he can see a blonde head walking towards the door. He hears the latch being opened, it's double locked, she's opening the locks to open the door. It is not Salime, is all he can think.

At first he thinks the woman who stares at him now is her. But she is heavily made up, dressed in a tight black top and miniskirt, red lipstick mascara and long, blonde hair. His stomach flips. He tries to speak, oh I'm sorry to bother you but I'm looking for Jean Ridley and Salime Douali. It dawns on him this woman is probably French and may not understand him. He is taken aback and relieved when she answers in perfect English.

I'm sorry they vacated this apartment oh at least four months ago.

So this is the right address, they did live here?

Oh yes, yes I was the landlady, I own this and several properties. I moved back here when they moved out. I lost my husband and didn't want to live in our other apartment so I moved in after they moved out.

The address, why did she put this address on the letters when she no longer lived here?

Are you a friend of theirs?

Yes, well a good friend of Jean's.

OK, well, I'm sorry they are no longer here.

I'm sorry to have troubled you. Goodbye.

She smiles and says goodbye, shuts the door and he hears her putting on the latches.

All this way, all this time and in just a few seconds, his hopes of seeing her come crashing down.

A total waste of time, you have come here, all this way and she is not here. Months ago she moved out. Why did she use this address on her letters? Now you can just turn around and go. Back to London.

He looks at the door. The light to the hallway has been switched off.

An hour later after walking around the length of the Boulevard de Clichy, he is tired, weary and depressed but he doesn't feel like leaving this place yet. He might as well make the most of his wasted trip and explore Pigalle, have a few beers, see what goes on here as the night begins to fall. He has booked into a hotel not far away so he might as well try to make something of the evening.

He finds a bar and as he opens the door he sees the place is dimly lit as if only by a small red neon light. A fug of cigarette smoke swirls the room which he can hardly adjust his eyes to. There appear to be no waiters, just a barman and a few people on high stools around the bar.

The rest of the room is tables with people sitting drinking and smoking on their own.

There's some soft background music playing quietly that he does not recognise.

He goes to the bar and sees pumps of beer offering drinks he is familiar with such as Carling and Fosters. It doesn't seem very French. He orders a pint and takes it to a table. It's difficult to make out faces clearly but they seem to be all older people, middle aged. In their 40s, 50s. A mixture of men and women.

Jake suspects it's some kind of place where people meet up to live out their secret lives. Loners who seek company in bars, over drinks.

But this is all very distracting. He is here because of Jean and he needs to think. If she has moved on and has no plans to eventually forward her new address, he will never see her again. He will never be able to write to her again. The finality of the situation leaves him cold and slightly angry that she always had that control, that power to cut herself off from him forever. Just a change of address and no communication and then she could just go, without a trace.

But why? Why would she cut him off?

The beer isn't going down well, his stomach feels bloated so he abandons it and orders a glass of red wine. Jean. Did she ever come here? On her own or with Salime? Would she come to a place like this?

The door to the bar opens, heads turn. A woman in a short black leather skirt. She walks to the bar without looking around.

He hears her order a drink and then she takes a table, virtually opposite his. She opens a small handbag and takes out cigarettes, places them on the table. She fumbles in the handbag and brings out a lighter. She sips her drink, it looks like white wine. He watches her, she doesn't look up.

She concentrates on lighting her cigarette. When she has it lit she takes another sip and then looks up, looks at him. He cannot make out the expression on her face, he cannot really see her face, but he can see she is blonde. A man walks to her table and says something in French but she appears to wave him away with her hand. The man walks away dejected, sits back at the bar from where he came but stares back at her. The woman smokes, sips, looks down at the table but then looks up again, at him, at Jake.

The woman gets up, he thinks she's leaving but her glass is still half-full and she is coming over to him. He can now see her face but still doesn't recognise the face he saw only a short time ago.

I saw you come in here, from my apartment window. You came to ask about Jean and Salime.

The woman at their flat. The woman who answered the door, who gave him the news, the woman who shut the door again.

You don't mind if I join you?

He had hardly registered her face when she answered the door. Now, even in this gloomy bar with all its smoke, he could see how attractive she was. Older than him, but an attractive woman.

I'm really sorry to have intruded on you this afternoon.

Not at all.

She looks around the bar, the silence is awkward until he says, is this your local? I mean, do you come here a lot?

She lights a cigarette and takes a sip of her drink and then looks at him intently.

I'm afraid I come here rather too often. But it gets me out of the apartment, I suppose. And sometimes you meet some nice people, though some can be a nuisance.

She nods over Jake's shoulder. Jake turns around and sees the man who had approached her earlier start walking over to them. When he arrives, the man, who has several days' growth on his face and a pot belly starts speaking to her in French. She repeats, non,non, then the man's voice is raised.

His face is right up to hers and Jake feels he must step in. He stands and grabs the man to pull him away. It happens in a flash and Jake feels the punch to his nose and sees blood. The man staggers away and leaves the bar.

Oh, goodness, are you OK?

Yeah, yeah, I'm fine.

Come on, let's get out of here. Come back to the apartment and I'll get you cleaned up.

He is standing in the lounge with tissues to his face to stem the bleeding. The woman, this stranger, is in the kitchen opening a bottle of wine.

He looks around the room. So this is where they lived. A palace compared to Nevern Place and so big. He would like to look around the rest of the flat, get the full feel of it but the woman, this woman whose name he does not know, this very sexy older woman, is back with a metal tray with a bottle of red wine and two glasses on it.

So do you live in Paris? she asks, bending down to a coffee table to set down the tray.

No, no, I live in London, I just arrived in Paris today.

To see Salime and Jean?

Yes.

Did they know you were coming?

He takes a sip of wine. No, I hadn't arranged anything.

Perhaps they forgot to send you their new address.

She takes a sip of her wine and says, I suppose they had a lot on their minds, what with everything that happened. I'm Caroline by the way.

Jake. How do you mean what happened?

Oh I shouldn't really say since you know them.

Caroline sips her wine and he senses she is slightly tipsy, that maybe she starts her drinking quite early in the day. The tone of her voice indicates she is going to tell him anyway. Things on her mind, things on her chest she needs to release even if to a total stranger. A lonely woman bereaved of her husband at such a young age.

She takes another sip of wine, he imagines she very easily gets through a few bottles of an evening. She lights a cigarette which makes him so at ease he lights one himself. He takes some more wine. He is sure that once this bottle is finished she will have another at the ready.

They had quite a few problems. I think Jean missed England. And then things got worse.

She drags on her cigarette. Another sip of wine before she continues.

She found out about Salime and I. He is a very handsome and charismatic man. I had been having problems since my husband died. Anxiety, depression, the usual stuff. I met my husband who was French in London and, similar to Jean, came to Paris to be with him and get married. I asked Salime if he would see me for a consultation. He said yes and it went well. I had a number of sessions with him and started to feel much better and Salime said my problems were over. Cured. He took me out for dinner to celebrate and came back to my apartment for coffee. He seduced me. I was flattered, welcomed the sex and we had a thing going on for a little while. It was risky because I had moved into the flat below to get away from the memories of my husband in our apartment a few miles away.

And Jean found out?

Salime told her. He said during one of their rows that she had not been devoted to him emotionally and accused her of still being in love with someone else.

Someone in Paris?

No, no, someone in England. When they had their rows I kept hearing him shout, you're still in love with the Englishman. It seemed to be a recurring theme.

She gives Jake an accusing look, like she's just twigged, Jake is the Englishman.

Did he get violent, physically I mean?

I can't be sure of that but I never heard things being smashed or screaming. I would have called the police had I thought someone was in physical danger.

Ask her the question, you know the question, the question that has brought your here.

Was Salime treating Jean for psychological problems?

She carefully places her glass on the table.

She looks puzzled. Why do you ask?

He tells her about his meeting with Salime, what he said, how Jean was ill and he needed to treat her, take care of her, that the story about her background and life was untrue, part of her illness, she didn't know who she was. How he said Jake must not see her.

Caroline looks perplexed, pours them both more wine.

I was not aware she had any psychological problems. She seemed normal, she came and went from here every day. She was doing a creative writing course. Salime was hardly ever here, rarely went back to this flat. If he wasn't seeing me he was out all night doing whatever. I don't see how he would have found the time to treat her and take care of her. I felt sorry for her but she seemed to just get on with life. She would spend a lot of time in La Jardine across the road drinking coffee, reading, writing in her notebook. She used to have a little brown battered case she carried all her books and notebooks in.

The old battered case. He can see it now. He can see that little brown case in the flat. Remembers asking her what she had in there. From Earls Court to a cafe in Paris. Her little brown case. Battered.

Did she look OK? Did she look down or distressed...or physically unwell? Bruised?

Gosh no. She cut a lonely figure and I felt dreadful about what happened between Salime and me.

Did she not confront you about that?

Strangely I met her in the cafe and told her I was so sorry. I expected her to be angry. But do you know what, she just looked at me, with a tear in her eyes I think and said, that is Salime, that's what I expect of him. It was difficult and I remember making an excuse that I had to go somewhere.

He can see her face, see those eyes with those tears. And the little brown case.

After his barrage of questions, her question comes out of nowhere.

You were her English lover, weren't you?

He feels disingenuous when he says yes, he's her English lover. After all she had written, after all she thought about Jake, how could he possibly claim to be her lover?

But was she missing him, did her heart still beat for him, as Salime had accused her of?

As he predicts, the wine soon runs out and and she asks if he would like some more.

He says yes, but regrets it as soon as she gets up to go to the kitchen. He is tired and feels slightly tipsy, his mind a whirl of alcohol and confusion.

Why did she put this address on her letters when she had been gone from here months ago? Nothing adds up, he thinks, nothing is normal or logical. From the moment he met her it has been a sandstorm of contradictions, complications, mystery.

The facts you have established from Caroline:

Salime was lying, Jean is not being treated by him for psychiatric problems. She is not happy with him – knows he cheats on her, repeatedly. He is hardly ever here, correction, was hardly ever here when they lived in this apartment. Jean "cuts a lonely figure". She does not live at the address she put on top of her letter.

Caroline comes back with more wine. As she pours he looks at her long, flowing blonde hair and her figure. She hands him his glass with a beautiful smile. She also has blue eyes, just like Jean. This woman is Jean in 20 years from now.

She asks him why he is here and he tells her he fears Jean may be in danger. Caroline repeats she does not think she is. She says, my impression of Salime is he is a deeply manipulative character. I think he likes to have control over people but I don't think he's violent. But why doesn't she just leave him? I suppose it's some kind of psychological power he has over her. Or just plain old-fashioned love. Mind you, although he doesn't look his years, she is rather young for him.

Jake sighs.

I don't know Caroline, I really don't.

He doesn't know whether it's the wine, the exhaustion, the frustration, but tears come to his eyes now and he begins to sob.

Caroline puts her drink down and comes over to him. She sits down next to him and puts her arm around him and pulls his head into her chest. She kisses the top of his head and this and the warmth of her, being held like this, makes him sob even more. When was the last time anyone had put their arm around him and pulled him into them, to bring warmth, to sooth him, to wrap him up in tenderness? All he ever wanted from the day, each day, was just someone close, someone warm, someone to hold him tight, make him feel wanted.

She lets go of him and he sits up, dries his eyes and says sorry. Caroline puts a finger to his mouth.

Shush, you have nothing to be sorry about.

She keeps her finger on his lips then slowly moves her face up close to his. She takes her finger from his lips and replaces it with her mouth. Tongues meet and they are kissing, just like lovers do, these two strangers who met hardly hours ago.

She pulls him closer, he can feel her breasts pressed against him.

In bed the love-making is slow to start with. She is on top of him, rubs herself against him, he cups her breasts and moves his mouth to her nipples. The love-making becomes more urgent, more physical, a shared mutual need.

They lay back and she tells him it was wonderful. She sighs, a deep, satisfied sigh and says, I think we both needed that

She tells him to stay the night. He snuggles up to her naked body and sleep overcomes him almost immediately.

I think we both needed that.

She is in her hospital bed, writhing in pain. A nurse rushes over.

A doctor comes to her bedside. He can see the pain on her face, a blonde woman's face, blonde with blue eyes. But around her eyes are bruises and dried blood.

He struck her down, kicked her, beat her.

She screams, and even though he is running away, he can still hear the screams as he gets further away, like the whole hospital, the whole building is an echo chamber of pain and horror.

And then he sees the strobe lights, hears the bum-bam pounding of the mega speakers. Ride on Time.

And it's Ok now because he is in an ocean of bodies, writhing, gyrating, windmilling, spooling together. He is with them, close to them, part of them, this shared heaving mass. And it all goes away. All the pain goes away.

He wakes up. It takes a few seconds for him to remember where he is. He sees her sleeping, he sees the back of her blonde head. He has to get away, he has to leave this apartment without speaking to her.

He slowly gets out of the bed, dresses and creeps out of the bedroom.

She left Jean's new address on a piece of paper on the glass table. He grabs it, stuffs it in his pockets and is out on the street seconds later.

Road cleaners are dousing the streets with water, the buildings form shadows in the half light of the emerging daylight.

He is starving. The contents of his stomach from the day before are just is just a sea of wine, he hardly ate. He will walk further down the avenue, get well away from the apartment.

He takes the metro to the address Caroline gave him and gets off at the stop she said was nearest. She warns him this is not a salubrious part of town and she is surprised Salime would want to move to a district like this. She told him that maybe Salime was not making too much money, they had fallen behind on the rent a few times and she suspected they were downgrading.

He ascends the stairs from the station and comes up into the street. It's a far cry from where he has come from. As soon as he hits the high street he can see it is run down, better days were some years ago. The typically French cafes, bars and restaurants do not exist, at least not in this street as far as he can see. There are a few dingy shops and convenience stores, the gutters are littered with cans and cartons, graffiti are the only colour in this dour street. From the blur of the night before he remembers Caroline telling him that he only has to turn left out of the station, then right and he will be in their street.

As he reaches it he sees the buildings are stucco fronted but cracked and discoloured, worn like a very old woman's face. Blinds are in most windows, others are just bare but too high up to see inside. Youths hang around smoking or drinking from polystyrene beakers, their faces expressionless, paralysed by their pathetic circumstances.

This is a ghetto, he thinks, this is where he has brought Jean. He looks at the numbers on the door. He has some walking to do before he gets to their apartment, or whatever abode it turns out to be and he is relieved because it gives him some minutes to think - this time he is in no possession of any grand plan, his adrenaline is low, the tank almost emptied. He does not know really why he has come here at all.

Why are they living here? Salime is supposed to be wealthy. So now as well as controlling her, he is broke, the life she thought she would have, the life she left him for. How did it come to this?

He needs to decide what he's going to do when he gets to the flat. He needs to decide when he's going to pack all this in and go home. But now he knows that Salime was lying and he has this to confront him with. He has come this far, he cannot go back now, he cannot abandon her. Rescue me.

He reaches their address. He stands on the opposite side of the street but before he has time to take it in he hears a woman's voice behind him.

Jake, oh Jake, thank God you are here.

He turns. It's Caroline.

Look, you must not go the apartment. I only realised this morning, Salime will know I gave you the address. And he will know it was me who told you. About them, about Jean's condition not being what he told you it was.

And would that be a problem? You said he wasn't violent. You said it was all over between you and him so what would be the problem?

Oh, I don't know, it's just he did not give me the address to give out to other people. I mean, I don't even know you are who you say you are. Look I know a half decent place away from here where we can get a drink. We had better go in case we are seen.

He follows her, she is dressed casually in tight jeans, her figure undiminished by informal garb.

She orders coffee for them both in a grotty café that smells of disinfectant. The only hint of style are old photographs, he presumes of the locale, that say they are circa 1930-something, he cannot quite make out the full date.

When the waiter has poured and left she says, you were in a hurry to leave this morning.

He feels a blush coming on, like red paint slapped on hard with a brush.

I'm sorry, I just wanted to come here. I haven't a lot of time. I will need to be getting back to London soon.

A smile crosses her beautiful face and he doesn't know what to make of it.

What are you going to do Jake when you see either of them?

He rummages for his cigarettes, offers her one but she nods no, he lights and says, that's it, I really don't know. Fuck, I'm so confused. If she is in trouble, if she is in danger....how would I feel if I just, went back to London without checking, without finding out?

Why are you so convinced she's in danger?

Because, what Salime told me was a pack of lies about her. About her not knowing who she was, where she had come from, her childhood, everything she told me, everything I knew about her. Why the fuck would someone say that?

Caroline nods, she looks at her coffee, he can see she shares a sense of bafflement, but she knows something, she's holding something back, as if she wants to tell him but something is holding her back. He catches her glance but looks away, he doesn't want her to read him, doesn't want to give a fraction of his thoughts.

Maybe they have moved on from here by now, maybe they are not here anymore, Caroline says, almost hopefully.

But there's only one way to be sure. I don't suppose they left a telephone number did they?

No, just the address. For the mail.

He wants to go home but needs closure, to be done with, to have done the right thing but to be told there is no more to do, no more to hear, no more to see, to be with Sylvie and Karim, drinking, dancing, smoking, to be a long way from here and all its mystery, all its confusion, away from being head fucked, away from all this, away from Jean.

He drains his coffee cup and wants to get away from Caroline.

I'm going back to London, it's not my business, if things are so bad for her she would leave him, why doesn't she just leave him if he's such a bastard?

Who are you angry with? Salime, with Jean, with Caroline, with Paris?

Jake tells Caroline he has got to go. He won't go to the apartment, he's off back to central Paris to return to London. She tells him there is a bus that will take him to the centre. The stop is around the corner from here.

Good luck Jake, whatever happens. And take care.

Thanks for all your help and for, well, you know, putting me up last night.

It was a pleasure.

Jake follows her directions to the bus stop. But instead of waiting for the bus he watches Caroline disappear before he goes back to Salime and Jean's street.

He takes the few steps to the main door. A panel of flat numbers and buzzers is to the side. Flat 4. Just one buzz, one press, he's come this far.

The main door opens, a young man with long hair is leaving, he holds the door for Jake, he says merci and walks into the building.

It's a long corridor of doors to the apartments, a musky odour permeates, the walls are speckled with ominous dark and green patches. He hears a baby crying, a man shouting in French, a woman shouting back.

He gets to flat number four. The door is open, just slightly, while all the other doors are closed, hiding the misery within. He looks behind him to make sure no-one is around. He moves closer to the ajar door and listens in but can hear nothing. He tentatively pushes the door and sees a lounge area with a sofa and a small wooden table in the centre of the room. But apart from these, the place looks empty. He enters.

It's a small dingy place, the white walls wear a heavy coat of nicotine and neglect. In the corner, a sink and a small stove. Next to that a door leads off into a bedroom and he can make out a bed that has only a bare mattress on it. Abandoned, vacant. His feet stick to the brown linoleum floors.

They are not here, they do not live here anymore. He shivers, the room is cold, a window looks out onto other apartment blocks. The place feels like a prison cell, no wonder they didn't stay here too long. He imagines the door slamming shut and being locked inside this hell-hole. He turns around and walks back out, down the corridor past the sounds of screaming rows and bawling children.

In the daylight relief washes over him like cold water splashed against the face on a hot sticky day.

A thunderbolt of decision hits him: This is the end, I'm through with this, I can do no more. She is gone, gone forever. All that I could do I have done. It is time to stop, time to rest, to move on and truly forget.

CHAPTER TWENTY-SEVEN

IT HAS gone midnight and he is walking down the Earls Court Road with Sylvie, Karim and a Danish guy called Mikhail who appears to have stolen Karim's heart. The Dane has his arms around her and is singing at the top of his voice, Yesterday, All My Troubles Seemed So Far Away.

Karim is giggling, tipsy, while Jake and Sylvie walk ahead laughing at the mad Dane.

They arrive back at the girls' flat to carry on drinking and popping a few Es. Mikhail is a Beatles fan and asks if the girls have got any to play. They haven't so Sylvie puts on Fairground Attraction.

After some manic dancing and chatting Sylvie goes into the kitchen, Mikhail and Karim sit on the sofa and without shame begin to kiss.

Jake joins Sylvie in the kitchen.

Looks like those two are getting on quite well, Jake says swigging from a bottle of Becks.

Sylvie smiles and looks into the lounge.

I think so, she says.

Emboldened by the E and drink, Jake puts his bottle of beer down and grabs Sylvie. He pulls her into him but immediately registers her resistance.

Sorry, I, I just got carried away.

No Jake, it is not that I don't like you. I do. But, well I don't want to get involved with anybody. I was going to tell you but I am going back to France at the end of the week. For good. I need to continue with my studies and I've been in London long enough now.

He can't work out whether the pangs of misery he feels are because of her rejection or the bombshell about returning to France she has just dropped.

I see. Well, I'll miss you. As a friend I mean.

And I shall miss you Jake. Maybe we can write to each other.

He's not sure whether he could handle another penfriend in France but just says, sure, and tells her they should have one last drink before she goes.

He says goodnight and disappears into the night, into Earls Court and back to Nevern Place.

They all seem to go, after such a short space of time, they all seem to leave you. Is it Earls Court? Is it something about this place that has no longevity, everyone just passing through, just a stop-over on a longer journey to a better place?

CHAPTER TWENTY-EIGHT

IT'S A large brown envelope with French stamps, his name and address written in her familiar but somehow haunting handwriting.

He sits at his desk with a mug of strong tea and a cigarette burning down in the ashtray.

Here she comes again, just as the clouds were lifting, just as the pieces of his new life, new plans were being glued together in his mind, here she comes again.

It has been three weeks since his sojourn to Paris. Two weeks since he had tearfully kissed Sylvie goodbye and moped around in sadness and regret over a love that had never even got started. And a week since he started his new job on a local newspaper in offices overlooking Eel Pie Island in Twickenham. A few small tentative steps towards A Life Without Jean running and rummaging through his head.

This is not a letter. It's a package. A package full of trouble, full of confusion, full of contradiction. To open it would be to open you up again, to allow the chaos that is her life to come seeping back into your mind just as it was beginning to show the first signs of drying out.

He feels around the edges of the envelope, the package, squeezes the middle. Not just a letter, the thickness was that of several pieces of paper, almost like a manuscript. He smells it, trying to detect an aroma from her he might recognise, might remember but there is nothing.

It's too big to set fire to in the flat. He could just toss it out with the rubbish. But what if someone was to find it and open it. It would be like he has exposed her secrets, her life, her troubled life. The contents were for his eyes only.

Curiosity builds. Would what is inside answer all the questions, solve all the mysteries, tie up all the loose ends? Is it her epitaph to him, a reassurance that she is being treated for psychiatric troubles, that he should not worry, that she was blissfully happy with Salime?

Well, that would be most unlike Jean. All he had ever known of her was confusion and mystery and he cannot imagine now that what is inside this big envelope will give him final closure.

Opening this envelope could be like opening a suspicious package – incendiary, explosive. But then Salime had lied. This much he knew.

He puts the package to one side in a far corner on his desk, goes for a run, tries to think of the stories he has to work on for the newspaper, thinks about his new colleagues, including a sexy blonde reporter called Alison, thinks of the book he is reading, thinks about how he will have a pint in Cromwells tonight.

Back at the flat he showers and shaves. He goes out and buys three broadsheet Sunday newspapers and reads everything that's going on in the news.

After he has read the Sunday Times and Sunday Correspondent, he grabs the Observer and takes it to Luigis in the Earls Court Road where he orders a carafe of red wine and a pizza. And reads the paper.

It's about eight o'clock when he sips his first pint in Cromwells which has a Sunday night feel of quietness and lack of punters.

He leaves for an early night – he will have to be up early tomorrow for the commute to Twickenham.

The day ends with a read of his novel for half-an-hour and then he switches off the light. The orange of a streetlamp shines on the brown envelope on his desk where it has not been looked at or touched for almost nine hours now.

Monday lunchtime and he buys a sandwich and a pint in the Barmy Arms overlooking the Thames after a morning of bashing out local news stories. He takes out the letter from his satchel and looks at it again.

He can see the river and a bridge. He could walk onto the bridge and toss this bundle of grief into the murky expanses of the Thames. Let it float, then as the water made it heavier, sink it, carry it away back to where the Thames began, out into the sea. Far, far away.

He finishes his pint, leaves his sandwich half-eaten and walks onto the bridge, the package in his hands.

Throw away this one. But there will be others. She will think this one is just lost in the post when you don't reply. She will send another. Will you have the strength not to open it? What if it's instructions, wanting you to meet her, to bring her home? Rescue me.

He looks at the river, then the envelope, her writing, *your name, your address.* The curls of the letters, the neatness of their formation. How can someone so confusing have handwriting so clear, so elegant, without scrawl, without a single letter indistinguishable?

Her face in Brighton on the night of their kiss, her smile, her voice, desperate voice, on the phone. She is a tide, she comes in, she goes out, and now she washes in again, crashing into his mind in great, all-engulfing waves.

Home, Nevern Place. His usual cold beer and packet of fags. He reclines in his chair with a sigh and he begins to read. He always does.

Dear Jake,

I hope you are well.

I am so sorry I did not manage to meet you when you came to Paris and I'm sorry I didn't write to you sooner but I did try to call you at Nevern Place. I tried to call you several times at home and when at last you answered the phone, the line broke up.

Salime did not want me to meet you - he said it would make my condition worse. I reluctantly told him when and where we had planned to meet. I have to tell him everything, he says. He told me he was going to meet you and explain the situation.

He says I need psychiatric help but he never gives me any. Just says I must do as he says and I will get better. I don't even know if I'm ill. I don't know what I think.

I don't know why I'm writing to you. I suppose I just need to talk to someone and writing is the only way I can do this.

I know he cheats. He says it is just meaningless casual sex that he needs and that he loves only me. Which is strange given that he once said he didn't do love. Fucking other people is just who he is, he says.

Sometimes I don't believe him but then when he holds me and tells me quietly how much he loves me, all the hurt just ebbs away.

Then he has his cruel moments where he bawls at me if we run out of things or the place isn't clean and tidy just as he likes it to be. He goes into rages and storms out and doesn't come back for hours. When he does come back he's all calm and holds me and the bad times seem worth it because the good times, well they seem so good.

I have thought about leaving him. When he goes off, I think, I could just pack a bag and go. But how can I leave someone who loves me so much even if he doesn't always show it? I've never had love like this, I don't think anyone can love me the way he does and I'm scared I'll never find it again if I did leave him.

He's stopped me from reading Jung and Freud, says they will just fuck with my head and I'm sure he's right. I told my friend at college, Isobella. She says he's a control freak and has no right to censor what I read. Isobella is a good friend but she's a bit of a feminist who has never found love so doesn't really understand men. She comes from a big loving family. But sometimes I hear her voice in my head when times are bad with Salime and I almost do it, I almost leave him.

The closest I came was last month but then he lost his job at the psychiatry clinic. He wouldn't tell me why. I thought he had plenty of money and we would be OK but he said we would have to move out of the beautiful apartment and downgrade. He found a cheaper place which was an absolute pit but he promised me he would find another job and we would move back to our old apartment in a few months. He knew how much I loved the place. I even put that address on the letters I wrote you thinking that I would be going back there very soon.

Now we are staying at an old friend of Salime's in Toulouse. Claude is his name and he is very nice to me. He is very wealthy and in his sixties and wants Salime to help him with his business – exporting or something.

But here is the bombshell. He wants Salime to run his operations in Morocco. It will mean us moving to Marrakesh!

At first I was shocked. Marrakesh. What an upheaval. But Salime says it's a devoutly Muslim country and he hopes it will be the end of him sleeping around, free from the temptations of Paris and then he can be with me and we can spend more time together.

A few weeks ago he had left the house and for no reason I decided to rummage through his briefcase. I found a diary. I had no idea he kept one. I got it photocopied and asked Isobella to translate – it was all in French. I could make out some words but Salime has always told me he doesn't want me to bother learning French.

I don't know what to make of the diaries. He talks a lot about control – controlling himself and me. Isobella says it confirms everything she suspected about him.

So, Jake, that's my news. How about you? I've put the Toulouse address on this letter. Send anything to that address.

Claude will forward them on to where-ever we are living in Marrakesh. We are going in a fortnight I think.

PS: Are you still going to raves? I heard things had died a bit on the rave scene. Would love to go to another rave again – like they used to be in 1989. I still remember our time in London, in Brighton, in Earls Court with fondness. I can picture us both now going crazy to Ride on Time. I still play it on my Walkman and it still drives me crazy. I hope you will stay in touch Jake. I don't ever want us to forget each other. Time can do that, let's not allow it to happen.

Lots of love
Jean
xxxx

Her mind, her logic is unfathomable, it always was. He does not know whether he feels sorry for her or whether he just wants to chuck this letter. Maybe he should have ripped it up and flung it into the Thames as he was going to do.

A thought crawls across his mind as he keeps re-reading her letter: She has now written more words and sentences to him than she has ever said to him in all the excruciating time he has been acquainted with her. So many words she has put down on paper, so few she has actually said through her sweet lips.

She is a lost cause. There is no hint in her letter that she is being physically harmed. There is no cry for help this time. She is depressingly, accepting Salime and the relationship she is in. I don't know why I am writing to you. I don't want us to ever lose touch.

What is she saying? If she is so in love with Salime, why does she want the distraction of someone else in her life, someone she met months ago and was hardly with? It was more of a drug-fuelled encounter of raves and sex. And then she went. He came into the restaurant and into her life and she found the father figure she had never had in her childhood. And this is what, who, she has now.

He sits with a pint in Cromwells and smokes, staring into space.

Another letter in his pocket. But he isn't going to read it again. Not here, not now. He has read enough and he is feeling some relief that he is beginning to understand the reality of Jean which is gradually going to lead him to cutting her out of his life.

But fuck, how many times has he had these thoughts? How many times has his inner critical voice thundered at him that the whole Jean 'thing' for want of a better word, is futile, soul-destroying, distracting him from the life he could be living. A life with someone, somewhere else, an easier affair.

It's almost a year since Jean Ridley came into his life. He cannot remember the exact date but he knows it was around this time.

He begins to write.

Dear Jean

Thanks for writing to me. It was good to hear from you.

I hope you are happy, it's a bit difficult to know for sure from your letter. You say that Salime cheats on you and that he seems to try to control you. Your friend Isobella thinks this too. I'm not so sure about anything. All relationships have good and bad points. I think though that the good points should be more prevalent than the bad and this is how I would decide whether a relationship was working or not.

I was disturbed that Salime told me you had serious psychiatric problems when I know this to be untrue and I met your old landlady who also said this did not seem to be the case.

Your relationship with Salime seems to be built on a foundation of fear – your fear. The fear of never finding someone who could love you as much as you say he loves you. But he told you from the start, Jean, he doesn't do love because he doesn't know what it is.

But why did he lie to me Jean? I find the lie terrible, to accuse someone of having mental problems they do not have. But the more important question has to be, why?

He stops you seeing someone you want to see. He bans you from reading certain books. I find all this bizarre and alarmingly so.

You say you don't know why you have told me all this stuff. You say you don't want to lose touch. I don't understand why. It will soon be almost a year since I even saw you, or we spoke. I know you more by the letters you have written than the words you have ever spoken to me or the time we have ever spent together.

I do care about you but I wonder to what extent I can be part of your life. I don't really know what you want from me, Jean.

I have had a few flings in the last year but have not found anyone long-term or serious. Which for the moment is fine, I'm still young, although I do eventually want to meet someone. Someone like you, maybe, but then I don't really know you.

To cut to the chase, I think you are in a relationship with a seriously psychologically devious man. I have no idea what motivates him, why he does the things he does, says the things he says (you being mentally disturbed) but I think whatever those reasons, they are probably going to become a more serious problem for you later.

I understand your insecurity, that you may not find anyone who loves you. We all feel this at times in our lives. You and I, with our backgrounds, are probably more vulnerable to feel this than others.

But love has to be love, unconditional and not controlling. It cannot be based on fear, it has to be because you love someone who you know, irrevocably, is in love with you and only wants the best for you.

My conclusion is that Salime does not really love you, he wants to control you, for whatever reasons. Maybe I will go to the library and read some psychology on why people have this need to control.

Jean, people don't cheat, like Salime cheats, on someone they love and are devoted to. He says it's his character. Well then his character is flawed, defective, for whatever reason.

I am not making a pitch here, but you deserve, no need, someone who truly loves you. I know you are going to find these harsh words cripplingly upsetting but as your friend, as a true friend and someone who has cared about you so deeply, I have to say the truth, at least as I see it.

The reality, Jean, is that you have not found love. You hope you have, you want it to be love but from all that you have said, from all that I have seen and heard about Salime, he is not the one. He will bring only misery to your life and will then try to sugar-coat it with words he knows you want to hear but words he does not really feel or mean.

Remember what he said in his letter before you went to join him in Paris? Some shit about he doesn't make love, he only fucks.

It is up to you, it is your life and I am not trying to tell you how to live it. You know Salime better than I do, I don't really know him at all. But then I don't think you do either. I don't think you have any idea who this man really is. He is an enigma, never there for you, living a double, mysterious life. A life that does not include you for the most part of it. You are whatever it is he needs and I have no idea what that is.

Jean, I have just re-read the paragraphs of this letter before this one and wanted to take a big thick green pen to it and edit it savagely, to take out some of the very strong and brutal points I have made. I feel I have written some cruel words in this letter, words you do not want to read. I started to write another letter, more subtle. I tried to do what Salime does, sugar-coat the bitterness, ease the hurt.

But that would not make it go away, it would not provide an escape route so I decided I would send you the original letter which is organic, from the heart, what I truly feel and think. This letter.

I imagine your tears as you read this and tears come to my eyes as fast as the ink is flowing from my pen when your sad vision comes into my mind. But we must say what we feel or we are lying, deceiving and I cannot do that to you Jean because that is what he is doing and if nothing else, you deserve some honesty, no matter how unpalatable that may be.

You may just burn this letter, rip it up and just carry on with your life. Who knows, you may find, deep within, some happiness. You may be able to make your life with Salime work out. The human spirit can be very strong, it can compromise.

It is up to you my darling and I am not trying to force you into ultimatums. I don't think you want anything from me and as I said, this letter is not a pitch for your love. I have no idea what I could offer a woman, least of all what I could offer you.

OK, I've made my point and I hope you understand my reasons for doing so. I hope that whatever you decide you will find love and happiness. Both exist, it is just a case of finding them and being sure that when you do find them they are the real thing. I hope you find all the love in all the world.

All my love,
Jake
xxxxxxxx

P.S. I have fond memories of last summer, too. Summer of 89 I won't forget, nor will I ever forget you. X

He thinks about how harsh his letter to Jean had been. But he is also relieved because he thinks this will either be the end of it between him and her – the most likely outcome – or Jean will see sense and get of out Salime's life. Either way, Jake has to get Jean Ridley out of his life because her last letter was, well, pathetic. He thinks of her upbringing, he understands she is looking for someone to replace her father, possibly, if you believe the psychology.

But he also concludes that his obsession with Jean is due to his own psychological flaws and childhood. Maybe he is looking for a mother.

This would be sick. A mother is a mother, a lover a lover, a girlfriend a girlfriend, a wife a wife. And Jean would never be any of these.

CHAPTER TWENTY-NINE

THE PLANE touches down at Menara Airport, Marrakesh. The blistering Moroccan sun almost scolds as soon as you descend the steps of the plane, stifling, oppressive and frightening when you have never experienced sunshine like this.

Lugging baggage across the tarmac saps the energy, sends sweat levels soaring under the arms, at the back of your knees, across your forehead, the need to be blasted with a shower of cold water overwhelms.

There are plenty of signs in English in this airport in North Africa so finding what you need – a taxi – is as simple as it is at Heathrow.

His rucksack is light, packed with shorts and t-shirts, not only appropriate garb for this place, but necessary if you are to avoid heatstroke or fainting. There are deserts in this country, heat you only ever read about, unimaginable in the mostly clement climes of England. London can get hot in summer, it did in the summer of 89, but nothing like this.

The taxi ride is through long roads with donkeys pulling carts mixing with rust-bucket cars, lorries and buses.

The buildings look dust-beaten, walls cracked, roofs made of corrugated iron. Scenes you see on the news from some war-ravaged or starved country, another world.

It is difficult to see where there might be a city, where there might be cafes, bars and restaurants and civilisation. The roads the taxi is driving along now seem as though they can only lead to some expansive sandy nowhere of a desert.

Soon the density of buildings starts to increase as the journey goes on. Small shops, the odd café or bar begins to appear, there's a feeling of getting there, but to where you do not know. Children with dusty hair and faces play in a ditch as the taxi stops at traffic lights.

The lights change and the driver stalls the taxi. He starts it up again and the vehicle judders into motion. All the windows are open but all that is felt is heat, there's just a slight breeze that doesn't seem to be trying too hard as the taxi picks up speed on an open slice of road.

He spots more small cafes and the odd convenience store but many of these buildings are just old houses and disused buildings from what he can see. The roads wind around corners and into streets now. Streets so narrow that the taxi is stuck behind a mule and a cart. There is no space to drive around and overtake it. The noise has also changed, from the unhealthy groaning of the taxi as it gathered speed on the open roads to the sounds of people talking, shouting, selling things, constantly interspersed by the wasp-like drone of scooters and motorbikes, a far more practical mode of transport for these arterial streets.

The driver pulls over and as he does, he says, 'Medina'. He remembers from the Lonely Planet guide book that this means the centre and presumably the Riad he has booked.

Jake had wanted to keep his rucksack on his knee in the taxi but the driver had grabbed it and put in in the boot.

Now he opens the boot and a man with leather brown skin and oil-black hair, not much older than him, steps forward and the driver hands him the rucksack.

The young man, in white t-shirt and jeans, beckons Jake.

Come on, I take you to the Riad.

The man leads the way, they turn a corner into an alleyway and Jake begins to feel vulnerable. Where am I being taken? This doesn't look like a main road, surely the hotel would be on the main road. He remembers though that a lot of the Riads are buried down alleyways in Marrakesh, but this knowledge does not ease his anxiety and the blistering sun makes him tired and weighed down by irrational thoughts.

They take a left down another narrow alley and the man stops and knocks at a black iron door. The door is opened by a dark rotund woman who tells them to come in.

The man leaves the bags near the entrance and stands smiling at Jake. He is waiting for a tip and Jake gives him a few coins which elicits a wider smile and a thank-you.

He is shown to his room which has only a curtain where a door would normally be. Inside he finds a bed with just a few blankets on it, a bedside table with a vase of flowers he does not recognise. At the other end of the room is the toilet and shower. The woman also told him that the room has a small safe and she has given him the combination number. He will probably not use it.

He lies on the bed to rest for just a few minutes and hears the soothing sound of a fountain trickling somewhere, the place is calming and he savours his new surrounds after the noise and bustle of the streets.

So he has got here, all this way to this country, here he is is lying on a bed in North Africa. He has never travelled so far or to a country with such a different culture. He pats his pocket to make sure he has his wallet and passport, he has been paranoid about losing them the whole journey and will take extra care when out on the streets.

After a reviving shower he packs his small shoulder bag with a bottle of water, his map and notebook and small camera. He imagines how foreign correspondents or war reporters feel when they arrive to cover a story in some far-off place. He feels satisfaction with his own organisation and preparation, it feels as though his life is in order, everything in its place, a place for everything and all of it secure, self-contained. Travelling, he had once read, is good therapy, and right now being here and organising himself feels just that, therapeutic.

Today he will explore the Medina and the Souks. The day to himself, the day before he is due to meet Jean, as arranged in her last letter.

Salime would not be in Morocco, he has gone back to Paris for a business meeting with Claude. They will meet in in Jamel fna, the main square of Marrakesh, in a café.

When he accepted her invitation he had no idea why. But then he thought a trip to Morocco would be good. He would go with an open mind and enjoy it. Jean would just be an interruption to the trip. He is expecting nothing, just to hear her out and to meet her again after all this time and, who knows, maybe for the very last time. Psychologists call it closure and this is really what he is hoping for on this trip.

Jean's letters and her naivety where Salime is concerned made him angry at first. But anger dissolved to leave a mix of sadness and pity he felt for this woman who couldn't be blamed for clinging onto something she thinks is love when she had been denied it throughout her young life. The only way he can really see how she is is to meet her and talk to her. The written word offers no real context, no human interaction, no tone. He needs to hear her voice, look at her face to see how she really feels.

He never believed what Salime had told him in Paris about Jean's mental state. And now Salime wasn't even practising as a psychiatrist. But there had to be something wrong with Jean to be so obsessed, to be so in awe of him.

The other voice told him he was making a mistake coming here. It is pointless, he should cut loose once and for all, Jean is a lost cause, was from the night you met her.

But the second voice seemed to reflect, calm down and see the merits of a break in Marrakesh.

He will meet Jean tomorrow but today he explores the Medina.

The sun seems even stronger as he steps outside the Riad. From the alley he reaches a small square and turns into Souk Smarine, which is covered in an iron trellis with slots across it that restrict the sun and offers him immediate relief from its heat. The shops and bazaars offer an array of textiles – shirts and kaftans mainly. He is forced to step aside as yet another screaming scooter comes by. The souk is noisy and crowded, a mixture of locals and lots of tourists snapping away with their cameras.

He comes to a square, Rahba Kedima, where stalls are set up in the middle selling baskets, hats and souvenirs. Around the corner he finds a stall selling cosmetics with tubs of strange coloured powders which he read in the guide are lip rouge and powdered kohl for darkening the edges of the eyes.

Another stall has leopard skins draped on tressles. As he walks further he comes to a passageway that leads to a bustling carpet-draped area, La Criee Berbere.

He is desperately thirsty and needs to sit down. He makes his way to Jemaa el Fna, the main square where he can get a drink and sus out where he will meet Jean tomorrow.

After the overcrowding and claustrophobia of the souks, the big open space that is the square is a relief. He walks through the crowds of tourists who are gawping at the snake charmers who bewitch their cobras with flutes.

He passes a stall displaying fearsome pliers and trays of extracted teeth. Another offers freshly squeezed juice the thought of which intensifies his thirst but he will resist, he really wants to sit down in a nice café and watch Marrakesh go by.

He finds a café tucked away in the corner of the square, near to the entrance of one of the Souks. He orders an orange juice, lights a cigarette and marvels at the busyness of the square. A wave of contentment washes over him. Here is so far away from England, from home, sitting in a square in this country he does not know. He feels free, relishes the isolation that allows him to decide what he's going to do next and where he is going to go.

One day I will be a foreign correspondent and travel to places like this. Or Paris, or Berlin, or China. Anywhere in the world.

This evening, he decides, he will go to one of the more upmarket restaurants and eat a typical Moroccan dinner washed down with a good white wine. Before that he will follow the guide to one of the few bars that sells alcohol. He will have a few beers before dinner and soak in the evening sunshine as he mentally prepares for his meeting with Jean. In the meantime, he takes in some of the Marrakesh attractions, the El Badi Palace, the Koutoubia Minaret which he learns is the most perfect Islamic monument in the whole of North Africa.

He tries to keep his mind off Jean, concentrates on the attractions, reads about their history and learns their origins. Plays the tourist.

Jean is just a sideshow here in this blazing wonderland, he tells himself, he will meet her as an old friend, he will possess no emotional attachment to her. Detachment. No hard feelings, no soft feelings. He would have come here anyway. Jean's invitation was just an excuse to travel.

The next day, he gets to the square early, refreshed after a good night's sleep which had been easy after the journey and his day of sightseeing. He tries to remember if he had dreams last night. Would his dream have been about Morocco, about Jean? Dreams. He remembered so little of his dreams, odd fragments occasionally came to him but they came and went before he could recount them vividly.

His meeting with Jean is not for another hour so he takes a seat at the café she told him to meet her at. He orders coffee and gazes onto the square.

Expect nothing from this. You are in Morocco on holiday, Jean just happens to be here.

Jean's last letter said she agreed with Jake about Salime. But she said she could not walk away, not now. She told him he didn't understand relationships because he had never had one.

At first this made him furious. She is not in a relationship either. She is in a situation in which someone is controlling her, exploiting her vulnerabilities.

But the ending of Jean's letter was what made his mind up to come here to Morocco.

She wrote: I think you are right, I think we should both let each other go. I will stop writing to you. I need to channel my problems, my emotions into writing a book rather than writing to you. I need to turn the negative experiences I have been having into knowledge, wisdom, fiction. But Jake, as you said, I have spoken to you mainly through letters. We have spoken through letters, through the written word. I want to see you again for one last time. I do not want to end it with a final letter. I know this is asking a lot of you, but would you come to Marrakesh? You could have a little holiday, make that your main reason for coming. And we could meet, briefly, just to check up on each other and properly say goodbye. Have real closure. There has been something between us, I still feel emotionally close to you. But I know I cannot use you as a sponge, to soak up all that I am, all that my life is. But I want to see you again, for one last time. I don't want it to be sad. I just want to see you. Think about it. I completely understand if you cannot make it, due to money or time, or for whatever reason.

But promise me you will think about it. I hope you don't think I have used you, I genuinely think we had or even have something special, even if it is not love or romance. I just need to see you, for one last time, that's all.

Love Jean

Xxxxx

Jake agonised over this letter. Why, what was the point of meeting for one last time? After several pints in Cromwells he decided to book his flight and accommodation and write back to her with dates. Despite the doubts, despite the inner voice, he just decided. He wanted to travel, Marrakesh looked good from what he had read. Why not go? What had he to lose?

Her reply was ecstatic. She told him which guides to read and gave him the name of the café where they are about to meet.

He is gazing onto the square, smoking hard and deep when the chair next to him scrapes the ground. He looks up but is blinded by the sun. Slowly a figure lowers itself to sit down and here she is, Jean. She smiles, moves her face towards his and kisses him lightly on the lips. He smells her smell, he feels her touch, her breath. A kiss on the lips. It probably means nothing, don't read anything into it.

How are you, you look well?

The lilt of her Liverpool accent has not receded even after all this time.

And it takes him back, takes him all the way back to when and where he has been dragging himself from. But it takes him back, takes him back to then.

I'm good. It's so good to see you at last. You look well too.

Have you been enjoying Marrakesh?

Yeah, seen all the main places and explored the souks and the medina.

He is relieved when a waiter comes to the table to take their order. They ask for green teas.

He feels uneasy by Jean's obvious nervousness, it's like some blind date, strangers meeting for the first time, even though he knows so much, has so much to ask her, so much he wants to know.

But it's all small-talk, formal, clichéd, anodyne. Questions and answers they had both written in their letters, questions they had already asked, answers they had already given.

The teas arrive quickly and Jake also asks if he could get a glass of wine. He asks Jean if she wants some but she waves her hand and says she is fine with the tea, He needs a sip of wine, he needs to loosen up, needs to taste something more stimulating than this green tea which he feels like he has consumed by the gallon since he arrived in this alcohol-dry city. But most of all he needs to get a grip of this situation, it needs to be more relaxed, he has to puncture this formality.

The thought of the wine coming relaxes him and emboldens him at the same time, enough for him to start his questioning.

So how is life living here, in Marrakesh, are you happy?

She is looking away, distracted by a little boy, the son of a tourist who is wandering around the tables, exploring, picking things up, the way toddlers do.

Eventually she turns to him. Tired eyes, a forced smile, not sure of the question let alone the answer.

Am I happy? Depends what happiness is Jake. I'm happy enough for now. But things have happened that have not made me happy.

She looks away as she picks up her tea and takes a sip. The wine arrives, thank fuck, he takes a gulp and lights a cigarette. He offers her one but she waves the packet away, says she has given up, she was smoking too much in Paris and decided to knock it on the head when she moved here.

She watches as he lights up. The wine is helping and he finds the confidence to ask her another question.

So, here I am. I just keep wondering why if everything is Ok you keep writing to me and why you wanted to see me. I mean, it's such a long time since, you know, we were together in London.

The mention of London ignites a smile.

London, God, it seems such a long time ago, she says.

She's dodged his question with a neat nostalgic diversion and then, do you still go to raves?

No, no, I went to a few last year but the scene has changed. It's not the same, been taken over by the big businessmen and gangs and all the feeling of what they used to be has gone. Shame. Plus, I'm probably getting a bit too old for raves.

A smile, or half-smile, as if it is taking her all her energy to show any interest, as if she really does not want to be here. It feels as though they have been a couple for a long time but have run out of things to say to each other, a relationship that has gone stale, lost its magic.

Silence as she looks onto the square again. *If she cannot answer your questions, can't she ask any of her own? Do you have a girlfriend? How is work, what are you doing? Are you still living in Nevern Place, in Earls Court?*

Then she asks, you flying back to London tomorrow?

Yeah.

The wine is running out, the glasses are too small here, he beckons the waiter and orders another one.

Jean says, you always liked your red wine

Still do, as you can see.

She looks away again which allows him to assess her. She looks pale for someone living in such a hot country, no sign of any tan. Her face is pained, distracted, withered. And when he takes a sizeable gulp of the wine he tells her what he thinks, thoughts he does not want to take back to London unsaid.

Jean, look at me.

Slightly startled, she looks, eye-to-eye. A breeze blows his hair over his eyes and he pushes it back.

I've come all this way and you just don't seem very interested in seeing me, talking to me. I know we were never really together, in any sense, for long. But all your letters, the time I went to Paris after you asked me and it's like I'm some kind of burden, some sort of inconvenience, like you'll just be glad when this is over and I've gone back to London. I'm so pleased to see you. And yet, yet you…I've missed you and I thought you missed me what with the letters and staying in touch and telling me about your life and your problems. Have you nothing to tell me, nothing to ask me?

Her stare is paralysed, her eyes don't move, her expression freeze-framed.

Another sip of wine, another cigarette. As mysterious and unfathomable as ever. Flashbacks to the final days of being together in Nevern Place. I am H-a-p-p-y, I am H-a-p-p-y…

She looks down at the table and plays with a mat, stares at her tea. His impatience becomes overwhelming. *What the fuck are you doing here? Wind this up, make an excuse to leave and then go and enjoy Marrakesh for the rest of your time here.*

She is still beautiful but it's different to how her beauty was in the summer of 89. Maybe he could still find love for her but now he sensed she is both unloved and unlovable, closed off, an emotional perimeter fence surrounds her. *It always did.*

In exasperation he looks away, looks out onto the square at the tourists, the snake charmers, the lanterns. Out of the corner of his eye he can see her still looking down at the table, as if the table harbours answers she cannot or will not give.

He sees tourists and couples walking by, hand-in-hand, talking, smiling, normal. Lives being lived, no clouds, no mystery.

Then it's as if a voice is coming from another table, it's so weak, so soft, but it is her voice.

Salime is dead.

Salime is at work. Salime is on holiday. Salime has a cold. She had said it in a tone that she could have used for saying any of these inconsequential everyday things. But the tone was not appropriate for saying, Salime is dead.

He turns slowly to face her. He looks for any sign of sorrow, grief, tears, but nothing.

I'm so sorry Jean.

It's the only thing he can say, it's the only thing you can say.

He puts his arms around her, tries to draw her closer but her body is rigid. She doesn't need him, his sympathy, his hugs. His love. *She never did, you idiot.*

Does Salime's death change anything? What happened? How did he die? Has she murdered him, fucking hell, has she killed him after all his abuse and mind games and control?

She looks up at him and says, why don't we order a bottle of wine? I feel like some wine and it's cheaper than buying it by the glass.

While they wait for the wine he asks her, how did he die? When?

I didn't kill him if that's what you're thinking. I know you think I had every reason to kill him but that's not what happened.

Of course, and I wasn't thinking that.

Liar.

The wine arrives quickly. He pours hers and she motions for him to stop when the glass is half full. He pours his own and takes a sip.

She holds up her glass, he picks his up again and they clink together and she says 'salute'.

Her blue eyes twinkle in the night-time light which is fading fast. But he feels she might now be loosening up, preparing to tell him everything.

It's all a lie. She had made it all up. It's part of her story, part of her writing, the life she invented. The lover she invented. It's all made up. Salime was her doctor, her shrink, never her lover.

His cigarette packet and lighter are on the table and she reaches out to take one and lights up. She breathes in the tobacco and exhales heavily, as though she is enjoying some relief from this cigarette.

At last a smile, a Jean smile, a 1989 smile, the summer seems to be rushing back – cigarettes, wine, that smile.

The wine, the alcohol, It's playing with your mind, it's making you see things you want to see rather than what is really before your eyes. It always does, it always did.

So what happened to Salime?

Ah, what happened to Salime Douali, the love of my life?

Another long painful pause as Jake thinks back to her letter, her letter about Salime. It was a month ago, Salime had been very much alive then so his death must be recent, in the last few weeks or even days.

She takes another sip of wine and stubs out her cigarette. He remembers her nails, always cut short, she never wore varnish.

She says, Salime killed himself, committed suicide. He jumped off a bridge into the Seine. His body washed up on the banks. A man walking his dog found the body. The police ruled out foul play and then they found a suicide note he had left for me. He had spent all the money his parents had left him which is why we had to leave Pigalle. Things became stressful for him but obviously he had deeper issues.

Jean, I am…so sorry.

She rummges in her bag and pulls out folded up A4 pieces of paper, straightens them out and hands them to him and says, at least he wrote it in English, not French.

Jake's hands shake as he takes the pieces of paper flapping about in a breeze that seems to be gaining momentum. The first breeze he has experienced in this humid place. *He begins to read. You are reading words composed on a typewriter. This is not someone's handwriting.*

My dearest Jean, I have known for some time how unhappy you are and how unhappy it seems we make each other feel. I thought I could love and help you. Give you the love your father should have given you and the love you deserved and needed. But to do that I would have had to have been of sound mind. But as I always told you, from the very beginning, I don't really believe in love in the sense that other people believe in it. I suppose you think that I would be of sound mind given that I am a psychiatrist. Well that was a lie my darling. I could never have given you psychiatric help because I am not a psychiatrist. I have never practised it or studied it. I had ambitions to become one, many years ago, but it never happened for lots of reasons. I pretended I was and it fooled many people, mainly women. I read a few books, learned some of the terminology, enough to convince people, enough to allow me to seduce many, many women, here in Paris and for many years in London.

You see my father gave me enough money to live where-ever I wanted, however I wanted without having to earn an honest living.

The fruits of his labour he called it and he wanted to make sure his only son never wanted for anything. And I never have, apart from, possibly, his love.

I have spent so long living the high life, fucking who I wanted when I wanted. I've spent so much time pretending to be somebody, something. But now I'm exhausted, worn down by the lies and shallowness of my existence. I have tried to bring usefulness to my life by running Claud's business. But it is not me.

My life has been one big lie, Jean, built around hedonism and luxury and the high life. Even the books I had with me in the restaurant I frequented in London were never read. I'm not even a reader, hate books. But it was all part of this persona I had invented for myself. The avuncular character who dripped with elegance and sophistication. My purpose was to have the power to do what I liked with whom I liked and whenever. Women fell for it every time.

When I was younger I told everyone I was an actor. Which was fitting really. I played a character that was not me, every day. At other points in my life I played the businessman, the entrepreneur. Oh Jean, I've played many roles, I really should have taken up acting.

Then as I got older I found women telling me their problems. Relationship problems, mid-life crisis problems, that sort of thing. The usual problems people allow themselves to get fucked up over. And so I reinvented myself as a psychiatrist. I managed to read a few self-help and psychology books and found I could just sound convincing by using some terminology. But mainly I listened and then advised them on what to do about their problem and they thought I was a genius.

When I met you I saw a beautiful young woman. And when I saw you I saw you differently to all the others. At the age of 50 I thought I should become an honest person, go straight and take care of you. You were my last chance of an honest, true, life. You were my future, not the past.

But I was afraid, Jean, afraid of losing you because I have had no experience of ever keeping someone, holding them forever in my arms. In fact I had no real experience of being in love. So I tried to control you.

I would have had more chance of holding on to you had I been honest, committed and become the man I wanted to become when I first saw you in London. But then I had gone too far with my story, my invented persona and I just did not have the guts to come clean.

And then I learned about Jake. I learned you were still writing to him. I found screwed up first attempts of your letters to him in the bin, the first drafts of your calls for help, your love letters.

I got angry about being written about, I failed to understand why you laid your soul so bare to him, someone you were with for only a short time, you said.

You told me Jake had been a fling, just a fling, in summer 1989, you told me you no longer even thought about him. Yet you were writing to him regularly, providing him with a regular bulletin of our lives.

But Jean, I am not blaming you. And right now I am not angry because now I see you had cause to need to confide in someone else. I gave you cause to still love him because I did not show you the love you wanted me to give to you.

So why end my life? Oh, my darling, how can anyone who does this answer that question before they go? There are so many reasons, reasons I cannot understand myself. All I know is it just feels like the only correct thing I have ever done in my life.

I hear you hum your songs, I hear you play your young music and all those tunes make me feel so old and irrelevant to you.

I suppose it is why I pretended to be a psychiatrist – because I wasn't really anything or anyone so I made up a persona, an identity. I remember at school having to read Dostoevsky in Notes From The Underground. He had the clerk write that he wishes he was something tangible, wishes even that he could be labelled a sluggard and a glutton. Then at least he would have had some sort of identity. Probably the only thing I ever remember reading in a book but I dug it out when I was feeling this way, feeling that I had come to the end. This is how I feel, how I have felt. All of my life.

I could write forever, I could write millions more words but they would not be enough to explain everything.

I was once in a jazz club in Paris. I was only about 22. A smoky place where everyone drank whisky and relaxed to the jazz songs.

There was a beautiful blonde singer – you remind me of her – who went by the stage name of Eva. She ended her act with a jazz ballad. The song ended sadly with lyrics that stayed with me and I repeated them many times when I was being melancholy or philosophical. I once said them to you back in London when we first met. These words, Eva's voice, would come into my head in these moods and repeat over and over again in my head. They were these words: 'The future….not the past.'

I tried to look to the future, I saw it was you, I thought, I believed it was you but I could not live in the present or the future.

But the future is there for you Jean, it's what you deserve. Jake is your future and in the other words of Eva's song: ' Go for it, make it last, the future not the past.'

Salime.

He knows as he was reading that she had not taken her eyes off him, watching his expression, his reaction to Salime's suicide note.

Another fucking letter. Why can't people just talk? To each other. Words, more words on a page. He only ever knows what people are thinking through what they have written. Words written that have never been spoken, feelings felt but never verbally, physically expressed.

Salime did not know who he was. His life was a lie, he invented himself because he could not find who he really was.

But who is Salime?

He puts the letter down carefully on the table and pushes it towards her. There are tears in her eyes now but there is something else, an angry expression on her face. That face, he has seen it before. In Brighton. The kid. Her reaction. He lights a cigarette, looks at their glasses and tops them up. He averts his gaze from her but he can feel her eyes burning into him.

The inner voice is her voice when it says to him, so are you satisfied now? Salime is gone? You think the way is clear now. That's what you think, isn't it? The way is clear, Salime has gone. I need you now.

A black guy comes to the table offering cheap cigarettes, Jake waves him away but he's persistent. Jake shouts, waves his hand and tells him to fuck off.

Jean looks at him horrified. The silence now has to be punctuated. *Say something, ask her something, for Christ's sake.*

So what are you going to do? I mean, go back to Paris…or London?

London. Why would I go back to London?

Well I don't know, I'm asking you.

He killed himself because he thought I was in love with you.

She is blaming him. *She is blaming you, this is your fault. Saime's suicide is your fault. Salime who does not exist.*

Were you still in love with me? He asks and this just comes from nowhere, the first reaction plucked off his emotional shelf that is bereft of anything else to take down.

She lets out a frustration-charged gasp, plays with the stem of her glass then grabs the pack of cigarettes and lights one. Long, slow, desperate inhalation.

The expression on her face is again the one he saw in Brighton. Do you want to go to this rave or what? The kid who got knocked over. Her cold-heartedness. But she had been denied love and love is like water, it hydrates the heart, keeps it alive. Her emotional state is a desert.

Then it comes, the crescendo of her contempt that has been building up, maybe since Salime died or maybe just in a few seconds since he asked the question.

Was I still, still, still in love with you? How could I still, still be in love with you when I never ever fucking loved you?

A cigarette, a swig of wine, red, red wine, her words pound at him, the inner voice. *You fucking idiot.*

Salime was complicated, controlling and I dealt with it by writing it down and sending my thoughts and my feelings to someone, anyone, it could have been anyone but it was you. But I never even had a picture of you, the person I was sending those letters to. I just used your name, your persona. I should have just kept a diary and locked it away in my little case. All I needed was to write it down. Why did I send it? Why did I send it to you?

Tears in her eyes, always tears in her eyes. There always were.

You were afraid of him. You wrote to me, you said you wanted to meet me in Paris. Maybe I need rescuing you said, or something like that. That's what you said in the first few letters. Don't you remember?

She sips and sits back.

So fucking what. Words, they were just words. Just the state of my mind. Shall I tell you something Jake? Every time I wrote to you I was as high as a kite on E. It made me lucid, it got my adrenaline flowing, it released my emotions. I wrote whatever came into my head and I just scrawled it down, as fast as I could, a million emotions crashing through my head. Some were accurate, some exaggerated, dramatised. For attention. To keep your attention because had I written that I was happy you would have lost interest, you would have got bored, you probably would not have even kept in touch. No story, nothing to see there.

Unfathomable. Unfathomable. She is and she always was.

He thinks of his flat in Nevern Place, thinks of his runs through Kensington Gardens, his pints in Cromwells and this is where he wants to be right now. If he could he would get a flight now and just go back. All this way, just for this.

He looks at her, she looks at him. Her voice quietens as if to sooth the wounds she has inflicted.

Of all the people in my life you are the only one who ever listened, hung on to my every word I said or wrote. Salime dismissed most of what I ever had to say about anything. But you listened, responded, believed me and I suppose I exploited that. The more I played with you the more gullible I realised you were. I tested it over and over again and just found you to be weak, powerless. You just soaked it all up without question. It wasn't all lies Jake, some of it came from the heart with a bit of help from the E. But you swallowed it every time.

He sips his wine, he grabs the cigarettes. *Tell her, tell her. Don't just sit here and take this.*

Ok, so I was gullible, I tried to do the right thing. I tried to care for you, I worried about you. I'm sorry you see that as weakness.

He is about to continue, to elaborate but she interrupts.

Jake, it's the way I see you and the way I see life. That's all. It's just me.

He tops his glass up and offers her more but she declines. He looks into the square now, it's getting late, people are drifting away. Everything is drifting away.

He hears the scrape of a chair and turns around thinking she is leaving. But a tall, lean man with grey hair, wearing jeans and a biker jacket and carrying a helmet sits at the table.

Jake looks at Jean then at the man then sees her arm reach out to him and touch him on the arm. The tanned arm, with the watch, the watch the man had worn in the café in Paris. The guy asks, is she ready to go. The accent is French. Not once does he look at or acknowledge Jake. They both get up, the man puts his arm around her. They walk over to a motorbike parked next to the café. He hands a helmet to Jean and they mount the bike, he revs the engine.

The bike moves away slowly then gains speed. It turns left out of the square and towards one of the souks.

Jake gets up, runs to try to keep up with the bike. He sees her back as he runs, runs, dodges people and other bikes. The bike is slowing down, the souk is not the quickest way to make a getaway. His running is good, he is just inches from the bike, then he is within reaching distance and almost touches it but there is a clearway in the crowd and now it picks up speed, he loses them, the souk is too crowded for him to sprint and now he has lost sight of them. They could have turned off anywhere.

You swallowed it every time. The more I played with you the more gullible I realised you were. It wasn't all lies. Not all, but mostly.

Islamic music plays from one of the stalls in the Souk, it is sad music, melancholy, it is the sound of the state of his mind, his raw emotions right now, raw, cut up, sliced up, discarded. His emotions are just slabs, chopped up. Cut up. He is thousands of miles away from where he wants to be, physical, geographically and emotionally. A long long way away.

CHAPTER THIRTY

IN A tunnel somewhere near King's Cross he gulps super strength lager and sits, slumped on damp ground. He can smell his own piss as he hunches his legs up. Girls, women, men lay comatose. Fucked by alcohol and drugs. Lives ebbing away as a train thunders over a bridge probably going north to near where he is from.

He takes an E from his pocket as he becomes paranoid that the last one is about to wear off. He swallows it down with the poison from the can. Super strength poison. It should be illegal. The urge to dance overcomes him and he switches his Walkman on. He pulls himself up and begins to move to the music. Ride on Time. As powerful and as pulsating as ever. There are girls here now who he could kiss, who he could touch who he could screw. Under this bridge not too far away from where it had all started. A gust of wind blows through the tunnel scattering drink and drug detritus, cans, needles, dirty fucking cans, dirty fucking needles. Poison. If his mother and or father could see him now. Up to his blood in E and alcohol. Ride On Time finishes and when he stops dancing he hears a laugh, a drunk female laugh and then a Liverpudlian voice.

Yer fucken mad youse is.

Sidney Youngblood's If Only I Could starts playing in his head and he sits down, sits down in this dark tunnel next to the girl. He puts his arms around her and draws her close. He feels her body compliant, in unison with his own need to be close to someone, anyone. He can smell his own stench, his own neglect and lack of strength and dignity and realises he is the last thing this girl in this King's Cross tunnel needs and she is the last thing he needs.

Poison.

He takes his arm away

Hey, you gor anymore booze?

He hands her his carrier bag with its tins of drink. She grabs it greedily, desperately, addictively. He gets up and walks the tunnel guided by a street light he can just make out at the end. He walks unsteadily but he needs to get out of this tunnel. He needs to get back on street level. He needs to see light.

In Nevern Place, the sight of the street is a blur, the sounds of the street a hum, like his ears are partially blocked. He opens the main door without difficulty. He ascends the stairs with a confident ease. Alcohol, drugs, they do not impede him now. He knows where he wants to be. Finally, behind the secure door of the flat he slumps on the sofa, but not for too long. He goes to the bedroom, strips off and hits the shower. He soaps his whole body, he lets the tepid water wash his dirt away. He lets the water cascade through his hair, pours shampoo in it and rinses. He towels himself dry, slowly, thoroughly, easily. He puts on some underwear and then a dressing gown.

He goes to the fridge and taps some ice cubes into a glass. He puts a moderate amount of whisky onto the ice, it clinks as the alcohol disturbs its frozen temperature, and then adds a generous amount of water from the tap, to dilute it, make it less potent, make it less harmful. If only you could do that with life, just add a little something to make it a little less strong, less fucking difficult. Jake laughs at his analogy.

Jake, you can, you can make it all so much easier on yourself.

He is still slightly pissed and is coming down from the E. He looks at the shelf and there they are. Mother and father picture and his picture of Jean and him. In Brighton. He slams down the drink. He goes to the shelf and picks up both pictures and takes them back to the sofa.

The pictures, staring back. A photograph is made up of ink and pixels, not atoms and neutrons and living flesh. He is looking at pieces of paper in thin wooden frames, not people, these are inanimate images. Dead. They have no meaning because they are not alive. They are just snapshots of people in another time. Then, not now. The past, not now, not even the future. Mummy, my Love. My mummy isn't my mummy because she has gone, a long time ago. Jean is not my love because she has gone. If she was ever here. No one is here.

PART THREE 2015, LONDON
CHAPTER THIRTY-ONE

IT IS unrecognisable. The old goods yards are gone, tall blocks of luxury apartments loom over him. The pavement outside King's Cross has been widened to create a piazza with bronze and metal benches and fountains. Shops, bars - not pubs - and designer boutiques, oyster and sushi restaurants surround him. But it is all so samey, so concrete, so grey, so corporate. Eurostar has moved to St Pancreas and the whole interior of the Gothic facade station now looks like an airport lounge. Shopping, eating, drinking. This was where, once, the runaways from the north would seek sanctuary from the cold and the pimps and the perverts, nursing tea or coffee from McDonalds or Burger King but they have been replaced now by the well-to-dos living it up in the amenities only they can afford.

He walks up Caledonia Road. The grotty old buildings are gone. Apartment blocks with big balconies have replaced them. The porn shops and the old striptease pub are long gone, no trace of them, as if they only exist in the recesses of his imagination. But they were here, they did exist, he tells himself. And not so very long ago.

He spots it, the turning into an alleyway that led to the warehouse. The warehouse of the rave in1989. But on either side of the alleyway are more shops and bars and cafes with tables outside. And at the end of the alleyway - exactly where the old warehouse used to be - is a corrugated iron arch. Above it carved in metal is a sign that says: Kings Cross Quarter. And beyond the arch a mini tower block of more apartments with more balconies. There is a wrought iron gate that is locked. You need to have a swipe card to make it open, to get beyond the gate and get to where the old warehouse used to be. Locked out.

You need to be a property owner. Everything now is owned, it belongs to somebody who can pay to own it. Pay to keep you out, keep everybody out. Time, it changes everything. It always does, it always did.

His train isn't due to leave for an hour. After his walk around the area, Jake decides he would quite like to sample the oyster bar and drink a cold glass of white wine in the new bijou Kings Cross.

In the bar as he takes bites of the fish, he checks his company emails on his smartphone which is safely encased in a brown leather wallet.

It's not a phone, it's a computer. Can't afford to drop it. All quiet on the western front as far as the emails are concerned. It was the fax machine in the nineties that had to be constantly checked. Great big fuckers that groaned to life then spewed out the sender's message. But at least you could escape it, you couldn't check it in the pub or in bed. You couldn't obsess about it. You could escape from its churned out bollocks.

He's on his way to see a client in Edinburgh. A new campaign, corporate brochures and blogs and emails; stuff he can rattle out now almost in his sleep. It's all marketing and PR nonsense but use the right words and you can make anyone or anything sound good. And people are so gullible and desperate these days. All you have to do is convince them they will more or less die if they don't have this or that and they will buy it every time. An app, an item of clothing, the latest technology. Doesn't matter. Use the right words and they'll bite, every time. And Jake knows his words. It's why he is now working for one of the biggest corporate PR companies in London. He writes words that sell even if, and he is the first to acknowledge this, they are words that speak bullshit in any real sense. But life now, in the world of consumerism, reality TV and social media shallowness, swallows it all up into its big fat stomach. In a world where a fault on the iPhone's battery is bigger news than what's going on in the Yemen or anywhere else for that matter. Yes, he could have been a brilliant journalist. But brilliant journalism is restricted to the brilliant few who get the media jobs through which college they went to and or who they know. The rest pump out talking cat stories and write picture captions about Kim Kardashian's arse and usually they are under 25 and working for peanuts that will never buy them a box room let alone a home here in London.

So Jake sold his ass to PR but it pays for a flat in Chelsea Harbour and as many oysters and glasses of the best white wine he can eat and drink.

It was never meant to be like this but it is. And it's a far cry from a studio flat in what was then grubby Earls Court. Earls Court where they have just torn down the iconic exhibition centre. Earls Court that used to be a magnet to travellers, Aussies, eccentrics, druggies, prostitutes, with its spit and sawdust pubs, hostels and BestBuy.

He still hates the phoney world of PR. But along the way of his career he had managed to endure it although he still regards himself as a writer rather than an account executive. And even now, he still doesn't feel like he fits in, like it's his real world. But he doesn't take it too seriously, doesn't worry about it or resent it as he did when he first came into the business. He has grown into it; time has made him easier about it even though he thinks every day that it really is the most contrived job you could do. In fact Jake is thankful that he is in a job he can do on auto-pilot because now he is just too tired to care. Everyone has sold out. To sell out is to have a nice place to relax in, lay your head, listen to your classical music, devour your books, sip your wine. Selling out is to be thankful you're not on the streets, or fleeing some war-ravaged country like Syria or Libya or flooded Bangladesh. Comfortable. Unexciting. But comfortable, warm, safe.

He puts his phone down and sips what is left of his wine. He fancies a cigarette but given you can no longer smoke in enclosed places he is glad he kicked the filthy and eventually grossly expensive habit a few years ago.

What was her name? Jean. Just a few yards from the oyster bar, where he was walking around, the warehouse where he met her. All those years ago. Ah yes, Jean. Ridley. He had always, in the intervening years, put an 'e' before the 'i' in her surname when he thought about the spelling. Ridley seemed too crude a spelling. It was like it deserved an 'e'. Reidley

Jean. She had stayed at the back of his mind all these years, especially when he reminisced about his early life in London. And he wondered where she was and what became of her. Twenty-odd years ago, almost three decades since 1989. Time. He never thought much about time then but time now worries him, he wonders where it will eventually take him and he wonders if the next decades will go as quickly as the last.

The inner voice is still there, it speaks to him all the time but it is more muted, he ignores it, he will not let it disturb the inner calm he has found for himself as he has become older. He read a book about something called mindfulness where you learn to control the voices and how you react to them. You don't let them control you, you hear them in a different tone so you can just say, ah, yes, ok, whatever. It works for Jake most of the time, but not all of the time. But it's manageable.

And how would she look now? Jean? He imagines she has matured into a glamorous middle aged woman who, like him, found herself and was at ease with herself after all her torment. Not completely purged of all those demons past, but managing them.

Was she still with Salime? Did Salime ever exist? Had they ridden off on that bike into the sunset of eternal happiness? Why had she lied? Where was she now?

He hoped, despite everything, she had found happiness and got her head sorted out. Maybe she just needed to grow up. Anyway, that was all a long time ago.

In the Edinburgh hotel room he prepares for tomorrow's meeting with the client. He wants to get this out of the way so he can go for a stroll, sample a few pubs and then get back to the hotel for a nice relaxing dinner and then an early night.

As he finishes the work he places documents in his briefcase, snaps it shut then checks his phone. A Whatsapp message from Vaneasa his ex-wife.

Can you call me urgently. It's about Billy.

He has not heard from Vanessa for a while. In fact he has not heard from Vanessa since his son Billy last got himself into trouble some months back.

He of course hates these messages when he is so far away. What's happened now? It has to be something serious, Vanessa only ever contacts him when it is. He picks up the phone and procrastinates in calling her, wondering and thinking what he should say.

They are in London, whatever it is he can do nothing. No matter what has happened he cannot possibly be there. But he will have to call her. He finds her number and presses call, utter dread courses through him. This will be bad, whatever it is, it will be bad, it always is.

Vanessa's number just rings and rings until it gets to her voicemail. He leaves a message to text him when she is free to take his call.

His mind fuzzes with worry and various scenarios. Billy knocked down by a car. Billy beaten up. Billy arrested. He paces the room and keeps looking at his phone to see if she has left a message.

Nothing.

May as well wait for her to call while having a pint, no point being stuck in this hotel room, he decides.

Jake met Vanessa Shaw in the mid-90s at a party thrown by some friends. Blonde, blue-eyed and petite but savvy with a bright sense of humour and an easy manner. She seemed sorted working as a psychologist. But what drew Jake to her was her compassion and understanding. Back then he was still a bit of a mess in terms of who he was or who he thought he was. Although he had always been cynical about Jean's psychology - mainly because it always seemed like a lot of parroting of stuff she had read in books - with Vanessa it was the fact she listened to him and never applied any judgement or theory to his psychological predicament.

He had told her on the dates they had, when she had asked him about where he saw his life going, that he had a massive problem. Her relaxed demeanour and a few glasses of red wine loosened him up.

He had told her, I just don't know who I am or what I want. I don't know who I want to be. I question everything I do and everything I decide. And there is always this other voice. I don't know where it comes from or who it is. Is it me? But then if it is me where does the first voice come from? Why do I have this voice that makes me so indecisive and so uncomfortable in certain situations, so uncomfortable I just want to get away, I don't ever want to be part of anything or to embrace it?

Vanessa had listened, had touched his hand when he seemed to be getting worked up. She did not tell him to slow down with the drinking when he ordered another bottle. She drank it with him. When he apologised for only talking about himself, she held his hand again and told him to stop being so self-conscious and that she was delighted he trusted her enough to tell her all about his painful, innermost personal angst even though, at that stage, they hardly knew each other.

In the infancy of their romance they did the usual things, seeing films, walking through parks, enjoying Sunday roasts, making love and then reading the papers together. But always, at some point, a bottle of wine would be opened - whether in a restaurant or at home, and conversation would turn to Jake and it would turn melancholy. It was as if every meeting would have to end with some psychological therapy session at which Jake poured all his emotions out while Vanessa, as part of the therapy, just listened and said nothing. Or maybe she did say something but by the time she did he had been too drunk to remember what it was.

After about a year in the mid-nineties they rented a flat together. It had been a wrench leaving Nevern Place and Earls Court and at the time it felt as though he was saying goodbye to his young self and early life in London.

But Vanessa had refused to live in the flat which she said was too small and more like a studio flat which is what it was. Her idea had been to move further out of London and they settled on Ealing where they rented a reasonable two-bedroom flat that overlooked the green near the Underground.

Jake found a new local and enjoyed being so close to the Broadway with its varied shops and eateries. For a year or two he enjoyed snuggling up with Vanessa or sitting on their balcony laughing at the drunks staggering to the Underground on a Friday or Saturday night feeling thankfully smug that they had left clubbing and staying out late behind and were settled in their cosy place and happy with a good meal and a bottle of wine. Life was good, they ate out regularly and spent a lot of weekends just as a couple and seeing nobody else. Happiness seemed to have found Jake at last.

It was the summer of 1998, he thinks, when Vanessa seemed to be somewhere else. She seemed withdrawn from him although it was at this time he was throwing himself into work and often working late and enjoying a drink afterwards, usually by himself away from people and the types he worked with.

One weekend they went to their favourite Italian restaurant. He had sensed something wasn't quite right for weeks and the visit to the restaurant was strained. Vanessa had little to say and Jake was beginning to sense that she was losing interest in him and that the relationship may be sailing into a harbour that would mark its end. It always does, it always did. The inner voice again, no longer as prevalent as it had been all those years ago but it became vocal whenever things were not going well, when self-doubt lurched at him.

He had had enough and he needed to confront her about how things were and ask her what was wrong. He had been meaning to for some time but fear of what the answer might be had deterred him. *She will be ok, she is just going through a period, people do, no need to put her one the spot.*

In the restaurant the atmosphere and her body language became intolerable to him. He refilled their glasses with wine but she told him curtly, no I don't want any more. She looked at him almost with repulsion as she watched him take another mouthful of wine. This was the trigger, this was the point when he could take no more of this, whatever this was.

Vanessa, what the hell is the matter with you these days? Have I done something wrong, something to upset you?

He hated the way he had asked her. So cliched, the sort of question a million people have asked their partners. How had it come to this, the conventional this, the this everyone seems to come to in relationships?

She looked at her wine glass and stroked its stem. Seen this before, was the first thought in his head. He pictured Jean doing the same all those years ago in Brighton. But fuck Jean. This was now, this was Vanessa.

Her reply when it did come was, to start with, along the lines of asking where the relationship was going. Why had he not mentioned marriage, why had he not asked her to marry him? Did he only see the relationship as temporary.? He didn't seem to be committed. They never talked about what they wanted in the future, their future together. After almost six years, they had made no plans, he had not talked to her about anything.

His answer was simple, darling we can do whatever you want us to do, we can get married, we can have kids, we can have whatever you want.

Jake, whatever I want? Fuck sake. It isn't just about what I want. It's like you're telling me I can...I can have whatever I want from...from this fucking menu.

She tossed the menu at him and he was relieved she continued to speak in almost a whisper so as not to create a scene in the restaurant.

It's about what we both want isn't it? And if we don't want the same things then it's not gonna work in the longer term. Don't you see, we have to talk about where we are going, what we both want. I'm in my 30s, the clock's ticking. I have to know we both want the same things. We have to talk. But you seem happy just to coast along, not think about this shit, just go to work, do well, have your beers, read your books. Jake, if that's how you see us carrying on then it's not going to work. I need us to move on to the next stage, to have a plan, to know what we both want. I mean, where do you see us going, where do you want us to go? Because at the moment we are standing still. At least from my point of view. Have you given any of this any thought, do you think about these things? I know you have had difficulties, what with your mother and your childhood and all that and I know it has had an effect on you. But Jake you have me now. Don't you think about what you would like to do with me and how the rest of our lives might be?

She finally stopped talking and grabbed the wine bottle and topped up her glass and took a gulp like a thirsty athlete at the end of a race.

He looked at her, he remembers looking at her, shell-shocked, as she just stared at something on the table. It was probably, as far as he remembers, the only angry outburst he had experienced with her and that made it all the more shocking. And as he looked at her he saw tears in her eyes and she sniffled and then searched her handbag for a tissue. She dabbed at her eyes. He touched her arm. When she had composed herself she at last looked at him. Looked at him in the face, her eyes searching his and she asked, do you love me Jake? Really love me?

Of course I do.

And he knew when he said it that it had not convinced either himself and certainly not Vanessa.

She wants a kid, she wants to be a mum, you know what she wants. A kid is a trophy of commitment. A product of physical unison. You make a kid together in an act of biological nature. It's the most together thing two people can do. She wants a kid. But do you, with this woman?

Though the inner voice only came in those days in times of emotional challenge when it came it was as interrogatory and judgmental as ever. As ever it had been in his twenties. And now it was asking him real questions, questions about the rest of his life.

Control the voice, give it a lighter tone, make it more friendly, don't let it control you. Manage it.

Being a father? He had never given it a thought. Maybe somewhere in his mind. And she wants him to propose. She wants marriage, she wants this to be permanent.

They ate and drank in silence. He had to ask her to marry him. But it had to be special, not forced and that night seemed the wrong time to do it.

Do you really want to marry her, do you really love her? Want to stay with her for the rest of your life or end up divorced?

One night after work he took in a few beers and came to a big conclusion. He needed to change his life. He needed to give it meaning and direction. He needed to marry Vanessa Shaw and have a family with her. To make a future, to lock out the past. He had never had a family as a kid, now he could have one as an adult, as a man, a real man, a father, a husband.

It was early and he sent Vanessa a text saying he would be late home because of work. The real reason: at that moment he had this uncontrollable urge to go to Earls Court, to Nevern Place. He could not explain it but he felt he was about to change his life irreversibly and forever and he just needed, right then, to glimpse his past, to be on the cold streets and to feel what it would be like if he was on his own again, like he was, like he felt all those years ago.

It was a February evening. Cold cold night. The Tube from Ealing to Earls Court would take just over twenty minutes. He drained his pint and headed for the station. On the train he watched a young family, mum and dad and little boy sat opposite. A sweet attractive couple with a lively blond blue-eyed son. The kid kept grabbing his father's spectacles and other passengers laughed. Jake didn't. He could only imagine how annoying a kid fiddling with your glasses would be. After a while the father picked up on Jake's staring so he quickly averted his eyes. The family got off at Acton Town and he felt a ridiculous sense of relief. Now he could carry on his journey to Earls Court without the distraction. Read his paper, read his book until he got there. He anticipated getting off at Earls Court and remembered those mornings he had waited there for the Tube to work. He remembered the little kiosks on each platform selling chocolate and water and nuts. Wooden, they were, wooden weren't they? He would always buy a paper, The Independent and a packet of Polo mints for the journey. And a pack of ten Marlboro Lights before he had progressed to caning packets of 20.

At Earls Court he climbed the once familiar steps up to street level. The Bakers Oven cafe he often had enjoyed many a breakfast in and cups of tea on cold winter afternoons was now a Greggs. New restaurants had opened, the big greasy spoon cafe that once fed Aussie travellers gigantic triple sausage, eggs and beans breakfasts was now an upmarket Italian restaurant. As he got to where Cromwells was he saw it was no longer Cromwells but the Earls Court Tavern. Its exterior was white and gold replacing the Cromwells plain red.

In Nevern Place he came to the flat and looked up. The stucco frontage of the building had been cleaned up and painted white. The window ledge that he had so often leaned out of now had a wooden blind pulled down in the window. He stared up at the window for a minute or two and flashbacks came to him of his days here in Earls Court. The very first days of his lonely arrival to the summer days of Jean and raves and being young.

But this is long gone, the past. What is here for you now in this little west London conclave you hardly recognise? It's cold, these streets are not what they were, time has moved them on, made them different. Could you really come back? Could you really bring those years, that year, 1989, back? You are cold and lonely now on these strange streets. Even the streets have moved on, adapted, changed, evolved. You walk these streets that now offer nothing, not like they did back then. You are cold, you feel lonely again and maybe those times were not so good after all. Oh yes they were, they were the best of times, never forget those times. They are your memories, they are your nostalgia. They shaped you, they pushed you in new directions, you learned, you formed, you developed. You got wiser, these streets made you wiser. It was your time, nobody can take it away from you, it is yours, you lived it, you earned it. Memories. Time, yours, your life, as it was, as it played out.

He stopped staring at the flat and pulled out his iPhone but there were no messages. Some push notification from all the news outlets about the worsening economic crisis, something about the Dow Jones tanking.

He got back into the Earls Court Road, crossed it and went into Cromwells. Or rather the Earls Court Tavern. His feet walked on wooden floors where all that time ago it was a dirty, sticky red carpet. The place was unrecognisable. The bar was ornate wood and mirrors, waitresses came scurrying out of a kitchen at the back bringing platters of food - steaks, pastas, over-priced fish and chips cooked in beer. The clientele was middle aged, the background music was soft, rather than the blare of the latest chart music from the old jukebox. Where were the youngsters, where were the prostitutes and travellers? Bottles of wine instead of pints of beer. Serviettes rather than beer mats. Everything different, everything changed.

He ordered a beer and paid more than five quid for it. A uniformed bar tender served him. He took a seat, which was a far too tall stool near the window as far away from the 'diners' as he could get which was not very far and not far enough.

He stared out of the window into the Earls Court Road and though it was dark, the lighting, the topography of the place had changed. The all night cafes and bars and supermarkets were now restaurants and boutiques. The flow of people walking by was more of a trickle. He sipped his beer and thought how this place had outgrown him, it had moved on. He felt Earls Court had been unfaithful to him, it had moved on and changed behind his back when he had not been here when he had not been looking. How could it? Why did everything have to change, even Earls Court for fuck's sake? Wonderful down-and-out rebellious Earls Court that back in the day was the shabby bad relative of the borough of Kensington and Chelsea. It had always been stubbornly incongruous to its posh neighbour South Kensington but now it had succumbed to boring, characterless conformity.

You might as well be sat in a cocktail bar in High Street Kensington with the knobs.

What would they think of it now, Sylvie, Karim and of course Jean?

He watched couples eating but not talking. Their mobiles were at hand and instead of chatting they were mesmerised by the electronic devices. The place had no atmosphere, no edginess. He noticed a group of four people, three guys and a girl talking loudly in between checking their phones. Probably in their twenties he guessed. What memories would they take away from this night, this night in Earls Court? Not the same as my memories, not as good or vivid or eventful as my memories.

He was where it all began but knew this was where his past really had to end. In a beautiful apartment on the green in Ealing he had a woman who now offered him, wanted, a future. He had no idea what that future would bring or whether it was what he really wanted. But if all you want is the past, the future does not stand a chance. He had to give it a chance because the past had gone, the past had deserted him and walked into another day, another month and now another year.

He left the pub and headed to the the exhibition centre. In the Warwick Road he could see it, an iron skeleton, it's facade eaten away as if it had been left on a beach for the vultures. No neon sign screaming Earls Court in red. No grand entrance that welcomed thousands of stars and people over the years. Just a skeleton, it's body eaten away by time, by change. There had been Facebook campaigns to save it but even social media is no competitor against power and money and time. He looked at it in the same way you would view a recently diseased relative in its coffin just before it was about to be cremated or buried. One last look before they finally took them away. His father sprang to mind for no real reason. Everything ends, everything finishes, you never think it will but it does.

It's moving, it's changing Jake, everything is changing and this is your last chance to change with it.

He buttoned up his coat, pulled up his collar and took the Warwick

Road entrance to Earls Court and took a Tube to the future. Not the past. At least that's what it said on the ticket. But really he had no idea where the train back to Ealing would take him. Time and only time would decide but it wasn't going to tell him right there, right then.

Jake married Vanessa. It was a basic registry office ceremony as neither of them were religious. The wedding itself highlighted how on his own he was. He had no family to witness him saying his marriage vows while Vanessa had a massive family that included both her parents and her two brothers and two sisters. There were her colleagues and old school friends. Jake had thought about asking a few people from work to come but he wasn't close to any of his colleagues, didn't even socialise after work with them. He had thought about asking his uncle but decided against it.

Vanessa's father was a successful businessman, in property and real estate, was arrogantly proud of his daughter. Mrs Shaw was a middle class snob of the highest order and though Jake had met her parents a handful of times he really hated their conceit on the day of the wedding. He felt no closeness and a few times caught the glare of both her mother and father who had expressions on their faces that said they had real doubts about Jake, this man their precious daughter was about to marry.

Billy was born a year later. Vanessa had said having a kid was the next logical step in the progression of their relationship. Jake loved the kid as a young child but also resented him in his deep subconscious. You have what I never had, a mother and a father. Jake would look at Billy sleeping and the enormity of his responsibility towards the kid overwhelmed him. He wanted to give the child all the things he never had. Other times he would look at the kid and resent him.

Vanessa doted on her son, she revolved their world around him and this was natural and Jake understood and accepted it but only to a degree. He failed to understand fully why mothers allowed a child to completely change everybody's life. But the problems began when Billy morphed into a teenager. Vanessa, he believed, was not allowing Billy to grow up. She treated him as though he were still a child even though he was on the cusp of becoming a young man. Billy's laziness both at home and at school infuriated Jake. But what really enraged him was Vanessa's liberalism towards him. She frowned on any chastisement Jake administered and it led to enormous rows.

It's 2010 the world is in a mess. If he doesn't work hard he is going to be fucked in later life. He will still be relying on us when he's in his twenties. He needs to grow up.

Jake, he's only 16, let him enjoy his youth. There's time for him to develop and realise he needs to work harder. But just give him some space.

Vanessa, he is lazy, he spends every hour on his phone playing dumb-ass games and watching rapping shite. When did you ever see him pick up a book or a newspaper? I was reading everything I could lay my hands in when I was his age.

When you were his age you were zonked up to the eyeballs on E. Have you forgotten what it was like to be young?

I still read, I still functioned, I still learned.

You were still going to raves when you were 23 for Christ's sake

But I had learned a trade, I was earning money.

He's seven years younger than you were. He's still a kid.

And the way you deal with him that's all he will ever be, a kid. He needs to pass his O levels he needs to put the work in. He can't do that listening to all that violent rap crap which is all he does. He's a fucking zombie.

That is, he is, our son you are talking about. He's not a zombie. What a dreadful thing to say about your own son.

Jake poured himself some more wine. Vanessa had stopped drinking since Billy was born. She looked at him as he took a sip.

You ought to cut back a bit in the vino, she said quietly.

Yeah and you ought to loosen up. Why the fuck do we have to stop enjoying ourselves just because of, just because we have a kid who should now be turning into to an adult?

His voice was calm but the words ignited Vanessa.

You never really wanted any of this did you Jake? Marriage, a kid. Billy and me were your last chance at a normal life, and well you just couldn't cope with it. In your forties and you still don't know who you are? Still don't know who you are when you're a husband and father?

His first inclination was to swig the wine and empty his glass and then storm out. It was the first time she had ever shown disdain or mockery about his psychological flaws and now she was so obsessed with the kid that she had abandoned all sympathy and understanding for him. Billy the kid was all she felt for now.

He looked at her but she just stared at the wine bottle. Have some wine, loosen up you bitch, don't just stare at it.

Words he felt like saying but then the truth of what she had said hit him face on. The truth of it. She really did understand him, too well and probably more than he understood himself.

It was about 9pm and they both heard Billy come in. Vanessa got off the kitchen stool and greeted him. Asked him if he had had a good day and was he hungry.

What the fuck is he doing turning up at this hour, Jake raged silently. He got up himself and took the wine bottle to the lounge. End of conversation with my wife, the mother's pride and joy had returned and he could not compete against him for any sort of attention or discussion.

Jake switched on the telly and watched the news as he finished off the wine. Europe on the brink of another economic crisis, people in Spain losing their homes, security services upping the terror threat. Young people in the UK leaving school unable to read or add up. He watched the breaking news ticker. Doom, gloom, 24-hour misery on 24-hour news. He had to stop watching the news and get back to doing some real reading again. Books were the answer, not all this rowing and dreadful incessant news.

He could hear the clatter of pans coming from the kitchen. Silly cow is cooking for him. At this time of night. Maybe her way with Billy would prove to be right. She was the psychologist after all.

But a few days later when Billy had been expelled from school for fighting another lad and putting him in hospital Jake decided that Vanessa was allowing the kid to sleepwalk into a life of trouble and failure.

When Jake pinned Billy against the wall and shouted why, why had he done this, Vanessa pulled him off.

You being violent is not exactly a good example to him is it?

As usual Jake retired to the lounge, undermined and weakened yet again. He listened to her talking to the kid, asking what happened. Psychoanalysis. For fuck's sake, he needs discipline, Jake muttered to himself.

He watched the television news and the wine subdued him into a mellowness and relaxed feeling. Relax. People, problems. They will wait for another day. Billy, Vanessa, work, life, they will all be there tomorrow. Nothing to be done now. The wine had blotted it out anyway. He heard a few words, he heard the odd raised voice, first Billy, then Vanessa. All in the background. He could not hear and he didn't have to.

A flick over to Newsnight but by now he hadn't a clue what they were reporting or saying. He could not take it in. He drained the glass, took the empty bottle and glass to the kitchen and felt Vanessa's stare. Billy was eating noisily and taking swigs from a can of beer. Jake mumbled that he was off to bed and bid them goodnight. Civilised but cold. Leave them to it. Nothing he could do or say. Mother and son. Let them deal with it. Man and wife, well that just didn't come into it, did it. He must stop drinking so much wine before bed. He should be able to sit up and read for half an hour before hitting the pillow. Yes, that would be his routine from tomorrow. A glass or two then up to bed and read for a bit. Like he used to way back then. In Nevern Place. A long time ago. Life as a father. Perhaps he would have made a better job of it if he had been allowed to.

Over the weeks and months Jake suspected and eventually convinced himself that Vanessa excluded him from Billy's adolescence because she knew that Jake was psychologically flawed and could not cope with the same flaws their son had. Billy was lost, just like his father and he concluded that she had concluded Jake could offer no help to his son. She had taken it all on herself and Jake became relegated to just the bread winner. He was good at his job but not at emotional stuff. He couldn't be, could he? As Jake sipped the remains of a second bottle of wine one night he took the bottle and glass, as usual, to the kitchen where Billy was talking to his mother about his latest crisis.

Jake made a point of slamming both glass and bottle down on the worktop. Mother and son had stopped their conversation when he had entered, as they always did. He said quietly and with a slur, don't know what the trouble is now but if it can be solved with money maybe I can help. Obviously that is my only way of contributing to any solution there might be. Billy looked up at exactly the same time as his mother, both frowned with looks of perplexity. Jake just left it at that, walked back into the living room, jabbed the remote control to switch off the telly then made the lonely drink-blurred ascendancy up the stairs and to bed. His head felt woozy and thick as he hit the pillow. A book he had bought for some bedtime reading lay on his bedside table, not a single page turned as he reached out to switch the bedside lamp off. Sleep came easily, the wine had medicated him and sent him into a deep slumber and on his way to another day. How many more days like this? This was his last thought before the wine and tiredness and powerlessness switched him off completely. Just like a television set. The wine and the weariness acting as the remote control.

One afternoon Jake arrived home after a few glasses of wine and found Billy slumped on the sofa playing some anodyne game on his iPhone. It was only 4pm and Jake had arrived home early because he lost his job. He had been told it was 'at risk' which meant that in a month he would leave the company without a job. He had drowned his sorrows. Oh what a fucking awful expression he thought as he got to the bottom of the bottle in some god forsaken poncy wine bar in Canary Wharf. Alcohol does not drown sorrows, it drowns souls.

Jake shouted at Billy, asked him why the fuck he was home so early. The teenager had headphones on and could not hear his father. Jake pulled the earphones out of his ears and shouted again. The lad was furious and shocked to find his father home.

When Billy told him he had been sent home from school, expelled, Jake's rage exploded. Uncontrollable rage. Lost it. All he could see was laziness and failure sprawled out on the sofa and he hadn't even taken off his muddy trainers. I have worked hard, so hard and now I've been kicked out of a job, with all the worry that brings and this little shit, the little shit I never really wanted, just lays idle on the sofa with his teenage shit on his stupid fucking smartphone. Not a care in the world.

Jake ordered him to get the fuck up and when he refused he grabbed him by the shoulders and pulled him. Billy got up and told his father to fuck off. As he was leaving the room still staring at his phone, Jake grabbed him and pushed him against the wall.

Go on, fucking hit me then, Billy implored his father.

Jake held his hand up about to strike a blow. But he put his hand down, let go and went to the kitchen in search of wine.

When Vanessa got home he was drunk and forlorn. He told her about the job. And about Billy. A row flared but Jake was past caring and her words were just a hazy echo. Something about how he had to get a grip, something about not taking everything out on the kid. Something about cutting down on the drink. His response to that was to refill his glass. Something deep inside him, even in this drunken daze, told him she was right but it was so deep down it would not come to the surface yet. Not yet, no time soon. As he sunk his head on the pillow thoughts of everything going wrong would not exit his mind. A wayward son, no job. It seemed to be building, morphing into something terrible, his life now. He pulled the duvet up tight and shivered. A vision of a dirty cold tunnel somewhere in London came to mind, he could feel dirt and wet, he could feel the cold of that tunnel and only sleep would blot it out, make it go away, as it did, as it always did.

CHAPTER THIRTY-TWO

JAKE SOON found a new job, he had to. When Vanessa told him she wanted a divorce as soon as possible he knew he would have to earn good money to survive. With the cash he had been left by his father – which had accrued a handsome return in interest – Jake was able to leave Vanessa the flat and set himself up in a luxury studio flat near the river in Chelsea.

He found himself back on his own again but there had been an inevitability about it. Vanessa had wanted different things, she was a different person, from a different background and had different ideas about bringing up a son, a son who he had never shared any desire to have. Jake realised he was not so much a bad father but a no-father in much the same way his own had been.

The split from Vanessa was amicable and she had even told him she didn't really want a divorce and if he was willing to change they could rescue the relationship.

Over several glasses of wine one night when she said this, Jake asked: Change? But what do you want me to change into? Who do you want me to be?

I want you to be happy, to be less confrontational, to stop drinking, to just, well, be happy to be a family with Billy and me.

He sipped more wine but was still baffled by what she meant.

I do care for you Jake and my biggest fear is that, well, you're going to end up being very lonely. I mean none of us is getting any younger.

I've been lonely all my life, Vanessa, I can deal with loneliness, it's all I've ever known.

What, you felt lonely with me, with us?

The voice. It just keeps saying to me, this is not who you are, this is not what you want, what you really want.

But why not get help with this inner voice. I've been telling you, there is therapy, there is treatment. You were managing it, you said you were managing. I told you I could get you more help with that but you said you were managing it, it was no longer a problem.

I don't think I want to be treated for it. You make it sound like this voice is wrong, that it's lying to me. But what if it's telling the truth?

Jake, it's stopping you from living your life, it's stopping you from, from committing, from participating in a normal life. How can that be right, how can that be good for you?

A normal life? What the fuck is a normal life? A big mortgage, a wayward kid, arguments, Sunday lunch with the inlaws who hate you?

They don't hate you.

Psst. Even my own son hates me. You hate me.

He sips his wine.

Oh Jake, you need help not self-pity. Nobody hates you.

Then why do you want a fucking divorce?

Because we cannot go on like this, for Billy's sake, for my sake and, in the longer-term, for all our sakes. Why don't you see somebody? You know I can't treat you.

Ah, a shrink. Not only do you hate me you think I'm a fucking nut-job too. 'Treat' me. I don't need treatment, I'm not ill. I'm just unhappy. You can't treat unhappiness. And don't talk to me about therapy.

Maybe it's more than that. Maybe the alcohol is affecting you.

Alcoholic nut-job now am I? Worst of both worlds. Mad and a drunkard.

Excessive alcohol is a depressant. You drink every night, you drink loads every night. You know you do. It fucks with your head. Jake, you go to bed, every fucking night, drunk. We have had conversations you later have no recall of because of the drink. You are susceptible, you have, well you have issues and they are made worse by drinking too much.

Vanessa became exasperated. It was their last sit-down together before he moved out of the Ealing flat. Billy watched him with contempt as he carried his suitcases to his car.

You're leaving, just like your mother did, all those years ago.

Abandoning a son, abandoning a partner, the people you are supposed to love. Love, it's what you have always craved, to love and be loved and now you are leaving.

Vanessa stood at their bedroom window, watching him go, wiping tears from her eyes. A broken family. Split up. Her mother would be round once she told her Jake had gone.

He stopped the car in a lay-by just outside Hammersmith. He had just left someone who had loved him, really loved him, for the first time. And Jake wept, hard sobbing shook a body whose limbs ached.

You might not have been happy but you could have worked harder at it, you could have tried harder to make it work. And now you are alone again.

He checks his phone to see if she has called. Still nothing. He makes his way back to the hotel, the Edinburgh night air a shock to his body after the warm confines of the bar.

In the hotel he tries to phone Vanessa again but still there is no answer. It is getting late and worry threatens to wreck a good night's sleep and preparation for the meeting with the client in the morning.

The minibar looks inviting and he pours a miniature whisky and sits on the bed.

Could fucking do without this. What the hell has the kid got into now? And no doubt it won't be his fault, no Vanessa will insist it's not his fault. And that's the trouble, that's always been the trouble. No fucking discipline from his mother. The kid is spoiled, mollycoddled, smothered in too much love and forgiveness.

You see it all the time. Modern-day parenting. The kids that are allowed to cry and scream on a train for no good reason. Allowed to ride down supermarket aisles on scooters while their mothers and fathers are oblivious to other people's safety. Allowed to go out at all hours of the night, drinking and drugging themselves stupid.

The parents, well they're on their smartphones, on Facebook trying to be kids again themselves. But hey, it's OK, because at least they had kids, they ticked the boxes. Now they can go back to playing with their smartphones.

The inner voice is working up nicely to a rage when at last his phone goes. Vanessa's name on the screen. On the smartphone screen. He answers.

Billy has gone missing. Been missing for three days now. She has called the police. He is now a missing person. Vanessa's voice is tremulous. She starts sobbing.

Yes, of course she's checked with his mates. No-one has seen him. He hasn't showed up at college. No, there are no signs he has packed his things, all his clothes are still in his wardrobe.

He manages to snuff out the urge to say, he's a fucking arsehole who you have let run wild, no wonder he's gone fucking missing. Instead, he feels for her and says, he's a teenager, Vanessa, he isn't a kid. He could have just, well, gone off for a while, to be on his own.

What, like his fucking father you mean? Wants to be all alone because he can't handle people or relationships?

He pauses. Then he is surprised at what she says next.

I'm sorry Jake, that wasn't fair. I shouldn't have said that.

It's OK, darling, really, it's OK.

Look, where are you?

Edinburgh.

Fuck. How long for?

I've got to meet a client in the morning. Then I'll come back to London. I'll come over to Ealing and we can deal with this together. What do the cops say?

Just asked the same questions as you. Will put out a description to the press and appeals, that sort of thing.

OK. Look, I'll try to be back for early afternoon.

OK. OK, thanks.

I know this sounds stupid, but try not to worry. There will be an explanation. You know what he's like, he's got a mind of his own.

He hears her sniffling, probably drying her eyes.

Yeah, well let's hope so.

See you tomorrow.

Yeah, goodnight, Jake, goodnight.

The trains hurtles through the north, and he looks up from his Kindle and out of the window and there it is, God's Own Country. They are about to go through York not far from where he was born and grew up. His uncle and aunt had died just a few years ago, his uncle first and then she followed about a year later. And now he hadn't a single connection with this place. He looks at the sprawling countryside, at the small stone farmhouses dotted on this green and never-ending landscape of solitude and freedom. Not a lot to get you into trouble here.

Twenty-odd years since he had left here. How might his life have been had he stayed and never gone to London? If he had got a job, met a Yorkshire girl, settled down. Maybe his father would not have taken his life. Maybe marriage and giving him grandchildren would have given him something to live for, compensate for the life he thought he had been robbed of. Maybe his mother would have come back to see her grandchildren.

But through the train window, Yorkshire whizzes by, a blur, just like the last few decades. Now he is on his way back to London, on his way back to trouble. Would Billy have grown up better here, or rather back there for the train had long gone past Yorkshire? But then would there have been somebody else, maybe not a Billy but a girl, to another woman. Another life at another time in another place.

As the train thunders through the Midlands, he realises he should be thinking about this life, and this son and this problem. Where could he have got to? Taking off like that and not telling Vanessa, putting her though all this after all she had done for him. Always backing him, taking his side, defending him. How could he put her through this?

But then the thought returns – it's her own fault. She has made the kid what he is, thoughtless, work-shy, irresponsible. Not enough tough love. Vanessa had fallen into the trap of trying to protect her son from the world, from any conceivable threat. She had given him too many chances, too many let-offs, not enough consequences for his actions or inactions.

He might be back now, he might be hugging his mother and his mother will be making him his favourite meal and putting cans of lager on the table for him. And she will have forgotten about Jake because now the son, her son, was back, the most important man in her life.

She maybe doesn't need you now. She never did before, she always took his side, she always gave him her undivided attention. Even when you were crying out inside, for a conversation, for some stimulation, anything that didn't revolve around bringing up that wretched kid was ignored. No need for you now. Billy's back.

It was wishful thinking. Jake arrives at the flat in Ealing and a sobbing Vanessa lets him in.

He follows her to the lounge and notices the décor and furniture is as it was when he left. It is like she has not made it her own, as if she is just waiting for him to come back, to his, to their home. It touches him at first but then he is jolted back to the present and the problem. The problem of a missing Billy.

Any news?

Vanessa shakes her head, tears in her eyes. So many tears. Tears over the years. He doesn't know whether it is appropriate to go to her on the sofa and put his arms around her.

You are divorced. The only thing you have in common with this woman is she is the mother of your son.

There's a long silence and Jake picks nervously at his fingernails and hopes she offers to go to the kitchen to make tea. He feels inadequate in his own silence, in his not knowing what to do or say.

Maybe he's gone to join ISIS in Syria. Fuck, he might be a jihadi. Spent loads of time – too much time – on the internet. Maybe he'll pop up in some video on the news threatening to bomb London and the infidels.

His other voice tells this voice to shut the fuck up and do not even think of saying this to Vanessa. And then he says it, maybe he's in Syria. You know, gone to fight. Become radicalised.

Her response is immediate, without consideration, I doubt it.

Well how do you know? It's all they've been talking about on TV and in the newspapers. Youngsters being radicalised and then going abroad.

I just don't think so. You watch too much news Jake.

I guess you're right. He's more likely shacked up with some woman in a squat. Living like a hippie on cannabis and wearing Jesus sandals.

He says it drily, not meaning to lighten the atmosphere but Vanessa looks up and smiles, then laughs.

Let's hope so.

What if he never comes back, what if he just disappears, forever? Of his own accord, to a new life. Or he's dead, never to be discovered. Or selling drugs and involved in some kind of gangland warfare and he's been cut up?

All these thoughts ride around in his mind like dodgem cars banging and crashing into each other. He's sure her mind is doing the same. He needs to get up and do something, he needs to stop thinking, stop his imagination taking him to hellish places.

He says, I'll put the kettle on and then we need to talk about this. You know, what his moods have been like, whether he's been locked in his room for hours.

As he pours hot water into two mugs, Vanessa says, the police have asked all those questions Jake already, that's what they do. They just ask questions. He was fine, he was beginning to work a bit harder, he's even started reading. He was always nice to me, did errands, seemed fine, seemed OK. I only looked at him the other day and thought how much he was beginning to grow up. I was thinking how much you would approve of him these days.

Jake's phone is in the inside pocket of his jacket. He felt it vibrate a few seconds ago and now he itches to take it out to check push notifications or emails, to connect with the wider world, the world that is not here in this room with Vanessa and her worries, their worries, their worries for their son, the only connection they have now they are no longer together.

He gulps what is left of his lukewarm tea and asks Vanessa if she is ready for another cup. *Make another cup of tea, get away from her, do something. Do anything, even an action as trivial as making another cup of tea. Take charge. Take action. Check the phone without her seeing you check the phone. You could check it now, in front of her, say you have to, it's work, you need to justify it by saying it's for work. People do it all the time.*

Vanessa doesn't want any more tea. But he gets up, goes to the kitchen and puts the kettle on. He leaves her in the lounge and as he waits for the kettle to boil he puts a tea bag in his mug. His phone vibrates again, he can feel it in his pocket, demanding attention. Its vibration will be another push notification of news that does not affect him – a BBC or Sky News news alert of another atrocity somewhere far away. Or an email from the office, a round robin email about something insignificant, something that, right now, he doesn't really need to know.

But it could be Billy. Maybe Billy wants to get in touch and has sent a text or a WhatsApp. For some bizarre reason he may want to re-connect with his dad. Tell him where he is. He has your number, he has a mobile, he could, if he wanted to, he could reconnect on his mobile phone to your mobile phone, to you.

The kettle is beginning to steam, it is reaching boiling point, it sounds like a small plane building up to take off. Its job is nearly done. Jake watches the kettle and moves his mug near to it, ready, ready for the boiling water for his tea. The kettle clicks. Stops boiling, it cannot get any hotter. The water is ready. He picks it up and pours water into the mug and watches the teabag float to the top. He leaves enough room for a splash of milk. He shouts to Vanessa, is she sure she doesn't want another tea. No, thanks, I'm OK. OK, but of course she is not OK. She is worried, where is he, where is her son? Their son?

If he comes through the door right now, she will hug him, pull him close, forgive him. And Jake will be relieved but then Jake will ask questions, demand to know where the fuck he has been and why he didn't tell anyone. And Vanessa will admonish him and tell him to calm down and not get at the lad. And Jake will get angry and storm off in anger and relief. She never learns, people never learn.

But right now, Billy has not come back, Vanessa is still frantic, Jake is still worried, still uncomfortable to be here with his ex-wife only because their son has gone missing.

He takes his seat again and sees that Vanessa is looking at her phone. Her face looks as though she is expecting to find something horrific on the device. He watches her, the temptation to check his own phone becomes stronger. Why not, she is looking at her phone. But she flicks the wallet cover of the phone shut and puts it down. He hates wallets and cases for phones. The iPhone is a purposefully designed gadget, slim and slick, it goes against the whole point of it by putting it in some cheap leather or plastic case. But people are insecure, scared they will drop it and in a world where all risks have to be avoided, you put a case on your super-slim phone in case you scratch it, in case you drop it. You just can't take the risk. Why risk it? People are scared, people don't want to risk scratching their phones or dropping them. Buy a case, protect your phone, protect yourself. Peace of mind. No need to worry, there is so much to worry about, you don't want the added worry of damaging your phone. Choose a case, choose a wallet, spend money on it, protect your phone, it could save you money in the long-run. Protect it, protect yourself, avoid the risk, get a case, get a wallet, ruin the fucking thing by surrounding it, mollycoddling it in cheap plastic. Or crap leather. Everyone does it, like they do with their kids. Protect them, keep them from potential harm, don't risk it. Smother them but keep them safe, it keeps them safe, it makes you feel better. But Billy is still missing, he's broken out of his case, he is at risk, he is not here, the protection did not stop him, all the love, all the understanding, all the forgiveness did not stop him from disappearing. Infact it probably caused it, probably made him break free because he was becoming smothered, unable to breath, too safe, too understood, too looked after. In a case. In case.

He moves his hand to the inside pocket of his jacket. Fuck it, he's going to check his phone. Then he feels her stare and Vanessa says, so how is work, how are things with you?

You cannot check your phone now. She is talking to you, she is asking of you. She is making conversation. At this difficult time. She is trying to divert her mind from the situation of Billy missing. She is showing an interest. She is showing an interest in you and how you are and how you have been. How are things with you?

Yeah, fine, busy at work, as usual. You know.

Vanessa nods, as if to say, yes, I know only too well and says, she is sorry but she wouldn't mind another tea after all.

Yeah, sure, I'll stick the kettle on.

He goes to the kitchen and fills the kettle, relieved to be away from Vanessa. And his phone vibrates again. *Check it, why not, you're only waiting for the kettle to boil.*

He takes the phone from his pocket. A firm grip, its metal is slippery, it is not in a case. He presses the home button. The screen is filled with push notifications, Sky News, BBC News, CNN, Paris 24 Hour News, Al Jazeera.

Gunmen rampage through Paris, seven dead, many injured. Breaking News.

Ongoing attack believed to be terrorism, early reports suggest ISIS responsible.

Terror returns to mainland Europe.

Breaking News.

Watch live now.

Events unfolding.

Terror.

Instant news, instant notifications. News on the go, whenever, wherever you are. You used to have to wait until the Six O' Clock news, or watch a News Flash or catch up on the Ten O'clock News. Now the news is here, on your phone, news is here all the time. Whenever, wherever, whether you want it or not. But no news on Billy. No breaking news on where Billy is or what has happened to Billy.

He scrolls the notifications. He sees the logos of all the news organisations pushing out the breaking news. But there is a logo that is not a news outlet. It is the Facebook logo. And it's a message.

Jean Ridley has sent you a friend request.

The kettle clicks to say it has boiled the water. But Jake does not hear it. He does not hear anything. He does not hear Vanessa's phone ringing. He does not hear her answer it. He does not hear her say, Billy, where the hell are you, are you OK? Oh, thank God.

Jean Ridley has sent you a friend request.

It is like the push notification is not just written words, it's like a voice, an urgent voice. Jean Ridley has sent you a friend request. And it echoes in his head.

Billy, he's Ok, he's with some friends in Brighton. He's coming back, he's coming home tonight, on the train. He's OK. Oh thank fuck for that. Thank fuck for that.

Jean Ridley has sent you a friend request.

The future, not the past.

CHAPTER THIRTY-THREE

HE IS in Earls Court and he takes pictures of the Earls Court Road on his phone because it might change, it might get bulldozed, just like the exhibition centre. He needs to capture what could only be faint memories, like 1989 is a fuzzy, vague memory that he wishes he could envisage more clearly, more vividly. Time warps memories and he wishes he could remember more clearly, more vividly.

From Earls Court he goes to Soho. Soho, the place he wandered around before he decided this city was the place where he had to be. But now, not far off three decades on it is changing, no not changing, it is being destroyed. When had he last ventured into Soho? Years ago. He had neglected it, neglected what had been his playground all those years ago. And though it is still familiar, so much has changed. Spot the changes. Spot the changes against your memory, your visions from almost 30 years ago. It is not difficult to see the changes but it frightens him that he can see so much change vividly but remembers so little and what he does remember is vague, a faded snapshot from the past.

He turns into Berwick Street. He has read how the market stall holders are battling for survival against the developers. This street where the market is more than a century old but now they want to wipe out history, replace the old with the new, the unaffordable.

He snaps the street from various angles. One shot takes in a fruit and veg stall, another captures a boarded up building that once accommodated 'models' with their neon red signs in windows. Red, the red light district. The peep shows, the strip clubs, the porn video shops. There are still a few but they are sandwiched by upmarket oyster bars and restaurants. They look unwelcome, they look like they don't belong. As if they are over-staying their welcome now in someone else's home. The home of corporate, high street branding, buildings made only of glass, transparent, lacking any mystery, tall and imposing.

He walks through St Anne's Court with the mysterious arch. This used to be a corridor of shops peddling filth or striptease 'theatres'. But apart from the odd triple X sex shop, the buildings are boarded up. Just about everything is boarded up. Soho's heart, it's boarded up, its character, what was its character, is boarded up. Fucking boarded up, bought, being prepared. For what? Another fucking glass penthouse. He snaps with his phone, he has to, this is all disappearing, it's all going, everything is changing, he needs to capture it before it disappears, before it all just fades away from memory, from sight.

Into an alleyway called Peter Street and in the doorway of a closed down shop a woman in a sleeping bag. She is awake, sat up but her eyes are vacant, her face is worn. Her hair is grey and matted. Agatha. It could be Agatha from all those years ago. Did she ever find him, her lover, what was his name? He tries to make out her face. It could be her. It could be that Brazilian girl he walked past and who called out to him and sipped a beer with him in Notting Hill and told him her story. All those years ago. 1989. Of course it may not be her. And she would be unrecognisable anyway. But if it is, would she remember him like he remembers her? He tells himself it's not her, that her story ended happily, this woman in the doorway, in the sleeping bag, cannot be Agatha. Agatha found happiness, Agatha found what she was looking for. Agatha is safe. He doesn't need to think about her, he doesn't need to go back there.

Peter Street, Wardour Street, Berwick Street, Old Compton Street, Meard Street. How did the streets get their name? Why are they called what they are? History, the past, he will look them up on the internet, he will find out because now it is so easy, now you just switch on your computer and you Google whatever you want or need to know. In an instant. Now you can know what you couldn't be bothered to find out before the world wide web. He wishes it had been so easy back then. What he would now know if Google had been around back then.

He is back in Wardour Street and walks past what was once the Intrepid Fox, the goth/punk pub he had wandered into the day he came down to London, the day he fell in love with London.

Now the Intrepid Fox is a long gone and he wishes he had frequented it more once he had moved to the city. But you don't expect things to disappear, you don't expect things to change so much. Why back then would he have ever thought that one day it would not be there? Why would he have thought then that in almost 30 years this place would change so much?

He crosses the road and enters a Nero coffee shop. He needs to sit down, take a look at the photos he has taken. He orders a latte. Latte, known back then as a coffee made with milk. Now it's a latte. Everyone knows what a latte is, everyone has had one.

The pictures on his phone look good, sharp, the product of wonderful modern technology. But they are pictures that make him unhappy because they confirm that everything is changing and these photos will never fade away. They are here, on his phone, which he can transfer to his laptop. He can keep them for as long as he wants, he can look at them whenever he likes. But what is the point? Once you have seen a picture once, you have seen it. Nothing else to see. Pictures never change. You might once, not that long ago, have put it away and brought it out in years to come when you are sorting through cupboards and having a clear-out. Now you can just click on them and look at them for no reason.

As he looks at the pictures it occurs to him that he could have gone one better and shot some video. His phone allows him to do this.

Then it flashes up on the phone's screen. A reminder. From Facebook. Jean Ridley has sent you a friend request.

He rides the Tube to Earls Court and heads for Nevern Place. He stands outside the old flat and takes out his phone and takes a picture of it. *This might all be gone one day.*

He walks to the end of the street towards the exhibition centre, or rather what was the exhibition centre. They have ripped it down, the cranes are in place ready to start construction of the latest glass housing development. For the rich, for the privileged.

Back in the Earls Court Road the Prince of Teck pub is still there but it's a gastro pub, the spit and sawdust long gone. Even the kangaroo with cans of Fosters hanging from it has disappeared. Gentrified. Corporate. Boring.

He goes to Cromwells, now the Earls Court Tavern, sits in the spot he used to and drinks a beer. It feels like he is sitting at someone's dining table where everyone is eating but he is just sitting there, drinking, out of place.

You are having negative thoughts about everything. Things change, it's called evolution. What have you against change? Things have changed from your father's day, and his father's. It is how the world works. You have been feeling so positive these last few months and now the voices are back.

He sits with his pint and he checks his phone. Has a look at what's going on at work, who is sending what to who. Any big announcements? Nothing, boring, but he doesn't really care anyway.

Why bother checking, why keep looking at this phone, this device?

He flicks to the camera roll and looks at the pictures he has taken. How many pictures are taken in the world, have been taken in the world, since photography was invented and available to the masses?

Pictures of weddings, parties, birthdays. In the old days you took your film for developing and were either disappointed or delighted with the results. You would look at the pictures and then put them back in the envelope and stash them away in drawers never to be seen again. Now you can snap away and see the results instantly. You look at them and then flick to the next and the next. But do you really look?

And isn't life a bit like that? You go from one phase, one year, the next and then forget about it. *Why can't you, Jake, why can't you just move on and live for the now? Your life is a carousel, it just goes up and down and round and round. The wrong way round.*

He sips his pint and looks around the pub. Sips his pint. How many pints would that be? Another pint, another day, another beer. Faces from the past are no longer here but they are vivid in his mind. He can see them. He can hear this pub's jukebox playing Marc Almond and Gene Pitney singing Someone's Got A Hold Of My Heart. Like a playlist his mind moves on to Adamski's Killer, Cher's It's In His Kiss and after that Simply Red's If You Don't Know Me By Now.

Why are you thinking of these tunes now? Why are you thinking about 1989 again? Why are you not thinking about now, about today, about the future. The future, not the past. Why are your emotions entangled in the so long ago, constricting you from reaching out to now?

He drains his pint. Christ, how many times have I done this, he thinks. And now I'm going to get another one and how many times have I done that? He goes to the bar and orders another, takes it back to his seat and looks at the glass.

Why, why have you ordered this drink? Because you need it? Because you really, really need it? Or because, well, you just did. Without thinking, without really knowing you did. It's just what you always do. You have another. Because you always do. And chances are you will have another, because you always did, because you always do. Without thinking, without thought. Like when you smoked. *You just smoked because one fag followed another. Not because you needed it or even enjoyed it. You just did.*

And like he always has, Jake lifts his pint and he takes another sip. I'm not an alcoholic, I just like beer. I just like wine. Lots of people do.

But what is liking? Why do you like another and then another. What does it give you, does it really make you feel better? Why do you drink beer, or wine, because you think it makes you feel better? Better than what? Better than how you felt before you drank it? Better than when you had your first pint? And then better again when you have the third which makes you feel better than when you had only had two?

Why do you think the way you think? Why do you think of then and not now? *Why do you still think of Jean Ridley? All the years, all the time, all the chances, all the talent, and yet here you are still stuck, marooned to the past. Why do you not see the future, why do you not see yourself moving on, settling down? You had your chance, with Vanessa, a beautiful woman who gave you a son, who tried to understand you.*

She wanted a kid and her body clock was ticking. And she saw me as a vulnerable target. Lost, so she could control, have what she wanted, a kid. A career woman who wanted it all. Vanessa saw me as a commodity, she saw me as a way of ticking all her boxes. Career, tick. Meeting the body clock deadline, tick.

She left me and loving me un-ticked. Nothing mattered to her when Billy was born apart from Billy. Billy was just something to protect, somebody to protect. Her son. my son. Possessive. A commodity, something, somebody who belonged to her. And that is all that mattered to her in the end. I was a means of achieving that and once my function was no longer required, I was nobody to her. If I ever was.

Is this fair, is this true? This is what all women want, a man, a child, a family, a future. And you, for some unfathomable reason, did not want this. Why? You do not know. Now, here you are doing what you have been doing all your adult life. Having another beer, embarking on another journey, back to the past. Because you cannot deal with the now, because you do not want to face the future?

I drink because it blots out you, I don't hear the voices when I'm drinking, when I'm drunk. I hear my voice. It may be a

237

drunken voice, but it is my voice. And when I'm drunk I know who I am. There is no conflict, there is no nagging, no questioning. Peace. Me. My voice. Like it was when I took the E and when I danced like a crazy bastard at the raves. They call it an out-of-mind experience and I am only me, only ever at peace, when I am out of my fucking mind. One voice, my voice, me. I'm speaking now, this is me, this is the only voice I hear. I wish this was the case all the time, through every hour of every day. But it isn't. When I sober up, when I face the real world, I hear the megaphones of conflicting voices. And I have no idea who they are or why they keep on speaking to me and confusing me. They always do, they always have. They stopped for a while but then they came back. And when they were gone I felt at peace. But now they are back. You are back. Here you come again.

Back at his place in Chelsea, Jake flips open his MacBook and logs on to Facebook and sees Jean's Friend Request. This time on a 12-inch screen rather than his phone. It looks even more dramatic, more enticing on the larger screen.

We were friends long, long ago. So why not be friends now and see what happens?

He clicks 'Accept' opens a bottle of wine and waits. Waits for any reply, any response. Now she can send him a message. Will she send him one tonight?

A bottle of wine later he is too tired and pissed to even remember why he opened his laptop. Its screen is dark, shut down, it has gone into sleep mode and that's what he does now. Switches off. If you ever do. These days.

The phone is on his bedside table. And as he falls into a deep sleep, another message comes through on his screen. It flashes up but then fades, it goes to sleep, piled up on all the other push notifications he will pick up in the morning when he opens the screen. As he always does. Just like everyone else, it's just the way things are. Now. These days. In this day and age.

In the morning, he wakes to the alarm of the phone. It is a week-day and work beckons. Not too many years ago he would get out of bed and put the kettle on for a massive mug of tea and cane at least ten cigarettes before he got going.

Now his mornings are still bleary-eyed but he fixes a strong coffee in a new machine he bought that dispenses coffee-shop quality latte and he eats muesli and a slice of high-bran bread toast. He makes himself a fresh fruit juice with the blender. He does all this before he splashes his face with cold water and dabs it dry. He takes a shower, savours the power-jet water all over his body and smells in the soap and lather from the shower gel. It revitalises him, makes him feel fresh and alive again and as he showers he thinks of all the simple things in life, like showering, that are so pleasurable, that make you feel better but are so basic, so uncomplicated.

Today he vows to cut down on the wine. A bottle is too much and he feels it every morning. The weariness of it, the lethargy and though now, at the moment, he can shake it off with his morning rituals, he realises it is becoming more difficult as the years roll by and it would be just so much easier to cut down. Sip it. To savour. Make a bottle last two nights. Go to sleep with his book, go to sleep sober, go to sleep normally and able to remember what he watched, what he read the night before. How many novels had he had to re-read because he had completely forgotten what he had read the night before? How many times had he watched intently an interview with someone interesting on Newsnight but completely forgotten about it by the next day?

I am not an alcoholic, I function, I go to work, I hold down a job, I know what I am doing. But I drink too much. Much too much. To stop it now. To grow up. To live. I gave up the E. No problem. I gave up the fags. No problem. Give up the full bottle a night. Should be no problem. Why would it be a problem?

He towels himself dry on soft cotton towels. He has time, time to brew a fresh pot of coffee and he takes his cup to the balcony that overlooks the Thames. He thinks of the day ahead. A couple of client meetings then a few projects he must write and complete by the middle of the week.

He goes to the bedroom and picks up his phone. The screen is an autocue of push notifications, mainly news. But there is another Facebook message. Its white-on-blue logo dominates all the other notifications as he scrolls the screen.

Jean again?

The coffee has wakened him and his copy editor's eyes can see the words do not spell Jean Ridley.

He clicks onto the Facebook app and onto notifications. Friend Request from his mother. His own mother. After all these years, after all his life.

Google has existed for as long as he can remember but it is the first time he has ever thought about googling his mother.

You could have done this years ago, you could have done it at any time.

He wonders why he never has, but then he wonders why he has, all through these years, never really even thought about his mother.

The truth is, he has thought about Jean all these years, more than his mother, probably more than anyone. And now, through what they call social media, his mother sends him a Friend Request. His mother, his own mother, wants to be his friend. His friend. *It is not a Mother Request. It is not a You Are My Flesh And Blood Let's Talk Request.*

It's a friend request. Just good friends. Mother and son. Abandoned son. Absent mother, deserting mother, the mother who left you behind, to find her own life, who just left you. And now she wants to be friends in the cyber world. She could not be there for you in the real world but here she is now, connected, because she can be. Because it just takes a click of a mouse, a 'send' function. All there is here is just words on a screen, a disconnected connection, not real, not meant, not right now. It's just dishonesty. She left you so long ago.

She left me. She deserted me. She chose another life. She left my father. I understood. I understood why she left my father but I will never understand how she could leave me.

And then there is Jean. After all these years. After all my life.

Two women, one his mother, one his lover. Time and years gone by when they should assume he would have moved on, even though he has not. Time without them, time with others, time that did not produce the happiness they would have surely wished for him.

Accept or block? Or decline? Block your own mother? Decline your own mother? Just one click to decide. The movement of a mouse, possible without any effort or thinking about it. Click accept and just see what happens. It will be interesting. Another facet of your life to wonder about. Embers that have not been stirred can be poked again. See what they produce, see what flies out. Nothing to lose. It's just a click. A mouse. A computer mouse. It takes no effort. You can always block, you can always decline. You are online. You are safe. You can decline, you can reject, you can block. You can do anything you want to if it gets too difficult.

Too difficult? Just block, just switch it off. Instant termination of whatever new emerges that you cannot handle it.

Is my mother on Twitter? Is she on Instagram? If I accept her request she will have photos? Photos of her life. Photos of her, how she is, without me. Old photos, new photos, her new husband. Well, not new anymore, because she left my dad years ago. She may have left loads of other men. She may have had many husbands, many kids. Her kid. Her son, her daughter, her child. The child she left behind will not be there but now I am connected. I could send pictures she could add to her photo album. I could even Skype her, talk to her, after all these years, after all this time.

Jake googles: He googles how old is Facebook? He googles, how old is the internet? Why has his mother waited so long to try to contact him? And why now?

Because she can. Because we all can.

He does not click Accept. He goes to work, he does what he has to do, he knocks out thousands of words of copy trying to sell something to someone. And his bosses are pleased as they always are. They tell him this in an email. Great copy, Jake. Client loves it. They never say it physically, to his face, they never come over to his desk and pat him on the back and smile and say, great work Jake. They send an email. From far away. Everyone is so far away. One click, that's all it takes, but they are so far away.

Back in his lounge, he opens his evening bottle. He loves the silence of being alone with his wine and his phone. He should be reading a book, as he usually does, but tonight he has a decision to make and he has to check his phone. He accepted Jean's friend request and has heard nothing since.

Now he must decide whether to accept his mother's. For some reason the wine doesn't work tonight. It does not give him that casual, why not, feeling. His mother's request seems sinister, he wonders what the agenda is. He realises that he doesn't really want contact with his mother because he has spent the last three decades trying to replace her. Trying to replace the love that was not there, trying to fill the void of her absence, the love that only a mother can give. And now she sends him a Friend Request. His mother wants to be his friend. Friend. Just a friend.

He is doing well so far with the wine. He has sipped it slowly but now he is half-way through the bottle and if he is to follow his resolution he will have to cork up this bottle, take it to the kitchen, rinse out his glass, gulp a mouthful of filtered water and go to bed. With a book.

The bottle stands on the table facing him. Looking at him, almost inviting him. Go on, finish me off. You know you want to. You know you need to. Your mother's just got in touch with you after all this time. It's a shock. You have a big decision to make. You deserve to finish me off.

The sirens of police cars racing across Chelsea Bridge disturb the silence. He looks out. He counts seven with their blue lights flashing, illuminating the white paintwork of the bridge. Racing to another incident somewhere in this harsh, violent, city. They are heading south. Towards Battersea where the power station is, the power station that is being turned into another high-rise glass luxury development.

He picks up the wine bottle and refills his glass. He wishes now that he had not given up smoking. The craving for something to smoke is overwhelming but for now, finishing off the wine will do. He closes down the laptop. He throws his phone at a cushion across the room. He knows it will not be broken, he knows he can look at it tomorrow. Addiction. But now, he must just sip the wine until he reaches semi-sleep, semi-stupor and can just go to bed and sleep.

The wine tastes good, it is soothing, he reclines in ultimate relaxation in his reclining chair. You recline because you can. There is at least another large glass of wine left in the bottle after he has finished this large glass. Is this where it all ends, is this what we come to? Just comfort, just doing things just because we can?

The sirens have stopped, the police cars have long gone. Now he hears the patter of rain on the windows, against the main large door of the balcony. Rain and wet outside, dry and warm inside. With the wine. With himself and with the memories that nobody can take away, that no-one can force him to stop remembering.

There is no voice, there are no voices apart from his own, the voice he uses to speak out loud: This is me, this is as good as I can get, for all my faults, for all my failings, for all my hang-ups, I cherish my memories and I speak now with this voice. Fuck it all, fuck them all. A glass of wine, a place to call my own, my own memories, my own time, now they want to come back to me, now they want me, but I am no more.

He goes to the bathroom. He sees the bottle of sleeping pills he was once prescribed when the voices kept him awake. He opens

the pills and takes one. And another. I don't want to wake up tomorrow. I don't want to wake up again. As he is about to take the fourth pill, he stops.

What the fuck are you doing?

He goes back to the lounge and picks up his phone. Message from Jean Ridley. He opens it.

Hi Jake, hope you are well. It's been such a long time. How are you? I'm living in London now. Would be nice to meet up after all this time. Xxxxxx

THE END

HAS THE PUBLISHER GIVEN YOU A STYLE GUIDE?

Printed in Great
Britain
by Amazon